THE
CHILD
MINDER

BOOKS BY HAYLEY SMITH

The Perfect Girlfriend
Such A Loving Couple

THE CHILD MINDER

HAYLEY SMITH

bookouture

Published by Bookouture in 2024

An imprint of Storyfire Ltd.
Carmelite House
50 Victoria Embankment
London EC4Y 0DZ

www.bookouture.com

ISBN: 978-1-83525-545-2
eBook ISBN: 978-1-83525-544-5

For my children: Nicola, James and Joel

THE CHILDCARE CIRCLE

MONDAY
Stacey (& daughter Coralie, age 7)

TUESDAY
Kim (& daughter Dulcie, age 6)

WEDNESDAY
Rhiannon (& daughter Freya, age 8)

THURSDAY
Nina (& son Bobby, age 8)

FRIDAY
Jarvis (& son Hayden, age 7)

PROLOGUE

Behave normally.

Smile if you can.

Mention the weather.

It's the first day after the half-term break and just a routine drop-off. No one knows what we know about last weekend. They can't possibly suspect anything; the tight-lipped stories in the local newspapers aren't giving much away yet, and their focus is clearly on a murder at one of the big houses in town rather than what happened at the beach house by the sea.

'Good morning, everyone, and welcome back.'

The deputy head opens the heavy gates, and we all filter through.

Usually, most of the parents would be quick to disperse, kissing their children and making a dash back to their cars. Not today though. Huddles form. People want information; they want to know what other people know.

The four of us, though, avoid eye contact as we busily fuss over our children: their book bags, lunchboxes, instructions for home time.

I hear *murder investigation* and *disappearance* – the words float to the top of everyone's conversation. Tess, the childcare circle co-ordinator, strides towards me.

'Any news?' she enquires. 'All the teachers have been asking.'

'Nothing,' I reply. 'I only know what's been reported in the media.'

I edge towards the school gate to make a getaway.

'Have you sorted out who will be covering the childcare with one of your team missing?'

Missing.

I force down the bile that has risen into my throat and blink away the image of blood running between the floorboards, soaking into the grain of the wood, pouring out of the wound like it will never stop...

'I'm going to do the extra day this week. I can put annual leave in.'

'OK. Well, keep me posted,' says Tess, and finally I can turn and exhale between my teeth, unclenching the fists in my pockets as the school gates beckon.

How did it get to this? How could an arrangement that seemed like such a good idea leave us in such a state of fear?

And how will it all end?

Because five parents and their children went away for a weekend.

But not everyone came back.

PART ONE

ONE

The Childcare Circle was an initiative that started at the primary school a couple of years ago.

It was a voluntary arrangement – a great alternative to expensive childcare – overseen by a co-ordinator who sorted everyone into groups according to their availability. There was an agreement to be signed and official background checks done for protection and peace of mind. Each group had a get-together before they started out, to agree a set of rules: things like not allowing age-inappropriate films or video games; respecting dietary requests; and preferred ways of disciplining the children.

Each member of the group was allocated a convenient day when they would pick up the children from school, give them a meal and entertain them until their parents collected them at six o'clock. This meant that everyone in the circle got four days of free after-school childcare.

It seemed like the perfect solution.

Before the start of term, seventeen interested parents attended a meeting with the co-ordinator. Stacey nervously hung around in the doorway until she felt a sharp tap on her shoulder.

'Hey, fancy seeing you here.' Rhiannon Ford beamed genuinely; her sculpted body was perfectly poised in a hugging blue catsuit.

'Wow, Rhiannon, you look great.' Stacey looked her up and down admiringly.

Suddenly, there was someone else beside them to muscle in on the conversation. 'What's this, a reunion of the Street Dance Winners' Team from... oh God knows when, I can't remember what year it was?'

'Nina!' Stacey rubbed a tic that had just started in her jaw at the sight of another blast from the past. It was 2006, she almost said, a year she would never forget. But she didn't want to talk about that; she didn't want them to remember what had happened. 'It's a son, you have, right?'

'Yes, an eight-year-old boy with the attitude of a teenager.'

Rhiannon rolled her eyes. 'A daughter for me, but yeah, tell me about it.'

Stacey laughed. She was relieved to see their familiar faces – being sociable with strangers had never been one of her skills – but she became aware then that she'd taken a step back and wrapped her arms guardedly around her body.

'I can't believe that the three of us are here again,' said Nina, tossing back her dark, glossy hair. 'Together after all this time.'

'With our own children, now,' said Rhiannon.

'And all searching for free childcare,' added Stacey. 'This circle thing sounds like a good idea, doesn't it, because childminders around here just seem like they're non-existent.'

Rhiannon nodded. 'I've contacted everyone registered in a three-mile radius to try and get a place for Freya and they're all full.'

'Look, I will have a word with the co-ordinator because she owes me a favour, and make sure that we get put in the same group,' Nina said with a wink. 'I'd rather someone that I know and trust take care of my Bobby, because if you just look around and see who you *might* get...'

Stacey and Rhiannon glanced in the direction that Nina nodded, at a heavily tattooed, greasy-haired woman with buoyant breasts spilling out of a tiny vest top.

'See what I mean?' she whispered. 'She was effing her mouth off at the headmaster last term, right in the middle of the playground. You wouldn't want *her* being your Wednesday childminder, would you?'

'Oh gosh, no,' Stacey replied. 'So yes, please do have a word with the co-ordinator. I'm in complete agreement with you.'

Nina, as good as her word, got it sorted, and they were all assigned into a perfect group with lovely mothers who had clean, expensive houses. Stacey would have nothing to worry about.

Unfortunately though, a few adjustments had to be made before the September term started. One of the parents in their original circle dropped out and managed to get a nursery place instead, and the other one's availability changed, so right at the last minute, and only three days before the children went back to school, Kim and Jarvis were shunted into their cosy group.

Stacey was straight on the phone to Nina. 'Can't you pull any strings? Because, well, it doesn't seem right, does it?'

'Yeah, I know. You've got issues with Jarvis, haven't you? He's a man, a single parent and we all jump to conclusions, don't we? We think that men can't care for children in the same way as us mothers. But all his background checks have been done and there are no problems with anything.'

'But I'm not sure how Coralie will respond to him. And what if she needs help with the toilet or anything?'

'Hey, don't get stressed. Coralie's fine with male staff in school, isn't she? Just think of Jarvis as a bit like a teacher. He's an instructor at that posh gym near the retail park, so he's a sort of teacher anyway.'

'I know you think I'm being irrational, but... I don't know. I just wish the others had stayed in the group. Because Kim, too... She's not really like *us*, is she?'

Nina laughed. 'You mean middle class?'

'I don't want to appear snobby or anything, but...'

'It will be fine, I'm sure. Let's give it until half term and see how it goes before we start complaining and asking to switch other parents in. Yes?'

Give it until half term. Just seven weeks.

Despite their early misgivings around the new members and their anticipated unsuitability, the arrangement appeared to work adequately for everyone. Stacey, Rhiannon and Nina tolerated Kim and Jarvis without being overly friendly – viewing the arrangement on wholly professional terms – and didn't let them too closely into their lives. As long as their children were safe and well cared for, they were happy.

'We should celebrate our success,' Nina declared, a month into the initiative. She was the events' organiser for Van Ryan's, a swish, modern hotel on the outskirts of town, and she only needed the most insignificant excuse for a party. 'A seaside break! The first weekend of the half-term holiday. It can be a get-together combined with a team building sort of thing. With alcohol, obviously.'

Nina always knew what would work, and was well-respected by a queue of clients who used her skills in putting on company conferences. 'There's someone who will do me a favour. A contact I've made recently through the hotel. He'll let us have his coastal property for a weekend, and it's awesome. A massive five-bedroom house right beside the sea.'

The best thing was that there would be no cost to anyone:

Nina had some reciprocal deals lined up with her contact, and as long as everyone left a good review when it got listed on *Booking.com* it would be payment enough.

'Where will we be going?' everyone asked. And kept asking.

Nina tapped her nose.

The location was a mystery.

'The first exercise of the team building element is trust,' she told them. It was her all over: she loved power, control. Keeping things close to her chest right until the last moment.

Only on that last Friday at six o'clock, when they all met up to collect their children from Jarvis's house, would she give them the postcode.

All the secrecy, the uncertainty.

It should have been a red flag; it should have stopped them.

But it didn't. They all went anyway.

TWO

STACEY

Monday – four days before the weekend away

Stacey pulled on jeans and a jade knitted jumper, tidy weekday clothes for the school run; she straightened her shoulder-length blonde hair; she brushed her pearly teeth with a faked demeanour of order and efficiency, feeling her customary sting of anxiety.

'Come on, sweetie, finish your breakfast,' she called out to her daughter, Coralie, from the downstairs cloakroom where she was applying make-up: the natural-looking type that gave her a glowing complexion and made her eyes sparkle, not the tarty kind that women wore for a night out – so that the teachers would clearly know she was a decent mother and not in the lower class of parents who slobbed to school in leggings or even pyjamas.

Her husband, Xander, was still upstairs, tweaking his appearance before he left for work. The amount of effort he put in always made Stacey uneasy. Aftershave. Shoe-polishing. Even smoothing his eyebrows with a dab of Vaseline. Stacey had watched his preening earlier with an uncertain sickness in the pit of her stomach despite keeping a smile on her face. But when she remarked with a light, throwaway comment, 'who's all this for?' he seemed to get furtive, turning up the radio and pretending to listen to someone being interviewed on the news. He was a good-looking guy and she knew that he must turn heads in his office, but still...

She couldn't help but worry about *everything*.

'Come on, Coralie,' she called again. 'We don't want to be late. Just four more Cheerios for Mummy, please.'

Her phone pinged with a WhatsApp notification. It was Nina, suggesting that their Saturday night away could be a good excuse for fancy dress. Stacey's heart sank. She tossed her phone into her handbag and grabbed Coralie's coat from the cloakroom.

It had just started spitting with rain when Stacey returned from school. There was a letter on the doormat: a brown envelope with her address typed onto a label. She suspected that it was one of the Childcare Circle Newsletters like the one she'd had last month, giving out activity suggestions and tips on how to make your own play dough and organically remove nits. She took it through to the kitchen and put it onto the table without opening it.

Another notification pinged on her phone. It was one of the other parents commenting on Nina's previous WhatsApp message about fancy dress:

Shall we have a theme? Halloween maybe? Then the kids could be involved too.

Oh dear, no, Stacey thought. It's one thing for the children to dress up, and she didn't mind that, but the parents? Really?

Stacey didn't want to go. But she didn't want to look like a party-pooper either; she was the sort of person that always liked to get along with people and not let them down. So, when everyone else seemed up for it she found herself being rail-roaded along.

Childminders and children, that's all the weekend was for. Five parents and five kids, with no partners allowed. It was supposed to be an opportunity for the adults to get closer. To do the cringy thing that people called *bonding*. Not that Stacey, Nina and Rhiannon needed it. They'd known each other since secondary school – there was even a time in the past when they would have described each other as *best friends*, they were so inseparable – so it was just a matter of letting Kim and Jarvis into their clique.

No. Clique probably wasn't the right word. They weren't like that. Stacey was friendly with everyone and always had a smile. She could take a joke and didn't mind being a bit self-deprecating as long as it didn't go too far. But she was dubious about bringing Kim into her social circle because it was clear that they were from very different backgrounds. And then there was Jarvis...

Stacey clicked the kettle on and took a deep breath. Checked her Fitbit to see if her heart rate was normal. It had gone up a little so she closed her eyes while she exhaled mind-fully and imagined herself walking barefoot in a lush forest.

Ping.

Anyone else? What do we think about a Halloween theme?

Another WhatsApp from Nina. She could be so pushy sometimes, forgetting that other people were at work, maybe without access to their phones.

Stacey ignored the message and poured hot water onto a camomile teabag in her favourite mug.

Sitting at the kitchen table, she started to make a mental list of things that needed to be packed for the weekend away as she picked up the envelope that arrived in the post earlier. She slid her thumb under the glued flap and tore it open.

It wasn't the Childcare Circle Newsletter; it was just a flimsy piece of A4 folded over.

She unfolded it and stared at the words:

I know your darkest secrets.

None of you are what you seem. How could you ever have trusted each other with your children?

You have five days to tell the truth. Or there will be consequences…

A black cloud swam in front of Stacey's eyes. Her heart thudded in her throat.

What was this?

Who sent it?

How did they *know*?

She read the letter again, feeling sick and breathless. It was typed in the same size and font as the address label on the front. Second class stamp. And no clue as to where it had come from.

Her whole body trembled; her tongue felt swollen, enormous.

No!

How could anyone know? It wasn't possible.

She snatched up the letter and envelope, carelessly knocking the handle of her mug. It smashed to the floor, splattering tea onto her feet and ankles. Numbly, she watched the hot liquid run into the gaps between the floor tiles, the sharp shapes of ceramic scattered around her feet.

Ping!
A text from Rhiannon:

Have you had a weird letter this morning?

Stacey's mind clicked back into action and she scrambled to dial Rhiannon's number.

'Yes, I've just opened a really strange note,' she breathed. 'It's freaked me out. It's as if it's threatening something... I don't know... that our children might be at risk if we don't confess to something we've done. Who sent it?'

'Well. I wondered...' Rhiannon sounded like she had a bubble in her throat. 'About everything that happened, all that time ago.'

'What?'

'*You* were there, weren't you?'

A pain shot through the side of Stacey's head and she closed her eyes as a migraine took hold. 'What are you talking about?'

There was silence. Four seconds. Five seconds.

Stacey had the sudden thought that the sender might actually be Rhiannon. Did *she* know about her secret, somehow? 'Rhiannon? Are you still there? Did *you* send the letter?'

'Of course I didn't! Why would I send something like that? I've just *received* one, same as you.'

'Oh. I just thought...'

'It must be some kind of prank. It's probably Nina, as part of her quest to get us to do fancy dress for the weekend. Some of her practical jokes are a bit bizarre, aren't they?'

'Yeah,' Stacey agreed.

'Perhaps we should throw the letters away and forget about them.'

'Great idea. Anyway, see you later at pick-up time.'

They ended the call. Stacey picked up the teabag and all

the pieces of shattered mug from the floor and put them in the bin. She wiped up the spilled tea. She scrunched up the letter and envelope together in a tight ball and threw it on top of her favourite broken mug.

It was nothing to worry about, was it?

Stacey went into the living room, wedging fists into her eye sockets and dropping onto the sofa, succumbing to the migraine that had suddenly taken full hold.

But what if the letter was real?

What if someone truly did know something?

Monday mornings really were the worst. They seemed to be a magnet for extra stress, when all Stacey wanted was for life to be normal, routine, boring even. She could cope with boring.

She looked at the photograph that hung above the mantelpiece: Stacey, Xander and Coralie with their arms around each other as they grinned into the camera. The picture had been taken in woods on a fresh autumn morning, on one of the weekends that they'd earmarked as family times. In it, Stacey's face shone with happiness. She looked secure and complete, as if she had forgiven herself for what she had done in the past.

And Coralie. Her beautiful daughter right there.

She was seven years old and the joy of Stacey's life. A slight frame with willowy limbs, turquoise eyes and soft brown hair woven into two neat plaits. She loved guinea pigs and donkeys, and glittery gel pens that had stained many items of her bedding. She was shy but always laughed exuberantly at the corniest of jokes. The childcare circle had benefited her enormously, giving her confidence and new friends that had become her closest allies at school.

The weekend away though... They wouldn't have their normal time together as a family. Stacey and Coralie would be spending it with the rest of the childcare circle.

Coralie was so excited that she was beyond herself with giddiness.

But Stacey...

Her previous reticence about the weekend away was nothing compared to how she felt now. Because this letter – *five days to tell the truth.*

She had a feeling that something bad could happen.

A strong feeling.

THREE

STACEY

Monday – four days before the weekend away

The high street was quiet. At the florist, Stacey picked hardy blooms out of a display bucket and waited while they were wrapped in cellophane. This routine that she alternated with her mother was something she did every month, since the death of her father almost a year ago.

She stepped outside with the flowers in her arms and spotted Jarvis coming out of the newsagent's across the road. Head down, she began to stride towards the car park so that he wouldn't see her. Avoidance was key with him; it was how they made the childcare circle work on a professional basis. But she didn't need to worry: he was absorbed in a task that looked like he was using a little notebook or something. Hang on, no, he'd got a scratch card. Stacey watched as he wandered absentmindedly, riveted to his coin-rubbing. He shuffled the card to the bottom of his pile and started on another one.

What a surprise. He had a nice car and a respectable house, and he swaggered around in expensive sports gear. He didn't seem the type to do that sort of thing.

Just before he reached the end of the road, a smile sneaked onto Jarvis's face and he turned with a skip, to go back into the shop. He'd obviously scratched a winner.

In the graveyard, Stacey spent time cleaning the headstone. She allowed herself to think about her dad, to remember how he'd loved and doted on her. He'd always been willing to take her and her friends to their dancing contests, waiting cheerfully in the car for them after their shows.

Until that one event where they went for the full weekend, and it all went wrong.

Afterwards, guilt got the better of them both; it was like a see-saw. He continued to be quietly mortified by what happened and the effect it had on her at school, but Stacey also felt bad that her dad's life had been so damaged by a favour he'd done for her and her friends.

Talking about it was out of the question; it was something shameful and best buried. She had to keep reminding herself that her dad wasn't normally like that; it had just been a one-off. Fingers on lips, keep schtum; Stacey was used to keeping secrets. That was how it had to remain for the sake of her mother.

He never went to a pub again, though. He never touched a drop of alcohol, even at home, even at Christmas. The humiliation of losing his licence and losing his job poisoned him, left him a shell of himself, and the light in him just fizzled out.

Poor Dad. Stacey felt her eyes pooling with tears. She arranged the flowers into the vase and took a picture with her phone to send to her mother.

There were three notifications waiting, texts that must have come through while she was driving. All from Nina.

Have you had a strange letter? In a brown envelope through the post?

Then the second one:

Do you think it's real?

Then the last:

It'd better not be you having a laugh because it's not funny.

Stacey shivered as she slid her phone back into her pocket, suddenly aware of the bite in the wind. So, Nina wasn't the sender of the letters: she'd received the same correspondence as herself and Rhiannon.

But if Nina hadn't sent the letters, then who had?

Early afternoon on a Monday was the best time to do a big shop at the supermarket. The aisles were clear and there was none of that hustle and bustle you get when you go after work on a Thursday. Stacey was methodical, working through her list, putting each item neatly in her trolley.

Outside, she loaded the bags of groceries into her car boot and went to return the trolley. A familiar figure at the cash machine caught her attention. The green parka that she always wore; the imitation Doc Marten boots in a dull brown. It was Kim.

Stacey watched her as she locked the trolley into the row. Kim was engaged in the screen directions, pressing buttons, removing her bank card and... Wow, withdrawing quite a lot of cash. Stacey watched her pull out the thick wad of notes and tuck them into her purse. Not wanting to become embroiled in a conversation with her because she might feel obliged to offer her a lift, Stacey turned quickly away to get back to the car before Kim noticed her.

Back home, Stacey rummaged in the bin to retrieve the letter. Despite her resolve to forget about the matter, she flattened out the paper and stared at it again, because seeing Kim taking all that money out of the bank had set her brain thinking in a different direction.

I know your darkest secrets...

Was this actually a blackmail letter? Had Kim received the same thing, too?

Stacey had a joint savings account with Xander. There was no fortune stashed away in it, just money saved regularly that would pay for holidays abroad or home improvement projects. If she were to withdraw a large amount – and it looked as if Kim had taken out *hundreds* of pounds – then Xander would be sure to notice.

Would there be further letters to demand some kind of ransom for not spilling her dark secret? Would it be easier just to give in and confess?

Oh gosh, no.

She couldn't possibly do that.

With the thought of Coralie's beautiful face in the front of her mind, she screwed up the letter again and dumped it in the bin.

Her husband. Xander. Could the anonymous letter be connected to him? Something about their relationship currently felt off. The worry had niggled her for a few weeks that Xander might be seeing someone. Maybe it was a work colleague: a couple of new people had been taken on in sales last month. There were inductions where Xander delivered a workshop, and then everyone went to the pub for drinks afterwards. Xander arrived home late and dishevelled, with his phone continually pinging with texts that made him smile pensively.

Stop it. Stop thinking like that. She seemed to be driving herself mad with jealousy.

Maybe a weekend break would be good for her, if only to take her away from her normal routines. Maybe she would come home with a fresher mind that didn't continually analyse Xander's every sentence and every silence. Absence makes the heart grow fonder and all that.

Maybe it wouldn't actually be the arduous experience that she was dreading.

The house was quiet. There was a patch of blue in the sky and the breeze outside had dropped. Stacey made another cup of camomile tea in her second-favourite cup and took it outside, to the small backyard area she'd created where she could inhale the scents from the potted aromatic shrubs: rosemary, lavender, sage and mahonia. This was her chillout space, her grotto. Wrapping a fleecy blanket around her shoulders, she sat in her hanging wicker chair and closed her eyes, mindfully listening to the soothing tinkle of the wind chimes and feeling the weak sun gently kiss her face.

Cast aside the stresses of your life, she told herself. And breathe.

The five children were in high spirits when Stacey collected them from school, talking excitedly about their forthcoming weekend.

'Our hotel is next to the beach,' Bobby told them. 'My mum showed me the pictures.'

'It's not a hotel though,' Coralie corrected him. 'Because hotels are where people get served with food. This is just a house where we are all going to share.'

'Can I share with you?' Dulcie asked Coralie. 'Can we have bunk beds?'

'I think it's been decided that all the children will be sleeping with their parents, because the rooms have double beds,' Stacey informed the children.

There was a collective groan of disappointment, and Stacey laughed.

'So we won't be able to have midnight feasts,' said Freya in a bitter voice.

'It's going to be a lot of fun, whatever we do,' Stacey reassured them. She grabbed hands with Coralie and Freya and swung their arms high as they walked along past the shops.

Hayden saw them and tried to do the same between Bobby and Dulcie, but Bobby recoiled and stumbled off the edge of the pavement.

HONKKKKK! A car screeched as it slammed on its brakes. A cyclist tipped sideways and scuffed his bike on the kerb in the traffic commotion. There was a scream from a woman at the bus stop.

'Bobby!' Stacey let go of Coralie and Freya and ran to drag Bobby out of the way.

'Keep your fucking kids out of the road,' a man shouted through an open car window. 'I could have killed him.'

Stacey was too stunned to respond. She watched with a thumping heart as the cyclist adjusted his seat and did a hopping motion back onto the bike.

'Mum?' Coralie was tugging on her arm. 'Mum, Bobby is crying.'

Stacey hugged Bobby with trembling arms. 'Oh, Bobby, are you all right?'

He nodded and whimpered, wiping furiously at his tears. 'I didn't mean to go into the road. It was Hayden who pushed me.'

'It was not,' Hayden declared, pale-faced and adamant, 'you did it yourself.'

'No, I didn't.' Bobby shoved a fist into Hayden's chest.

'Boys, come on, stop it. We don't want an argument.' Stacey got between them.

Dulcie watched them all, chewing on her thumbnail. 'Are you going to tell his mum?'

'It wasn't my fault!' Bobby shouted.

'We won't tell anyone,' said Stacey. 'Luckily you haven't been hurt, so we'll go home and do some baking and forget that it ever happened.'

'Do we have to keep it a secret?' said Dulcie.

Stacey shivered at the word *secret*. She looked around. Had anyone seen what happened; was anyone taking note of her trustworthiness? Was anyone out there *watching* her? Quickly, she herded the children away from the road to walk carefully towards her house.

The kitchen table was littered with baking bowls, spoons, batter dribbles and flour. Cupcakes were in the oven, eggshells on the floor as Stacey sponged a stain off Freya's school skirt.

There was the sound of the front door, and then Xander appeared, waggling a bottle of wine.

'Hi, you're early.' Stacey's face lit up as she moved over to kiss him. 'This is a surprise.'

'Meeting got cancelled. So I just thought, early finish.' Xander pulled off his tie and looked around at the mess. 'All right, kids?'

'Bobby nearly got killed by a car,' said Freya.

'Shut up,' Hayden said as he stirred the melted chocolate.

Dulcie poked Freya on the arm. 'It's supposed to be a secret. Remember?'

Xander raised his eyebrows at Stacey.

'It's nothing. Bobby tripped off the pavement, and a car beeped its horn. That's all.' Stacey took the bottle of wine from him and put it in the fridge. 'I just thought it wasn't worth mentioning to the parents. Well, to Nina. You know what she's like.'

Bobby looked up. Xander threw him a half-smile. 'I think I'll go and get changed. Might just stay upstairs and watch a bit of TV while you lot are doing this.'

He retreated from the kitchen as Stacey opened the oven to a cloud of steam.

There was a sudden hubbub as Dulcie knocked the jar of coloured sprinkles onto the floor.

'It's OK, don't worry.' Stacey rushed to reassure her as Freya told her she was stupid.

Chaos had overtaken the session. Stacey looked at the clock: it would be another hour before the parents collected their children, and all she wanted to do was sit in her garden grotto with a glass of wine. Would it be so bad to just stand outside for five minutes and take a breath?

But she knew that she wouldn't. Because if the other parents couldn't trust her to look after their children, how could *she* trust them to mind Coralie?

'Come on.' She galvanised the group with a small spark of remaining energy and picked up the dustpan and brush. 'Let's start clearing up in here.'

Rhiannon was the first to arrive, two minutes early. All the children were waiting in the hall with their coats on, holding a decorated cupcake in each hand.

'Mummy!' Freya proffered a sticky bun towards her.

'That's lovely.' Rhiannon smirked towards Stacey, before conspiratorially lowering her voice. 'Any more thoughts on the thing we were talking about earlier?'

'What, that letter?'

But they were unable to discuss it further, as Jarvis and

Nina arrived at the same time. Bobby glanced nervously back at everyone as he was led out towards his mother's car skewed up on the pavement with its hazard lights flashing. No one mentioned the near-accident earlier.

Kim was sprinting gracelessly down the other side of the road as Jarvis took Hayden out.

'She's a bit late again, isn't she?' Dulcie acknowledged that her mother always seemed to be the last one to arrive.

'Only five minutes this time,' said Stacey, loud enough for Kim to hear as she reached the door, panting heavily and trying to apologise between breaths.

'Sorry. It's been a mad day.'

'Tell me about it,' said Stacey, even though she didn't really want to know. 'See you soon, sweetie,' she said to Dulcie, encouraging her out of the front door with a hand on her back.

There was an uneasy silence for a few seconds and Kim looked like she was about to say something important but then changed her mind.

'Thanks, Stacey.' She led Dulcie away, and Stacey closed the door firmly behind her.

Coralie called up the stairs. 'Daddy, you can come out now!'

Stacey went to the fridge for the bottle of wine.

FOUR

THE WEEKEND AWAY

Friday – the first night of the weekend away

'What on earth have you done to your face?' says Nina when she arrives at Jarvis's house on Friday at six o'clock to collect Bobby. 'You look like you've been hit by a bus.'

'Running injury: face plant on the kerb,' Jarvis replies, touching his hand carefully to a patch of extremely painful bruising. 'I should've tied my trainers with a double knot.' He holds up his left hand to display the Elastoplast on his knuckles and attempts a flippant wink, but it's not happening with the state his eye is in.

'Well, what you need to cure that is sea water and wine. And this weekend you'll have both. I hope you're all packed and ready to go.'

'Absolutely. As soon as you give me the postcode.'

Nina tosses back her dark hair and wags a finger. 'Hold your horses. I'm going to tell everyone as soon as they get here.'

She's been hanging on all day for the details which have only just come through as she pulled up outside Jarvis's, and she's copied them out onto slips of paper for everyone.

They don't need to wait long. It's only a matter of seconds before Stacey's car pulls up, closely followed by Rhiannon's.

'Guess who we're waiting for?' says Nina, with more than a touch of sarcasm. 'Again.'

But just as she has spoken, Kim appears, plodding along the road with a heavy rucksack on her back.

'OK then,' Nina says with a smile. She hands out a piece of paper each to Jarvis, Rhiannon and Stacey. 'There you go. Postcode for your satnav. There's apparently plenty of parking on the road at the front of the place which is called Kittiwake House. Safe travels, everyone.'

Jarvis studies the letters and numbers quizzically. 'Is that a postcode for the Hull area?'

Stacey hasn't looked at hers yet. She is rearranging her car boot so that Kim's rucksack can be slotted in. 'Hull? We're going on holiday to *Hull*?'

'Oh my God.' Rhiannon bursts out laughing. 'Is this another one of your pranks, Nina?'

'What? Hull?' Puzzled, Nina gets into her car and punches the postcode into her satnav, wondering if the owner of the holiday home is playing some kind of joke on her.

'You're scaring me now. I hate surprises.' Rhiannon's hand is tugged by her daughter, Freya, who is desperate to get into the car so that they can set off.

Jarvis and his son, Hayden, are ready with the engine running. 'Well, see you there, everyone.'

* * *

Stacey and Kim have run out of polite small talk within the first seventeen minutes of the journey. The decline of the high street. The busyness of the Friday commuter traffic. The weather forecast for the weekend and how bad the impending storm might be. The excitement of the children: they've talked about nothing else all week, haven't they?

A bulky silence hangs between them after that as Stacey follows the satnav instructions. She still has no idea where their journey will end. Somewhere near Hull, she supposes. The children, Dulcie and Coralie, chat effortlessly in the back seats, about school, about a dance they have been doing at Rhiannon's house, about the fun things that they will do on the beach.

'I'm so looking forward to this weekend,' says Kim. 'Aren't you?'

'Well...' Stacey shrugs. 'I could think of better things to do.'

'Oh. I thought it would be a good idea: that's why I suggested it to Nina.'

'*You* suggested it?'

'Yes. Didn't she say? It was my idea from the start. She just took the lead on organising.'

Stacey sniffs. 'Well, that's Nina. Trying to take the credit for everything.'

'Oh well, it doesn't matter. What's important is that we're all going to be together.'

Stacey doesn't reply. She is wary of letting Kim assume that they are more than just members of a group that has a mutual arrangement.

'You seem to know Nina and Rhiannon quite well,' says Kim. 'Are they good friends of yours outside of the child-minding circle?'

'I've known them for ages,' Stacey replies. 'We were at secondary school together. We were all in an award-winning dance trio. Can you believe it? Although afterwards we went off and did other things for' – she checks over her shoulder as she pulls onto the motorway – 'well, for about thirteen, fourteen years at least, until Nina and Rhiannon returned to live in the town. So, we're not *close* friends, like when we were teenagers.

This will be the first socialising we've done together since the days of our school discos.' She lets out a bubble of a laugh.

'And did you know Jarvis before?'

'Before what?' Stacey slams her brake on suddenly as a car pulls into the gap in front.

'Before the childcare circle.'

There's a pause as Stacey checks the rear-view mirror. 'No.'

The silence is back again although the kids are still prattling away behind them. Teachers they like. Teachers who tell you off for talking. Some boy called Euan who mooned in the middle of PE even though neither of them actually saw it happen.

Stacey switches on the radio then turns down the volume until it is white noise. Kim gnaws at her fingernails as she gazes out of the passenger window. The world slides past them: trucks moving stacks of pallets around; cars with drivers singing their hearts out; a family despondently standing on the hard shoulder beside their flat-tyred vehicle.

Then the rain starts pelting down. Stacey puts the wipers onto fast and reduces her speed.

'What nasty weather,' remarks Kim. 'I hope it's not coming with us.'

They travel carefully along, with the sound of the water battering the car and the gusty wind sloughing them towards the middle lane. Kim looks into the back seat to make sure the girls are belted up properly.

'So, tell me about you,' Stacey says. 'Have you always lived locally?'

'No, no. We only moved here a year ago, because the town had things that suited me. House. Work. A good school for Dulcie. Her previous one wasn't up to much.'

'So where did you live before?'

'Where *didn't* I live?' Kim counts on her fingers. 'Born in Lincoln. Then moved to a dive of a place in Nottinghamshire.

Followed by Sheffield. Then Grimsby. Then Derbyshire: the top crappy bit where all the drugs are. Then... hang on, did I mention Doncaster? No, so Doncaster was after Grimsby.'

'It sounds like you moved about a bit,' says Stacey. 'My parents never moved anywhere. I went away to uni but only for a year because I got homesick and dropped out, then I came back and lived at home again until I got married, and we bought the house where we are now. I'm a bit of a homegirl really.'

'I wish I could have been a homegirl.' Kim shrugs and looks down at her newly bitten nails in the half-dark of the car. 'My mum died when I was seven, so I ended up in care.'

'Oh no, that's awful, Kim. And is that why you moved around so much?'

'Yeah. Foster homes, children's homes, bedsits. It wasn't a great life. So, I've been determined to give Dulcie the best that I can. Get her into a nice school. Work for a living instead of relying on benefits.'

'Well, you're doing great. Dulcie is a lovely girl.' Stacey has a yin-yang moment where she feels bad about judging Kim, but is enjoying gathering this new information, knowing that it will cause a stir when she passes it on to Nina and Rhiannon. 'So, things must have turned out good for you house-wise? I've been hearing rumours that you live in the nice bit of town.'

Kim snorts. 'Is *that* what people are saying?'

'Well, I just heard...'

'I'm a bit of a magnet for rumours, aren't I? Always have been. People see me and make assumptions, usually not in a good way. I bet people don't do that with you, do they?'

Stacey's face has flushed and she can't answer. She turns up the radio a little and tries to hum along to Robbie Williams' 'Rock DJ'. Kim chews the nails of her other hand. The girls in the back are playing Rock Paper Scissors.

The satnav tells them that they are fifty-one minutes away.

Relentless, the rain throws itself towards them as if it's trying to prevent them from reaching their destination.

* * *

'Read out the letters and numbers to me, sunshine, so that we know where we're going.'

Freya gives Rhiannon the postcode in a clear, serious tone and she puts it into the satnav, waiting for a signal. When it's loaded, she minimises the screen to see the end location.

The place name is there in front of her. Her chest constricts. A phantom burning sensation in her throat makes her gag.

Christ, no. It can't be.

'Come on, Mummy.' Freya fidgets around in the back seat. 'Everyone else has gone now. We're going to be the last ones to get there.'

Rhiannon exhales and rubs her hands harshly over her face. She can't possibly return to *that* place.

'Mummy? We need to get going.'

'Freya, sunshine, I don't know... Maybe I'm not feeling too great, but...'

'No! Mum, we need to go!'

'But I'm not sure now if I'm feeling well enough to do the journey.'

'No! You can't cancel our holiday. It's going to be so much fun.' Her face crumples with the threat of tears.

Rhiannon reaches to the back seat to caress Freya's leg. 'Listen, we could do something nice tomorrow instead, like go out for the day and get ice creams. Visit the farm park? You like it there, don't you?'

But Freya is crying now. Full blown heartbroken waterworks.

Breathe, breathe, breathe, Rhiannon tells herself, closing her eyes.

'Mummy, I want to go with the others.' Freya sobs out the words. 'Everyone else is going.'

Am I just being selfish and irrational? Rhiannon thinks. Because, really, what will happen if I go back there? Won't it just look worse if I don't turn up?

'I don't want to go to the farm park. I want to be at the seaside place with all my friends.' Freya's face is red and wet, hurt with disappointment.

How can Rhiannon let her down like this? How can she be afraid of a *place*? It can't *harm* them. And it's not as if she'd be arrested there after all this time, is it? The whole incident has probably been forgotten, existing only in her remorseful memories.

'OK, sunshine. OK, don't cry. Look, I just had a moment, that's all, where I didn't feel very well and I wondered if it might be best to stay at home. But, no, I'm fine now and we'll go. We'll have a holiday at the seaside with all the others.'

Freya's mood changes in a snap. 'We're going? Yay!'

'We're going,' says Rhiannon. 'So, get that sad face cheered up right now.'

* * *

There's a catch in the back of Nina's throat as she pulls the car off the drive. That place. They're going back to stay in *that* place. What are the chances?

God, the memories of it all. Nina, Rhiannon and Stacey eighteen years ago: the three of them plastered with make-up, crop tops, shorts over tights, lips in pouts as they performed what they thought was the coolest dance in the show.

Nina recalls the scene wistfully. The exhilaration of winning, of having the weight of a medal around her neck.

It could have been the best weekend of her teenage years. Should have been. But then there was all the drama with Stacey's father: had she really never noticed what was going on with him and that woman who seemed to turn up at most of their contests? How could Stacey have been so blind to what was obviously an affair?

That will be a topic to avoid. He's dead now, isn't he?

She will be gracious and not mention it this weekend. God, she hadn't even known that they would be going back there, to *that* place. It was just a bizarre coincidence – wasn't it? – and she would never have arranged it if she'd known.

Never.

Because... well, because.

She shivers and flicks on the windscreen wipers as the first raindrops start to splatter down.

'Mum, did you bring my shorts for the beach?' Bobby taps at the back of the driver's seat.

'Yes, chick, I packed everything. It might be a bit cold for swimming though.' Nina has two enormous holdalls in the boot, along with all the boxes of food and drinks. She has brought enough alcohol to stock a city centre bar.

'I could paddle though, couldn't I?'

'You sure could. And there are some nice little rock pools to play in.'

'We'll be able to just go out of the house and onto the beach, won't we?'

'Well, it's on a cliff, but there might be a path down from the house.'

'And we can just go on our own without the adults, can't we? Because you'll be able to see us from the windows.'

'Er no. You don't go anywhere on your own. And certainly not the beach.' Nina has a proper flashback then. The heavy, wet sand; the hysterical laughing that turned to sobs; Rhiannon's screams at the sight of the police.

'I bet everyone is going to love this place. They will, won't they, Mum?'

Nina pauses. She thinks rationally about what memories it might dredge up for Stacey and Rhiannon. Good ones and bad ones. Then suddenly she wonders how *she* will feel when she's back in that town, or on that beach.

Bobby prompts again. 'They'll think it's the best holiday ever, won't they, Mum? Because it will be, won't it?'

Nina coughs out a cold laugh as the doubts start to plague her. 'It will be what we make it, chick.'

The satnav butts into their conversation then. *'Keep right at the next junction.'*

She slows the car to forty: visibility is appalling and the wind keeps skewing them over the white lines.

'Won't it be funny,' says Bobby, 'if it rains so much that it floods all the roads and then we get stuck at the holiday place for weeks and weeks?'

'It would be pretty disastrous if that happened.' Nina shudders and bites her lip. Touches her foot to the brake again.

* * *

'OK there in the back, dude?' Through the rear-view mirror, Jarvis checks out Hayden, who is watching a cartoon on his tablet.

Hayden nods. 'Are we nearly there yet?'

'Half an hour to go.'

'Why have you still got your hat on? It's boiling in here.'

'Well...' Jarvis laughs, thinking quickly. 'I don't have as much hair as you and so my head gets colder.'

'You keep touching it though. It looks weird when you do that.'

Jarvis has been feeling around his injured, throbbing scalp throughout the journey, mapping out the lumps and crevices, pressing the tender bruising, checking for any wetness that might suggest his wound has reopened, and wondering if his skull might be fractured.

'Oh, I just like the feel of the fabric, that's all.' Immediately, he regrets saying that, because it's the sort of thing that Hayden will take the mickey out of.

'Have you been to the barber's and they've made your hair look stupid?'

Jarvis laughs. 'No, I haven't had a haircut.'

'I bet you have. I bet you've had it shaved off. Let me see, let me see.' Hayden lurches forward and tugs the hat off his dad's head.

'Ouch!' The pain is blinding as Hayden's hand knocks against the deep laceration, and Jarvis reacts instinctively by slapping at his arm.

There's a squeal from Hayden, and a screech of tyres followed by a livid and lengthy beep from a car in the outer lane as Jarvis swerves over the white lines.

'Give me my hat back.' Jarvis's hands tremble as he realises that he almost hit another vehicle. He could have killed them all: the family in the car beside them, plus himself and Hayden. He really needs to get his shit together and calm down. 'Give me my hat back, please.'

Wordlessly, Hayden tosses it to the front of the car.

Jarvis grips the steering wheel rigidly, agitated, clammy-handed.

'Sorry, dude,' he says to Hayden. 'I didn't mean to go off like that. I'm just stressed.' He carefully arranges the beanie on his head again, and Hayden returns to his cartoon.

Through the driver's side mirror, Jarvis spots a flashing blue light. He checks his speed, lowering it so that he's running just under seventy. The emergency vehicle gains ground until Jarvis can see that it is a police car.

What if it is looking for *him*?

What if it is going to pull him over and arrest him on the hard shoulder, dragging him out to handcuff him in the thrashing rain right in front of his son? His heart pounds ferociously as the car reaches them, and then it pulls into the outer lane so that they are neck and neck, and the two officers in the car actually turn and look at him as he is visibly shaking in anticipation...

Then they're past him, a car's length in front, two cars, three cars, zooming along through the rain and road spray until Jarvis finally grasps that they are going after someone else.

Not him.

He slumps with relief. On the satnav it says that they are twenty-four minutes away from their destination.

Hayden squirms in the seat behind him. 'Are we nearly there yet?'

FIVE

KIM

Tuesday – three days before the weekend away

'A word in the storeroom please, Kim.' Mr Borg, the coffee shop owner breezed past, tapping her on the shoulder.

This was likely to be bad news. Words in the storeroom were never about anything positive. Kim wrung out the mop and left it by the bucket.

'I've just got to have a quick meeting in the back,' she whispered to her daughter, Dulcie, who was busy colouring at one of the tables. 'Don't go anywhere. I won't be long.'

She tucked her hair behind her ears and went to the storeroom, which was actually a garage in the back yard. Mr Borg was leaning up against a freezer, tapping a message into his phone.

'You wanted a word?' Kim said in her brightest voice.

Mr Borg held up a finger while he scrolled around, then after another half a minute of delays he put his phone away and looked at her.

'Yes. I did.' His face was stony, as always. 'It's about your holiday request. Unfortunately, you didn't give enough notice so it can't be approved.'

'But I don't normally work Saturdays anyway. I'd only swapped with—'

'It's not really my problem that you've swapped. We need weekend cleaning cover and your name is on the rota.' Mr Borg didn't let her finish.

'I have the opportunity to take my daughter to the seaside and we don't normally—'

'Not my problem,' he interjected.

'Please, Mr Borg.' Kim hated having to beg. 'Please, if you could just allow–'

'I already allow too much. I let you swap shifts, I let you have flexibility so that you can do your other job, and I let you have your daughter here while you work. Maybe you should try to find another employer that will do these things.'

Kim knew that she had lost the argument. But the holiday was too important to give up.

'What if I could arrange to swap back again? Would that be OK?'

'If you want to sort it out then it's up to you. But it's not my problem. So, back to work. I want that floor spotless before you leave here today.' Mr Borg shooed Kim away like a dog.

'Is everything all right, Mum?' Dulcie asked when Kim returned to the coffee shop and picked up her mop.

'Everything's fine, darling.' Kim slopped the murky water around, wondering how she could rearrange her shifts. They *needed* this holiday. Almost more than she needed this job.

Kim Taylor had to juggle three jobs. There was her position at The Blue Bean coffee shop, cleaning five mornings a week, with an additional two lunchtimes washing pots. There were random evening shifts working in Bart's Burgers, a grim and greasy takeaway in the shadier part of town. And for three afternoons a week there was her job doing cleaning and personal care for an elderly client, Mrs Coates, which was a private arrangement where she was paid in cash.

And then there was the childcare circle. But that was only for a couple of hours after school on a Tuesday; she liked the kids that she minded and Dulcie benefited from being around them.

So, her life was busy, and very different to the other parents' lives in the circle. Kim listened to Stacey, Nina, Rhiannon and Jarvis as they constantly claimed to have stressful lives, complaining about things like their online shopping order, and how disgraceful it was that they had their fresh pasta switched for easy-cook rice. Or how the air conditioning kept glitching in their new car. Or how they wished they'd had a proper York-stone patio laid instead of composite decking because, even though it would have been ridiculously expensive, it would have been more in keeping with the style of the house.

Kim listened all the time, knowing that she could never afford the things that they bought.

But she didn't mention that to the others. She felt lucky to have a home and work and a healthy, gorgeous daughter. She had never been to university or had the same opportunities as the other parents. Her upbringing had held her back, stifled any aspirations, any thoughts of higher education or a well-paid career.

Something might change at some point in her life, she often told herself. Things might improve, and then she could buy better food or nicer clothes or even a proper haircut at a hair-dresser's. She kept her ambitions achievable so that she wouldn't be disappointed. She kept herself to herself as much as she could.

It was Kim's childcare day and so she checked the weather forecast regularly to see how cold or wet it would be when the children came out of school. She knew that she wouldn't be able to do her sessions in the local park for much longer because the nights were drawing in.

So far, her childcare plan had worked well: she had organised activities to engage the children such as games of rounders, mini-Olympics, den-building and hide-and-seek. All the children said how much they enjoyed playing outdoors, and luckily it had never yet rained on a Tuesday. But after the half-term holidays... well, she would need to look into using the local play centre and there would be a cost to that.

At nine thirty, when her shift ended, Kim returned home to prepare for the childcare session. She'd had the idea of doing a scavenger hunt and getting the children to collect such things as an acorn, a dandelion leaf, a feather. With a pen and five pieces of paper she started to write a list for each child. A piece of bark. A conker. A smooth pebble.

She added more items until there were twelve: that would keep them busy for a while. Then she had to go and prepare their picnic. She left the lists on the table. Next to them was that other piece of A4, the one that made her nauseous every time she set her eyes on it.

I know your darkest secrets.

None of you are what you seem. How could you ever have trusted each other with your children?

You have five days to tell the truth. Or there will be consequences...

What would she do about it? She couldn't bear to think of

how to handle the situation and it had eaten away at her all night, leaving her light-headed and groggy. She imagined the others all opening the same letters, although no one had mentioned it in their WhatsApp group. No one had mentioned it when they all went to pick up their children from Stacey's house last night either. Had they even received them?

Kim's darkest secret sat in her soul like a rock. The regret never left her; it was as constant as the sun, reminding her daily of what she did all those years ago.

She picked up the letter quickly, to scrunch it and throw into the bin bag of rubbish waiting in the hall.

Mrs Coates, Kim's elderly client, lived on the far edge of town, a good half-hour's walk for Kim. Carmel, her house, was nestled among a cluster of imposing trees at the end of a long, neglected drive. It looked like it had once been an opulent residence, but indoors it reeked. Age, damp, an infestation of rodents, and Mrs Coates's deteriorating toilet habits had all impacted on the ambience of the place.

On her first visit, Kim had held her breath and pinned a smile to her face, making positive comments about the impressive fireplace. Within eleven minutes of the interview, she had bagged the job without having to complete any forms or go through a criminal records check.

Mrs Coates told her afterwards that it was because she had shown a zealous interest in Vincent the parrot – a large African Grey whose party piece was shouting 'shut the bloody door'.

'There is another condition to your role here, though,' she had insisted firmly. 'Which is complete confidentiality and discretion. I don't want you to tell anyone that you work for me. I'm a proud woman. I don't want all and sundry thinking that I can't look after myself. So, I will pay you in cash weekly and no one else needs to know about anything.'

Initially, Kim was unsure how to approach this new post, having never worked with elderly people before. It was apparent that the woman needed assistance with personal care: she smelled like she hadn't had a bath for months, and her clothing was badly stained. Her diet was poor and comprised mainly biscuits, and tinned soup that she heated in the microwave.

Diplomacy and caution were key. 'What would you like me to start with?'

Mrs Coates tentatively proposed reorganising the kitchen cupboards, but Kim had the sense that it wasn't really what Mrs Coates wanted. It definitely wasn't what was needed.

'Would it be all right if I suggested some chores? Because I don't mind getting stuck in. I'd really like to do jobs that would make your life more pleasant.' Kim smiled. 'And obviously, make Vincent's life nicer, too. Do you think he might like that?'

'Vincent isn't as sociable as he used to be. I think he's embarrassed about himself because he has accidents and sometimes goes in the wrong place.' Mrs Coates lowered her eyes and twisted a huge emerald ring on her index finger.

Kim was sensitive to the tone of pain in the woman's voice and chose her words carefully. 'I don't know if it's because you've not been out for a while and you've become accustomed to it, but I'm finding it a little bit whiffy in here. Maybe Vincent is the culprit? I could clean out his cage, open the windows and air the place. He might benefit from a gentle misting to freshen up his feathers. And then I could maybe give you a shower and a little pampering, too?'

'Miss Taylor, that sounds like a perfect proposal. I think Vincent and I would very much appreciate that.'

This skilful conversation was what began the process of Kim taking on the role of personal carer to Mrs Coates. Tactfully, and through the third person of Vincent, Kim began to restore the dignity of her employer.

And so, on every visit, Kim started her work by scrubbing out the parrot's cage, then gently spraying him with water. 'Shut the bloody door,' he squawked, inching backwards and forwards on his perch.

The room still had a background fug of fust and urine, but Kim had plugged in some fresheners and always opened the windows while she cleaned. She prepared meals to leave in the fridge: sandwiches with the crusts cut off, pork pie with pickles and coleslaw, mushroom risotto that could easily be reheated. She did the laundry, and ventured into the front garden to hack back the bushes that scraped threateningly on the windows. And Kim also liked to cosset her employer by washing and blow-drying her hair, painting her nails, dabbing her cheeks with Olay moisturiser. Apart from the covert nature of her role, this was probably the most important part of her job specifica-tion. This was how she gained Mrs Coates's respect.

'The temperature seems to be dropping now, Miss Taylor,' was the first thing that Mrs Coates said when Kim arrived just before midday. Sun was streaming through the huge Georgian windows, but the warm rods of light didn't reach as far as Mrs Coates who was sitting on a velvet chair at the end of the room. She was draped with a gaudy crocheted blanket and wearing some kind of fox-fur stole around her neck.

'It's not too bad for the time of year,' said Kim. They always had to start with small talk for the first five minutes. 'I haven't seen any frost in the forecast yet.'

'It was very wet and windy last weekend. It can't have helped the horse racing.'

'No, maybe not.' Kim collected Mrs Coates's empty crockery from the walnut table next to her walking frame. Then she went to the huge kitchen at the other end of the house where she boiled the kettle and set out a tea tray. Mrs Coates liked her rituals.

Kim had got the job after replying to a handwritten advertisement in the newsagent's window six months ago.

Lady's Maid Required for Immediate Start. With some additional light cleaning and cooking duties. 1.00 p.m. – 5.30 p.m. three afternoons per week which may be flexible.

The eccentricity of the old lady had previously seen a number of employees vacate the post within a short period of time. But Kim had settled into her role and knew her place. She loved her job and respected Mrs Coates's wish to remain in her draughty old house surrounded by the dark antique furniture and the company of her parrot rather than go into a modern care home. 'You won't get me in one of those horrendous prisons for the elderly,' Mrs Coates stated regularly, 'I will die here, thank you very much.' At the age of eighty-nine, her flabby body was prone to rheumatic aches and pains. She struggled to walk, and her bed was located in what used to be the dining room. But her mind was still sharp with a rude sense of humour. Her hair was a white halo of fluff that she often tamed with a silver tiara, and she always made the effort to wear lipstick. She had outlived three husbands – the second had been very wealthy and had left her the house and a small fortune – and still occasionally spoke of the possibility of finding a new gentleman to fall in love with. She'd never had children, describing them generically as *sticky* and *unruly* and *calculating*. Once, when Dulcie had been mentioned in conversation, Mrs Coates rolled her eyes and made a vomiting gesture, so Kim had avoided the subject of children since then. Her only surviving relative was a vague great-niece of indeterminate age – 'I seem to think she's called Naomi, but how would I know when she never visits?' –

and she regularly talked of rewriting her will so that all her assets would go to the World Parrot Trust.

'Would you mind terribly if we didn't bother with the shower today, Miss Taylor?' Mrs Coates held a quivery, leathery hand to her chest.

'Is anything the matter, Mrs Coates?' Kim was surprised at the abandonment of their routine. 'Are you feeling all right?'

'I'm a little under the weather. Maybe daunted by the onset of winter.' There was a rasp in her voice that Kim hadn't noticed before. Was it the first sign of a chest infection?

'Well, if you don't feel like it, that's fine. We'll save it until Thursday then.' Kim pulled a chair up to the side of her employer and sat, taking her hand. 'You feel a bit cold. Would you like me to light the fire? I could bring a few logs in and get it roaring in no time.'

Mrs Coates shook her head and closed her eyes for a few seconds. 'Let's wait until November before we start lighting the fire. I can manage until then. When did you say the tree surgeons were coming to take those branches off?'

'Sometime later in the week. The man said maybe Thursday or Friday. So if I'm not here to deal with them, I've left the money in the drawer in the hall table. You'll be able to sort them out, won't you?'

'Of course I will. They do know what they're doing, don't they?'

'I went round the garden with them and showed them which trees need chopping back and they made a note of everything. I know you weren't completely comfortable about it, but it will give you peace of mind to get them trimmed. The neighbours were concerned that heavy winds could bring down the overhanging branches onto their conservatory. And you don't want to get sued for damage to their property, do you?'

'Yes. Yes, I see. It's for the best. I do realise.'

They sat in silence for a while, listening to the comforting tick of the grandfather clock and the sound of Vincent weaselling around the obstacles in his cage.

Suddenly, Kim had the sense that she needed the wisdom and life experience of this elderly lady. 'Could I possibly ask you something, Mrs Coates?'

'Of course, my dear. As long as it's nothing to do with sexual matters. I would prefer to keep those sorts of things private.'

'If you got an anonymous letter claiming to know something about you, some dark secret, would you take it seriously? Or would you just throw it away and ignore it?'

Mrs Coates turned and fixed a stare onto Kim.

'I'm just curious. Would you tell anyone about it? Or take it to the police, for example?'

'Are you being blackmailed, my dear?'

'No. No, it's nothing like that.'

'Shut the bloody door!' Vincent broke into the gravity of the discussion.

'Do you think the police could get fingerprints off a letter?'

'I should imagine so. But whether they would bother is another matter. Unless it was a serious threat to someone's life.'

'Hmm. So if it was more of a vague threat you think they wouldn't?'

'Is this about something in your past? Something that you've *done*?'

Kim tried to distract herself by looking at Vincent, hanging upside down with his beak poking through the cage bars. She wanted to rid herself of the images in her mind, the pictures that appeared without warning, of the small, lifeless body. She tortured herself, holding in the secret as if it was a breath. For the past eighteen years she had desperately wanted to talk to someone about it.

Kim nodded. Maybe it was time. Maybe she could come clean. Maybe Mrs Coates was the one that she could offload her darkest secret to.

'Shut the bloody door!'

Mrs Coates suddenly groaned and reached for her walking frame. The crocheted blanket slipped to the floor. 'Would you mind helping me to the toilet, Miss Taylor? I think those short-bread fingers are causing me some trouble.'

The moment was gone. Kim stood and took Mrs Coates's elbow.

SIX

KIM

Tuesday – three days before the weekend away

In the park the kids embarked wholeheartedly on the scavenger hunt. Kim waited on a bench in the centre of the grass, telling the children to keep her in their sights at all times while they were collecting the items on the list. *Don't talk to strangers, don't touch any dogs, don't eat anything you've picked.*

'And don't go near the lake,' Dulcie added.

'Of course.' Kim confirmed this rule, just the same as she did every Tuesday.

Bobby – Nina's son – asked if they could trade things with each other, and Kim agreed to allow this before all the children set off running towards the shrubs and trees.

Ten minutes later, Kim was still on the bench, keeping the children in her line of vision. There were excited squeals and the scene was becoming confused with a new group of children among the trees who were throwing balls to two boisterous spaniels.

Kim stood and shaded her eyes from the sun that was dazzlingly low on the horizon. Dulcie, Coralie, Bobby, Freya, she mentally ticked off. Where was Hayden? She picked up her rucksack, moving closer to the children.

'Hayden?' She hoped that he hadn't strayed too far. He was wearing a red coat, she remembered. Ah, there he was. Relieved, Kim hitched the rucksack onto her back and returned a wave to Bobby who was shouting that he only had to find three more items.

Then she saw the spaniels jumping around Hayden, heard a shout of, 'get down, Oakley, you're muddy', and realised the child was not Hayden; it was just someone else in a red coat.

'Hayden!' she bellowed, running towards the shrubbery, towards Dulcie and Coralie who were squatting on the ground with their collection of leaves and twigs and berries.

'Where's Hayden?' Kim shouted to them, her urgency making them scramble to their feet.

'I don't know,' said Dulcie. 'I thought he was with Bobby.'

Coralie's chin started to wobble. 'Are we in trouble?'

'No, no.' Kim sprinted into the rhododendrons, screaming out Hayden's name so that all the children – even the ones she wasn't minding – stood rigid and fearful as they watched her.

The moments of pure panic stretched out. Pigeons scattered guiltily from the higher branches, and a smattering of leaves zig-zagged onto the ground.

'HAYDEN!'

Kim panted and stumbled over exposed roots. What if Hayden had been taken? She looked around, unable to see any of the children in her care. Oh God, what if something had happened? What if something happened to one of the others while she was searching for Hayden?

Then Bobby appeared at the other side of the bushes.

'Have you found him?' Kim shouted.

'No. I think he might have gone down to the lake.' Bobby's face was white, troubled.

'Oh shit,' said Kim, despite her recent participation in the

WhatsApp debate about how the childcare circle members shouldn't swear in front of the kids. 'Shit, shit.'

She checked her watch. The scavenger hunt had started over twenty minutes ago. How long did a child need to be missing before Kim had to inform the police? Or – no, no, she couldn't bear to think about it – before she had to inform the parents?

'Bobby, go and get the others,' Kim told him firmly. 'All of you go back to the bench while I look for Hayden. Here, take the bag and be in charge of giving out the sandwiches.'

Bobby, just like his mother, was the type of kid that enjoyed responsibility. With a serious expression he put the rucksack on his back and went off to supervise the other children.

Kim tore through the woods towards the lake. Please, God, no. She blocked her imagination from visualising a child floating in the water. Which direction? She heard voices in the distance and through the trees spotted a flash of red.

'Hayden!'

Oh, no! NO! There was a dark-haired man with Hayden, holding his hand, pulling him along the path. The backs of them both were moving further away from her.

'Hayden!' she screamed, and his small pale face turned in alarm towards her.

Suddenly, she tripped on a rock, then she was flying through the air, arms out ready to break her fall...

Thud.

Her teeth bit into her tongue and a metallic tang flooded her mouth. She floundered on the floor, hands, chin and clothes scuffed with mud, hesitant with that initial shock and pain, beads of blood yet to break from her grazed skin. She pulled her sleeve away from a bramble. Fleetingly, everything went black and she forgot what she was supposed to be doing.

'Ouch. Oww.' Kim brushed earthy detritus from her face

and scrambled onto her knees; her jeans were ripped, and she cursed herself for ruining her only decent pair.

Behind her, there was the sound of heavy footsteps. Quickly, she stood, her body quivering. Embarrassment, fear, her hands stinging from the rough gravel. Then she remembered: she needed to find Hayden.

'Hey, what's going on?' A male voice, threatening yet recognisable.

She turned. 'What the... What are you doing here?'

'I could ask you the same thing.' Jarvis's piercing eyes burned into her. 'And I could ask you where all the children are that you're supposed to be looking after.'

'They're by the bench. We were doing a scavenger hunt.' Suddenly, Kim saw the flash of red behind him, the small peering face of Hayden, and her shoulders slumped with relief as she realised that he hadn't been snatched; he was safe.

Jarvis swivelled Hayden out and put him on show for Kim to see. 'Is this who you were looking for? My son, lost in the woods?'

Her cheeks were flushed with shame. 'They were all playing together. He wasn't gone for long and I came to look for him straight away.'

'He could have been abducted! It's this sort of incident that makes me think I can't trust you with my child.'

'I'm so sorry. It's never happened before. I don't take my eyes off them: you ask the others.' She began to move back towards the bench as Jarvis and Hayden followed her. 'I'm always completely responsible with the children.'

'Dad, it's OK. Kim is good at looking after us and we do fun things. We *like* her.' At least Hayden was on her side.

'Please, don't mention this to anyone else. Please?' She reached out to touch Jarvis's sleeve but he shrugged her muddy hand away.

They reached the clearing and the park bench where the

children were sitting with the sandwiches that Kim had made for them.

'Hey, Hayden, you're back!' Bobby waved. 'Come and eat your food.'

'Can I?' He turned to his father, who let him run and join the others.

'Why were you there?' Kim asked Jarvis. 'I thought you were supposed to be at work. That's why I look after them all on Tuesdays, isn't it?'

'Early finish. And I had to go to the shop so I came through the park and found Hayden wandering around on his own.'

'He wasn't just wandering around. All the children were on a scavenger hunt in an area where I could keep an eye on them. You shouldn't have just taken him without telling me.'

'Oh, it's my fault now, is it?'

'Mum! What happened? You've got mud all over you.' Dulcie jumped off the bench and ran towards her mother.

'I'm fine, petal. Just a little accident with a tree stump.' Kim turned and hissed to Jarvis, 'Please, let's not argue about this in front of the kids.'

Thankfully, he held up his hands and stepped back. She checked the time: it was twenty past five already and they needed to start walking back to the point from where the kids' parents had arranged to collect them.

'That was great work, Bobby, sorting out the picnic for everyone. Thank you.' She ruffled his hair as he beamed with pride.

'Did I get the most things in the scavenger hunt, too?' he asked, and Kim had to hurriedly count up all the activity debris in order to declare that yes, Bobby was indeed the winner.

She felt Jarvis's shadow over her, demeaning, judging the way she handled the kids, and sneering at the cheap food she'd prepared for them.

Well, she thought, at least she bothered to make the effort to entertain and feed them. On *his* day – Fridays – he usually just sat them in front of the television or let them kick a ball around the garden. No forethought went into his sessions, and the kids only ate microwave burgers or hot dogs. Dulcie had told her that he spent most of his time on his phone or laptop.

'I may as well take Hayden now. Then you'll only have the four of them to watch.' Jarvis was beside Kim again, coming to zip up Hayden's coat and jostle him off the bench.

Kim didn't reply. She gathered up all the rubbish from the picnic to stuff into the rucksack, seething at Jarvis's snide remark.

'Hey.' Jarvis caught her wrist and pulled her round to face him. 'Look, I don't really want to say anything to the other parents. We've all got to rely on each other to get by with work. But... I just need to know he's safe with you.'

Kim spoke with a tight voice. 'Of course he is.'

Jarvis glanced behind, rubbing a fist over his lips, deliberating. 'Look,' he said quietly, 'I know this might sound weird, but I just wondered if you got something yesterday.'

A breeze had started without warning and mobs of sycamore leaves stormed across the grass. Kim pulled up her collar as her heart started pumping in her throat.

'What?' she asked, but she already knew the answer.

'A letter,' said Jarvis. 'You got one too, didn't you?'

Kim walked back through town with the four remaining children. She was extra careful crossing roads, keeping them all within grabbing distance. A lesson had been learned at the park: Jarvis had caught her out and she didn't know how much she could trust him.

She saw him most mornings in his sportswear as he took Hayden to school. Trainers, leggings, tight-fitting T-shirts that showed off all his muscles. He was permanently tanned – prob-

ably from a UV sunbed – a deep golden colour that worked well
with his dark cropped hair, and he always smelt nice. Good
teeth. There was no doubt he was attractive and she watched
with interest at how women giggled and flirted with him in the
playground. He worked in the big gym on the retail park. Kim
had never been – you needed an expensive membership that
she couldn't afford – but there was a swimming pool and spa as
well as yoga and aerobics classes, and Rhiannon taught a hot
salsa group there on a Wednesday.

'If anyone wants a discount membership just let me know,'
Jarvis had put into the WhatsApp group during the early days
of their childcare circle. 'I can do fifteen per cent off with my
staff code.'

Only Nina had responded, throwing money at a full annual
pass that she'd barely used.

They were all still working out a pecking order, Kim
realised. It was obvious that Rhiannon, being a minor celebrity,
was at the top, closely followed by Nina. Money and assertive-
ness spoke volumes. Stacey and Jarvis were more difficult to
place, but Kim knew where she was. Right at the bottom.

Stacey was waiting outside Bart's Burgers when Kim
arrived with the children at five minutes to six.

'Hi, darling, did you have a good day at school?' Stacey
fussed over Coralie, zipping her coat up an extra inch and
tucking her hair into her hood.

'We did a scavenger hunt, didn't we?'

'Oh, that sounds like fun. Let me see your hands, sweetie,
they might be muddy.'

'Come away from the road,' Kim said to Bobby. 'You could
slip and fall into the traffic.'

Bobby obediently went to stand by the door of the takeaway. 'Why don't we ever go to your house? Why do we always
have to wait in the street?'

'Well, it's just easier this way after we've been to the park.'

Kim's face reddened, then she spotted Rhiannon's expensive new car pulling up. 'Look, Freya, your mum's here. Are you ready to jump in the back?'

Rhiannon put her car window down. 'So, are we all looking forward to the weekend? Do you have transport sorted out, Kim?'

'We'll have to get a bus if no one can give me and Dulcie a lift. But I can't book tickets until Nina lets us have the postcode. So, I'm hoping that she'll tell us before Friday.'

'Aha, who's mentioning my name? Nothing bad I hope?' Nina strode into the huddle from nowhere, auraed by a blaze of musky perfume.

'We're just discussing the weekend. How we're getting there. And when you're going to tell us the location,' said Stacey.

Nina tapped her nose. 'Patience, patience. All in good time.'

'But Kim needs to book bus tickets: she hasn't got a car like the rest of us,' Rhiannon added, reminding everyone what a loser Kim was.

'Ah.' Nina scratched her head. 'I didn't think.'

'Can't they come in *our* car?' Coralie was listening in to the conversation. She pulled on her mother's hand because Stacey appeared not to have heard her suggestion. 'Mum? They could come with us, couldn't they?'

Everyone turned to Stacey apart from Kim, who looked at the floor. The delay was excruciating.

Stacey shrugged her shoulders. 'Well, I don't know how much space we'll have but, yeah, we could try to squash you in.'

'There's *plenty* of room,' said Coralie as Stacey visibly squeezed her wrist.

'Obviously, we could get the bus if we knew where we were going.' Kim looked at Nina.

Stacey looked at Nina, too. 'Well, yeah. If we knew where we were going.'

Nina held up her hands. 'Wait and see. And car sharing is good for the environment.' She steered Bobby away from the group and down the road.

Stacey stood back to let Rhiannon's car move away.

'Is that OK?' Kim said, sheepishly, dodging out of the way of a Bart's Burgers customer. 'You know, about a lift on Friday? I don't mean to be—'

Stacey flapped a hand at her. 'Don't worry. It will be fine. Just don't pack loads of stuff.'

'OK. Thanks, I really appreciate it. And sorry about the mud on Coralie's hands...'

But Stacey had already turned to leave, had already dragged Coralie away from Dulcie, who was skipping down the alley beside the burger shop.

Kim blew out a breath, relieved that their transport had been sorted.

Suddenly, her phone pinged in her pocket and she took it out to read the text.

Time is ticking away.

Have you confessed yet?

Would you rather pay a fee than have your darkest secret exposed?

If so, just reply by texting the word YES and you will be sent further instructions.

Kim's knees buckled for a second.
WHAT?
What was all this? Who had sent it?
She checked the sender's number but it wasn't in her contacts.

'Mum!'

Kim was knocked out of her involuntary panic by Dulcie's voice, and she scanned the street around her: people on their way home from work, people waiting for buses, people going to buy food. No one obviously watching her.

She reread the text; a muffling, throbbing sensation in her throat threatening to choke her. Confusion rattled around her head: this was obviously some kind of addendum to yesterday's letter. But what did the sender know? What did they know about *her*?

It wasn't a joke, was it?

It was real. The situation had just gone up a gear. It felt... dangerous.

'Mum! Come on, let's go home,' Dulcie shouted. 'It's freezing out here.'

What do I do now? Kim asked herself.

Someone was seriously messing with her mind. She looked around again. Was she being stalked? Was she being targeted? Blackmailed? Maybe she was being watched from a darkened upstairs window, or from a security camera.

Someone certainly knew something.

The weekend away had been all she'd been able to think about, but this new development had disrupted everything.

With a trembling, guilty thumb she quickly deleted the text and turned to follow Dulcie.

SEVEN

THE WEEKEND AWAY

Friday – the first night of the weekend away

Jarvis is the first to arrive at the beach house. He pulls on his handbrake as the windscreen wipers sweep away sheets of torrential rain, and he peers at the looming property. With the woeful help of the energy-saving streetlight, he can see that its once-white render is rust-streaked and fragile. One of the second-storey windows is boarded up; the television aerial dangles intrepidly from the front chimney. The garden contains an overturned dustbin and two broken plastic chairs. It's like a haunted house from *Scooby-Doo*; he thinks it is hard to see how the interior is going to match up to the impressive photographs that Nina has told them about. He can imagine that many years ago the place would have been a smart Victorian home with a delightful sea view, but now...

Hayden looks up from his tablet. 'Is this it?'

Jarvis grunts and shrugs, unsure. He double-checks the postcode on the slip of paper that Nina gave him, then googles it on his phone, too. He reluctantly ventures out of the car and into the rain, scanning up and down the road: maybe there's some confusion with the location and the correct property is a bit further along. But he can see nothing apart from a small wooden chalet-bungalow wedged into the hillside up the road.

'Come on out.' He raps on the car window. 'We'll go round the back and take a look. Put your hood up.'

Hayden scrambles out of the back seat, disappointment evident on his face. 'It looks a bit spooky.'

Jarvis puts his phone into torch mode, and just as they step onto the drive there is the sound of another car arriving to park up behind his own. He looks back to see Nina getting out, her face a picture of bewilderment under the streetlight. She flings an umbrella up over her head before approaching him, one hand trying to hide her aghast expression.

'What the actual fuck?' she mouths to Jarvis, obviously assuming that Hayden can't lip-read. 'This can't be it, can it?'

'You tell me. You booked it. I'm going to have a look round the back. Perhaps we're not seeing its good side.'

'Actually, it *is* the place.' She points to the front door, where the name is displayed on a board above, in flaky paint. Kittiwake House. 'This is the right one. Oh, my goodness.'

'Well, let's check it out. It might be better from a different angle.'

Nina shouts to Bobby, who follows them around the side of the house to the back garden where they are blasted even more by the rain and sea spray.

'God, this is bracing,' says Nina, battling with her brolly. 'And the last bit of the journey was horrendous. Did you have to drive through all that water just before the caravan park? I thought my car was going to give up in the middle of it.'

'I know. It was pretty hairy, wasn't it? They could do with putting some kind of diversion in place because it's only going to get worse.'

'I'm not sure if that's the only road into the town. Let's just hope Stacey and Rhiannon make it through or we could be having this luxury place to ourselves.' Nina puts her face to one of the windows and cups her hands around it, but it is too dark to see inside. 'There's supposed to be a key safe next to the back door. Can you see it yet?'

'Yep, it's here,' Jarvis replies. 'What's the number?'

Nina gets her phone to locate the text which had the number on it. 'Hang on a minute, my phone's ringing. I'll just have to take this call.' She instructs Bobby to stay under the porch with Jarvis and Hayden while she makes her way back to her car, out of the hideous weather.

'Hi!' She answers as brightly as she can while considering how to manage this faux pas of a holiday booking.

'Hello, is that Nina Ronson?'

'Yes, speaking.'

'I'm calling from the Royal Hospital...'

'OK...'

'I'm calling about your aunt. We have you down as her next of kin.'

'My aunt?' Nina tries to reach into her memory regarding her family tree. 'I don't have an aunt.'

'Mollie... she was admitted...' The intermittent line crackles and breaks up. '... a fall and... injury...'

'Oh. Yes, OK. She's actually my great-aunt. My grandmother's sister. I've never really had anything to do with her. To be quite honest with you, I assumed she'd died years ago.'

'...Found   unconscious   by   a   tradesman...   ambulance... records we have... next of kin...'

'Sorry, you're cutting out and I can't hear you properly. You're not wanting to discharge her and send her to my house, are you?' Nina says in horror. 'Because she can't come to me.'

'No... duty to inform you... prognosis isn't good... you might want to be here with her.'

Nina checks her watch, knowing that everyone else is going to be arriving at any point soon and she's going to have to deal with their questions, their blame. 'Well, I'm afraid I'm away this weekend so unfortunately I'll have to decline. Sorry.' Nina ends the call abruptly, and she groans as she sees the beam of headlights behind her from Stacey's car.

It's probably best if I just face Stacey and Kim head-on rather than listen to their whinging observations of the obvious, she thinks. It's how I would handle this kind of situation at work.

The rain has subsided a little, and she steps out of the car and into the road at the same time as the other two women, sweeping an arm out to introduce the house to them.

'OK, ladies. Clearly there has been some kind of cock-up with the property. It appears that I was sent the wrong photographs, so I sincerely apologise to you both for something that is out of my control and not my fault.' Nina delivers her statement confidently as Stacey and Kim take in the uninviting vision of their weekend holiday retreat.

'There's no wonder he let you have it for free,' says Stacey. 'Is it even furnished?'

'Have you been inside yet?' Kim asks.

'I was hoping we'd come to the wrong place,' Nina replies, frantically scrolling through her emails. 'But no. This is it. Jarvis is round the back with the boys.'

'Maybe it's best if we just go home,' says Stacey as the girls jump out of the car with their bags.

Kim stands there, looking embarrassed. 'But we've driven such a long way.'

Nina's phone starts ringing. 'Oh, you can fuck off.' She jabs at the decline button as the Royal Hospital number appears on her screen again. 'Excuse my French. I've just had news that some distant elderly relative has had a fall. Like I really want to deal with that in the middle of all this.'

'Dulcie, get off the road, there's a car coming!' Kim rushes to drag her daughter onto the pavement as the lights from another vehicle sweep up the street.

'It's only Rhiannon.'

The car manoeuvres aggressively around to park in front of Jarvis's, before Rhiannon gets out and stomps confrontationally towards Nina. 'Oh my God, we nearly died trying to drive through that flooded road. I dread to think what all that water has done to my new car. And I can't believe you've brought us back here, to *this* place. What point are you trying to make, exactly?'

Nina blinks emphatically. Shifts into a hand on the hip stance. 'Point? Like memories, reminiscences, old friendships? Having fun and winning the dance competition all those years ago, which is what basically set you up for a career in choreography? If I'd done this deliberately then that would be the point, because it would be a nice thing to do. I've put time in voluntarily to organise a free weekend for everyone. But as the location was a mystery to me too, I don't think you have any right to make accusations.'

The streetlight catches Rhiannon's expression of awkwardness as she tries to backtrack. 'I'm sorry, I didn't mean... I don't know. It's like we all have different ways of remembering coming here, don't we?' She looks around at Stacey for support.

'It was a shock for me, too,' she agrees. 'But, yeah. Mixed feelings and all that. I certainly wouldn't have *chosen* to come back to this town.'

'So, anyway...' Rhiannon claps her hands together in fake jollity. 'Well, let's get into the place then and crack a bottle open. Make the best of it rather than standing out here getting soaked.'

Stacey grimaces and nods her head towards the forbidding silhouette of their holiday home.

'No!' Rhiannon casts her eyes over the squalid exterior. 'No way. You're having us on, aren't you?'

'It might be nicer inside,' says Kim. 'We've not had chance to have a proper look yet.'

Rhiannon dances and pumps her hands in mock excitement. 'Well, what are we waiting for? Come on, girls!'

She leads the way as they all traipse along the side of the house to meet the whining squall of wind that awaits them.

Dulcie clasps her mother's hand. 'Do you think it will be all right? Do you think we're still going to have a nice time?'

Kim squeezes her daughter's fingers reassuringly. 'Don't worry. We're going to have a *great* time. I can't wait.'

EIGHT

RHIANNON

Wednesday – two days before the weekend away

'I need the key for the dance studio.' Rhiannon popped her thin, angular face around the office door where Jarvis was on the computer typing an email.

'Oh, hey, yes.' He unclipped a key from a bunch hanging on a lanyard around his neck. 'Everything OK? Looking forward to the weekend?'

Rhiannon wiggled a flattened hand. 'Yeah. So-so.'

'I know what you mean.' Jarvis laughed. 'I hate surprises. Why can't Nina just tell us where we're going?'

'It's how she is. She's always been like that. A power thing, I suppose.'

'Hmm.' Jarvis's expression turned serious as he beckoned Rhiannon inside. 'Come on in. Just pull the door shut for a minute.'

'What?' Rhiannon, her lithe body clad in red Lycra, squeezed through into the untidy space. Was this something about the anonymous letter and text?

'I hate to ask for help, but I'm in a bit of a predicament. I lost my bank card yesterday and so I've had to cancel it. Only thing is, I don't have any cash and I need to put fuel in the car and do some shopping so that the kids will have something to eat on Friday.'

'So...?'

'So, I wondered if you could just give me a small loan until I get things sorted?' Jarvis dropped his head into his hands. 'I know, it's a crap situation and I hate having to ask favours from people.'

'So where did you lose it?'

'Probably in the park last night. I had it at the shop but haven't seen it since.'

'Ah yes, Freya said she saw you in the park yesterday. Have you been back to look?'

'Well, that's not the point, is it? I've cancelled it now. But I need money to tide me over. I'll give it back as soon as my new card comes through.'

'How much?' Rhiannon reached into her tote bag for her purse. 'I've got twenty quid if that's any use?'

Jarvis put on an apologetic expression. 'I could really do with more than that. I mean, just the petrol...'

'Well.' Rhiannon jiggled her toned shoulders and looked up to the ceiling. 'It would mean having to go to the cash machine after my salsa class.'

'If you could, that would be fantastic. I'd be eternally grateful.' Jarvis bowed his head and prayed his palms together to show his appreciation. 'A hundred should be enough.'

Rhiannon unlocked the dance studio feeling mildly irritated with Jarvis. Surely there must be someone else he could have asked for a loan. Family, friends, other work colleagues?

She didn't doubt that she would get her money back. It was just... well, it felt a bit wrong being asked. Technically, he wasn't even a work colleague: she only hired the studio once a week for her class and they'd never socialised together.

But... whatever. They were all going to have to muddle along at the weekend and hopefully it wouldn't be too painful. She'd go to the cash machine at lunchtime and get the money for him.

The dance class was full, as usual. Having a reputation like hers with the elements of stardom meant that there was always a waiting list. Rhiannon welcomed everyone with a smile as they put on their dancing shoes.

A thought suddenly struck her. The anonymous letter. Then that additional text last night. Could the sender be someone from this class? A disruptive student, jealous of Rhiannon's success. But why would they target Stacey and Nina too? Unless they also knew that they were together at the dancing contest all those years ago...

Rhiannon watched the dancers carefully as the music started, as she called out the instructions. Some of them had a high level of ability, as if they had done dancing before. What if someone *did* know about Rhiannon? What if one of these students had been *there*, that fateful weekend?

'One two three four cross body turn.' Rhiannon demonstrated with an invisible partner before picking someone out to do the move with.

A fixed smile on her face, she taught and encouraged the class. The music continued and the couples laughed and danced, crossing and turning, until they were breathless and sweaty, ready for a break where they reached for their water bottles.

Rhiannon took out her phone and opened up last night's text:

Time is ticking away.

Have you confessed yet?

Would you rather pay a fee than have your darkest secret exposed?

If so, just reply by texting the word YES and you will be sent further instructions.

Unsure of how to handle it, she had not yet responded.

She looked up. The class was waiting for her to start the music again. Rhiannon swiped away the text and smiled at her poised dancers as she resumed her playlist.

The lesson continued, and Rhiannon, in true professional mode, put her worries to one side and led everyone through their steps in the routine. At the end, they changed into different shoes and gathered up their bags.

Rhiannon watched with suspicion as her students filed out of the class.

Who could it be?

The unknown, anonymous sender had wormed their way into her head to rake up the past. How should she respond?

What could she do to prevent her safe, privileged life from being ruined?

Lunchtime was a small tub of green salad topped with chopped walnuts that Rhiannon ate in her car as she listened to her mindfulness app. Afterwards, she dashed to the cash machine to withdraw the money for Jarvis before returning to deliver it to his office. He was still on his computer and clicked quickly out of something that looked like a card game.

It's great when people can sit in an office and play Solitaire, she thought. Some of us have to do actual work.

'Oh my word, you're not just a celebrity; you're an absolute star,' he said in a cringy way as she handed the cash over.

'That's OK, just don't leave the country.' She recoiled as he stood to attempt a clumsy hug.

'Let me get you a drink or something,' he said, fussing around the mess on his desk.

Rhiannon backed out of the room. 'No need. I've just grabbed lunch and now I've got to drive into Nottingham for a meeting with a theatre group about choreography for their panto. No rest for the wicked, as they say.'

'Wicked?' Jarvis lifted his eyebrows. 'Have *you* got a dark secret, then?'

'What?' The words pressed a button that made her heart stumble over a beat. 'What do you mean?'

'I'm assuming you got a letter and a text like me and Kim did, and presumably Nina and Stacey too?' Jarvis's words punched her in the gut.

'So, all of us got them? It's got to be a prank, hasn't it? Something for Halloween, like a kind of murder mystery game. Don't you think?' She didn't want to be reminded of how she might be unravelled and exposed; she was still trying to convince herself that it was some type of scam.

Jarvis tipped his head. 'Hmm, it's not really how I saw it.'

'No?'

'Have you done anything about it?'

'What do you mean? Responded to the text? Of course not. It's obviously not real.'

'Well... I'm not sure.' Jarvis grimaced. 'So, you think it's something to do with the weekend? Like Nina, messing around?'

'I could imagine her doing that sort of thing.'

Jarvis folded the slim wad of cash from Rhiannon and tucked it into his pocket. 'Hmm. Secrets, though. Are you going to tell yours to anyone?'

Rhiannon felt the prickles at the back of her neck, the

phantom burn in her throat. 'Absolutely not. Anyway, I'm in a rush.'

She let the door slam behind her and marched to her car. Tosser. As if she'd confess to anyone else. Not even her partner Katya, her soulmate, her biggest confidante, had been allowed access to her darkest secret. She kept it locked away because if it got out and found the light it might just destroy her.

It was only as she slipped into the stream of traffic on the motorway that she recalled the conversation with Jarvis, and started to wonder... could it be him? Did he suspect something about her and was trying to tease out more information? Was he looking to expose her? Maybe he was jealous of her status and wanted to see her brought down.

She ruminated on this possibility as she drove, considering how their lives might have overlapped all those years ago. They were similar ages: he could so easily have been there at the dancing contest, or known the victim.

Suddenly she was back...

Back to eighteen years ago, remembering the police siren and the flashing light as Stacey's dad's car was stopped; the fear and knee-jerk guilt she felt as the officer peered gravely at them all in the vehicle. She remembered her own panicked reaction: screams, flailing arms, the way her manic eyes scanned the road as she threw off her seatbelt and tried to force her way out of the back door of the car. Stacey and Nina had been terrified, had tried to hold on to her, reassuring her that nothing was wrong even though something was obviously very wrong. Stacey's white-faced father was summoned out of the vehicle to be breathalysed and arrested.

And then there was the waiting. The uncomfortable plastic seats in the police station where they were made to stay for an interminable amount of time – something like five or six hours – until her mother came to pick them up.

Rhiannon's chest constricted and that old stabbing pain was suddenly back like it had never been away. She imagined the smell of bleach scorching her nostrils.

She remembered the heavy ball of nausea that had rolled around in her belly as she sat between Stacey, sobbing and inconsolable, and Nina, visibly hyperventilating, in that stuffy corridor where a female police officer with squeaky shoes wouldn't let them out, even though Nina kept begging and begging, saying that she'd left something behind.

It was this incident that ended the close friendship between the three of them. They had gone away to the dancing contest and won, yet their victory felt wrong. They returned to school dejected and damaged. Gossip was rife; shame and backstabbing split them apart.

But thankfully, the years in between had removed the sting of their childish disputes. Now they were mature adults, responsible parents, closer than ever.

Weren't they?

NINE

RHIANNON

Wednesday – two days before the weekend away

After a short and unproductive meeting about the pantomime, Rhiannon pulled off the motorway and was soon back on the outskirts of town. The trees – a riot of carmine and gold and russet – had only just started to shed their leaves, and the enviable houses on the suburban streets had their windows lit to show off their extravagantly sparkling chandeliers. Long drives, stone statues and tall chimneys were features of the mansions around here – The Elms – which made up the sought-after area for the wealthy. As a local celebrity, she should have been residing here; her level of stardom however hadn't yet placed her in the super-rich bracket.

She could have been living in one of these desirable residences, Rhiannon thought, somewhat ruefully, if her long-term relationship with Hans, a high-earning consultant in financial services, had succeeded. Finding him introverted and boring, though, she had unintendedly neglected him until he sought love elsewhere. It had been ironic that she'd found herself pregnant with Freya just a month after he had moved out and relocated to the Netherlands.

These days, though, on the whole, she was satisfied with her life. She'd been with Katya for six years and they were perfect for each other: creative, innovative and liberal. They'd met on the set of a musical where Katya was the lighting technician, and, after dating fervently for a year, bought an old garage site and project managed the building of a blocky modern eco-property that was clad on one side with copper.

Freya had never visited her father abroad, but she chatted with him weekly on FaceTime, and Hans made the effort to visit every six months, when he took her to the Meadowhall shopping centre to buy her a new wardrobe-full of clothes. Give him credit, he'd never shied away from his financial responsibilities.

But to have one of the millionaire mansions along this road, nonetheless...

Rhiannon daydreamed as she slowed down to gawp at the Georgian windows and stone-pillared porches.

Suddenly...

No way! It couldn't be her, could it?

There was Kim, further down the road, striding along, swinging a bag of groceries.

What business did *she* have around this affluent part of town? Rhiannon crawled along, watching with intrigue, as Kim turned into one of the sweeping driveways and pulled a bunch of keys out of her pocket.

Really?

Rhiannon craned her neck as she passed the house, observing Kim unlock the huge front door. It was a massive old place with loads of character, but quite dilapidated. Properly renovated, it could be worth a couple of million.

Shit!

She slammed the brakes on and her car skidded on a patch

of fallen leaves, stopping just in time to avoid the injured black cat lying helplessly in the road.

'Oh, no, the poor thing.' Rhiannon dashed out to tend to the animal. It tried to lift its head as she gently touched its fur, and she saw immediately that it was bleeding badly from one of its back legs. The pet needed to be taken to a vet quickly if it was to have a chance of being saved.

Rhiannon ran to retrieve an old coat that was left in the boot of the car for emergencies. But when she returned to the animal its eyes were closed and its body was lifeless. No, oh no! She stroked its silky fur dejectedly before lifting its floppy body onto the coat. Helpfully, there was a collar around the cat's neck, and a chrome tag displaying its name and address.

Georgie. 6 The Elms.

Poor Georgie, she thought. She would have to go and break the sad news to its owner. Maybe it was the place where she'd seen Kim.

* * *

It wasn't, though; it was the one next door. Rhiannon carried the cat up the long driveway and rang the brass bell on the entrance porch.

'Oh, is this my Amazon delivery?' The woman had a puzzled ridge in her brow as she opened the door.

'I'm so sorry.' Rhiannon's voice quivered as she offered out her coat that contained the deceased pet. 'I've found your cat at the side of the road. He was injured and I was going to take him to the vet but then he just...'

'My cat? Oh no, not Georgie. Are you sure?' The woman folded back the edge of the coat, revealing the soft black fur.

'He died just now. He must have been hit by a car sometime earlier. He looked like a lovely pet.'

The woman hugged her arms around herself as she blinked and pursed her lips. 'Oh no. The kids are going to be so upset. We got him as a kitten.'

'I'm sorry. I didn't want to just leave him on the road. You could maybe bury him in the garden.' Rhiannon looked around at the expansive front lawn, the rusting shrubbery, the tall, mournful trees.

'Yes. Yes, we will.'

The woman took the cat out of the coat and placed it on the ground to gaze at it respectfully for a few moments.

'Do you know your neighbours well?' Rhiannon nodded towards the side wall of the house next door, to where a thick rope of ivy had clambered up onto the roof.

'Not really. We've only been here just over a year and what with work, you know. I've only ever seen a youngish woman there and she may well be on her own, but... The place really needs something doing with it because it lets the street down, doesn't it? I did go and put a note through the door recently about her trees overhanging our conservatory, but I've heard nothing back; it's as if she just doesn't care. I mean, I'm not the sort who *wants* to get solicitors involved, but...' It was obvious that the woman had an issue with the neighbours and welcomed the opportunity to vent, despite just finding out that her cat had died.

'Hmm. Well, I hope your children will be all right about the cat. Please pass on my condolences.' Rhiannon couldn't waste any more time or she would be late picking up the kids from school. She jogged back to her car and cast her eyes towards the dark windows of number four, The Elms, just before she drove away.

A twist of unease rummaged in the pit of her belly as she headed towards home.

Kim was such a devious character, she thought. What was going on with her? There she was, pretending she was poor and only ever taking the children to the park, when all the evidence pointed to her having a rambling old house that was worth a mint.

Perhaps *she* was the one they shouldn't trust with their children.

Rhiannon's modern home had a dance and exercise space in the basement. With one wall fully mirrored, a built-in sound system and top-notch vinyl floor, it was the ideal place to take the children to burn off energy.

She started by running through their normal warm-up routine which involved flossing and star jumps, before they moved onto a choreographed piece that they had been learning every week. Through her phone, Rhiannon controlled the music – she put on 'Roar' by Katy Perry – and she adjusted the coloured lighting so that reds and purples flashed with the music.

'What does everyone think about performing this dance at the holiday place this weekend so that your parents can see how brilliant you are?' She roused them in her practised, enthusiastic voice. 'How good would that be? Yes? You're all up for it?'

'YES!' the children shouted back in delight, bouncing around the room.

'Great! Let's do it then!'

They ran through the routine over and over for the next forty minutes until it was perfect, and then they went to wind down with some TV and freshly made smoothies which they were allowed to garnish with pieces of fruit.

Dulcie was the last one in the queue for the fruit, by which time all the strawberries had gone. But she didn't complain; she was happy to dress the top with sliced banana and segments of satsuma.

'That looks yummy,' Rhiannon commented as she stood by the refrigerator watching her.

'Are these grapes?' asked Dulcie, pointing to the blueberries.

'No, sunshine.' Rhiannon laughed. 'Don't you ever have blueberries at home?'

Dulcie shook her head. Her face was flushed.

'I saw your mum today, at a house on The Elms.' Rhiannon watched Dulcie for a reaction, but she just looked at the floor, tracing a toe along the edge of a tile. 'Is that where you live? The Elms?'

Dulcie poked her finger into her smoothie, giving a shrug of her shoulders. 'I think our house has a number four in it.'

'Really?' Rhiannon couldn't disguise the excitement in her voice.

'...but I don't know what you mean about elms. But it might be elms.'

'Is it an *old* house, where you live?' Rhiannon tried again.

'It's quite old. There are some mouldy bits in my bedroom.'

'And do you have to go up a long drive to get to your house?'

'Well, you have to go a long way down there, along the side' – Dulcie demonstrated with a snaking hand – 'and then you get to some old steps up to the door.'

There were definitely steps up to the pillared porch, Rhiannon remembered. Stone steps that had weeds growing out of them. She was absolutely sure that this was where Kim lived.

A blast of boisterous laughing filtered through to the kitchen, and Dulcie looked up at Rhiannon. 'Can I go now?'

'Yes, of course you can.' Rhiannon gave a little shoo with her hand, and Dulcie scurried out of the kitchen to go and join the others.

This new knowledge about Kim felt important. Rhiannon

scrolled back through the WhatsApp messages right to the start of the group where all the parents had added in their pick-up points for the children on the different days.

Everyone had given their address and postcode. Everyone except Kim, who had dropped a pin on a Google Map, showing the front of Bart's Burgers. No one had thought to question it at the time; they had all been naïve in thinking that Kim's routine of taking the kids to the park for games and activities and a picnic was a great way of giving them some exercise and fresh air, and massively preferable to plonking them in front of a television screen.

Now, though. Something felt wrong about it. It felt deceitful.

It felt like Kim was keeping some kind of secret.

Stacey was the first to arrive, fifteen minutes early. But this was because she wanted to confide in Rhiannon privately, before everyone else got there.

'Look at this.' Stacey unfurled her fingers to show Rhiannon an earring in the palm of her hand. A gold dangling flower with an amethyst in the centre. 'I found it in Xander's car, just under the passenger seat. And it's not mine.'

Rhiannon took a breath and tried to think of something diplomatic to say. 'Don't just jump to conclusions. It could belong to a work colleague.'

'Yes. It *could* belong to a work colleague. That's my worry.' Stacey put on an intense face. 'I've seen the Instagram pictures of one of his *work colleagues*.'

'Well, have you shown him the earring? Asked him about it?'

'How can I? I don't know, I just want to keep things normal. I don't want to end up triggering arguments where he might walk out.'

Rhiannon crinkled some sympathy into her face. She remembered how she hurt when Hans left her.

Dulcie skipped into the kitchen. 'Is my mum here yet?'

'No, sunshine,' Rhiannon replied. 'Five more minutes and then you can put your coat on.'

'Guess what I found out today.' Rhiannon closed the door after Dulcie returned to the lounge and leaned her head towards Stacey's. 'About Kim.'

'What?'

'She lives in a big house on The Elms.'

'The Elms? No way. You're joking, aren't you? I thought she lived somewhere near the burger place and that's why we have to pick the kids up from there.'

'I know. That's probably what she wants us to think. But I saw her going up the drive to number four, swinging her keys like she owned the place, and I also spoke to the woman in the house next door who confirmed it, and then I had a little chat with Dulcie earlier about where she lives. Kim Taylor lives in one of the mansions. But she doesn't want us to know about it.'

'Why?'

'Well, you tell me. There's obviously something going on. All that pretence when she must be loaded.'

'Ahh!' Stacey's eyes lit up. 'Ahh, well that makes sense now. I saw her at the cash machine outside Sainsbury's the other day and she was withdrawing a *lot* of cash. I mean, a big thick wad of it. Like what's the maximum you can get out? Five hundred pounds?'

'Hmm. Why would you take out that much cash? Particularly when she's trying to give the impression that she's always broke.'

There was a sudden rap on the door, and they both jumped out of their gossipy huddle. It was six o'clock. Rhiannon let Nina and Jarvis into the kitchen, and they collected their children's belongings from the table where they had been tidily placed.

'Kids! Come on, it's home time,' Rhiannon called breezily through to the lounge, and a flurry of bodies blundered through to put on their shoes.

'I'll keep you posted,' Stacey nodded to Rhiannon as she squeezed out of the throng with Coralie.

'Mummy!' Dulcie was on the doorstep in her outdoor wear as Kim appeared breathlessly behind Jarvis's and Nina's parked cars. She was four minutes' late.

'Come on, petal.' Kim took Dulcie's hand and gave Rhiannon a wave of thanks before disappearing, followed by Nina and Bobby.

Rhiannon was left with Jarvis and Hayden standing in front of her.

'Been a mad day, hasn't it?' Jarvis said, zipping up Hayden's coat.

'Yeah.'

'I'll get that money sorted for you, I promise. It was really good of you to help me out.'

'No problem.' Rhiannon ushered them to the door. She half-wondered about talking to him about Kim and the information she'd discovered, just in case he knew anything more, but he was already outside, zapping the lock on his car.

She closed the door and took her phone out again to open up the offending text. In a split second she had decided what to do, how to respond.

She hit the *reply* button.

A distraction was what was required. There would be no blackmail payment from *her*: she wasn't that stupid, wasn't that much of a pushover.

Instead, she would spill the beans on Kim.

TEN

THE WEEKEND AWAY

Friday – the first night of the weekend away

The childcare circle members huddle closely under the back porch with their children, hoods pulled up tight, as the rain comes down harder.

'This is not what I expected,' Rhiannon says, pressing her back to the wall.

Jarvis is waving his torch beam around, checking if there is something wrong with the key safe. 'Read the number out again.'

'It's six eight four four.' Nina pushes him aside as she tries to line up the digits, but nothing is happening. The box still won't open. A playful squeal comes from one of the children as high spirits result from their boredom, and Bobby and Hayden break away from the group to dodge and tag each other.

'Why don't you try ringing the owner? Maybe he's given you the wrong number.' The suggestion comes from Rhiannon.

'We shouldn't have to be doing this. Not in this awful weather. Let's just hope there's a signal.' Stacey is still wanting everything to be cancelled so they can all go home.

Nina dials the number of Paul, her client, while Jarvis fiddles around with the key safe. Everyone else is trying to keep warm.

'Bloody answerphone, can you believe it?'

'Try again, just give it another go.' Kim attempts to keep a positive tone.

The kids are definitely getting fed up now. They've all left the adults crammed under the porch while they dart about in the darkness, on the patch of lawn at the side of the house. It doesn't matter though; they can't get any wetter. Once they're inside they can all dry off and settle down.

'No, it's just gone to answerphone again.' There is a crescendo of frustration in Nina's tone.

'Maybe it's six *nought* four four?' Rhiannon suggests. 'Have you tried that? Because you might have heard it wrong when you wrote it down.'

'No, Miss Know-it-all, I haven't tried that. Because he actually texted me the code. And it's six *eight* four four.'

'There's no harm in trying though, is there?'

Kim chews at her nails again as Nina redials the mobile number.

'Oh, hi, Paul.' Relief is evident. Nina puts a hand to her wet forehead and smiles at everyone. 'Paul, we're here at the property and the number for the key safe isn't working. Can I just check, please, that it's the correct one? Because I'm not sure if the mechanism has jammed or what.'

There's a pause, and they all hold their breath.

'OK, so you're saying that it's six eight five five? Because that's not what it said on the text.'

Suddenly, there is an ear-splitting shriek from one of the kids.

'Muuummm!'

Kim dashes around the side of the house to see what is

happening. It's almost pitch black apart from a few fading solar lights dotted around the shrubbery.

'HELP! Help me!'

'What's happened?' Kim shouts, grabbing randomly at Freya's sleeve.

'Over there. The path at the end just collapsed, and he's gone over the side. He might be in the sea!'

Kim switches on her phone torch and instructs the four silhouetted kids to go and stand by the wall of the house, out of the way, while she tentatively edges towards where she can now see the garden abruptly ends. The sound of a scream blends with the roar of the sea, and she can hear that the tide is in, crashing over the rocks below.

'Help me! Help me, I'm going to fall into the sea and drown!'

'I can't see you. Where are you?' Kim swings the beam of light down and around, leaning carefully over the broken edge, until a contorted, terrified face peers back at her.

'Hold on,' Kim says, noticing fingers grasping onto a tree root that had previously been part of the garden.

'I can't! I'm going to fall.' Feet scrabble ineffectively on the side of the cliff. 'I can't get back up.'

Kim squats down and shines the light into his frightened little face for another two seconds as the rain belts down on both of them and the sea below growls like a predatory monster.

'Help!' Bobby screams as a rock tumbles down the cliff. 'Don't let me fall.' Sobbing, begging, pleading.

Kim smiles at him.

'Get me up! Don't just keep staring.' His shoes claw uselessly at the side of the wet, slippery ledge.

Kim squats down, feeling the force of the sea hitting her face.

'Please...'

She grabs his arms tightly. 'Come on, pet, you hold on to me. You're safe now. I can pull you back up.'

It's a close call.

Another moment later and he would have been dead.

* * *

There are lights on in the house. They have managed to crack the code and get the key. Kim and Bobby, both bedraggled and muddy from the cliff edge and the weather, are the last ones into the fusty-smelling kitchen.

'Oh great, look at the state of you,' Nina says when she sees her filthy, tear-stained son. 'I think a shower is needed. What happened?'

'He had a bit of a scare and slipped down a ledge at the end of the garden.' Kim rubs at the sludge on the knees of her jeans.

'Isn't this like a notorious place for coastal erosion?' Stacey chips in. 'Can you remember when we came for the dance contest and there was that storm that took part of the cliff down? Someone said there were caravans and all sorts that ended up on the beach.'

'Well, that's good to know,' says Jarvis sarcastically. 'We're staying in a place that could be in the sea by morning. Great booking, Nina.'

Nina's cheeks are red, even with thick make-up on. She ignores the comments and leads Bobby upstairs to get cleaned up.

'Well, the place is just about habitable. I'm not sure what happened with the photographs that Nina was raving about,' Rhiannon whispers as she looks over her shoulder, 'and I think she's been well and truly conned by this Paul guy if she's done work deals with him on the basis of getting this shithole for the weekend.'

'If I could make a sensible suggestion,' says Stacey, 'it would

be that we all just go home. What's the point in staying in a
dump like this where the weather is awful? And according to
the forecast, it's not really going to improve.'

'But I'm not sure how safe it would be to try getting through
that flooded area near the caravan site. It was pretty bad when
we arrived,' says Kim. 'At least a foot deep and rising. I don't
know how Stacey managed to get the car through. I mean, the
thought of doing that again...'

Jarvis sighs. 'We can survive here. It's not the end of the
world. Looks like it's been unused for a long time, but we can
light the fires and there are some electric heaters in the
bedrooms. And it's only for two nights. The kids will have fun,
so let's just make the best of it for their sakes.'

Rhiannon is scrolling through her phone. 'Actually, I don't
like to be the bearer of bad news, Stacey, but Kim might be
right about the flooding. I've just had an alert that says
they've closed that road, so we'd have to find another route
home.'

'There isn't another route,' says Jarvis. 'It's a one-road-in,
one-road-out place unless you've got a boat.'

Stacey's face drops. 'No! What about getting home? We
can't get stuck *here*!'

'Well, the forecast says that the rain should stop around four
o'clock in the morning and then there's another storm possibly
arriving early evening on Saturday, but Sunday actually looks
like it will be quite a nice day.'

'So, it's likely that everything will be fine by Sunday
evening. We may as well just resign ourselves to having fun.'
Kim is unusually cheerful.

'Exactly! That's the spirit!' Nina turns up and joins in with
the conversation. 'Let's get the food and drink unpacked.' She
removes two bottles of bubbly from a box and slides them into
the fridge. 'Stacey, would you unpack that box there, babe? It's
got all the nibbles in for tonight.'

'So, what's the situation?' Kim asks. 'Has everyone picked which room they are having?'

'I've allocated the bedrooms,' says Nina. 'I'll show you where you and Dulcie will be sleeping.'

Kim follows her up two staircases to a room in the loft that runs the width of the house. There is a small double bed wedged up against one wall. A tatty rag rug sits forlornly on the bare floorboards, and a single glass pane in the rotting window frame is letting a draught howl in and billow the thin net curtain. No pictures on the walls. No effort made with the décor.

'Looks like you've allocated me the Savoy Suite,' Kim laughs drily. 'No radiator in this room?'

'All the rooms are pretty similar. It's not like we got the best ones before you,' says Nina. 'And I'm not sure if I'll want the heater on in my room anyway because there's a horrible dusty smell to it.'

Kim shrugs and smiles. 'Don't worry. It's not as if I'm used to luxury. Anyway, I'm quite happy to be up here out of the way.' She drops her rucksack onto the floor. 'I'd better get changed. Is it cocktail dresses tonight?'

'I don't think we agreed on any particular...'

'I'm joking. I've got the choice of fleecy pyjamas or another pair of jeans, and I'm thinking pyjamas. With socks.'

'Well, I'll leave you to it. I'm going to go and deal with the food, so come back down when you're ready.'

Kim has already unpacked and stripped off before Nina is halfway down the second staircase. She pulls on her pyjamas and feels a quick surge of adrenaline run through her body.

This is it.

The start of the weekend that she's waited so long for.

ELEVEN

NINA

Thursday – the day before the weekend away

Nina sent a text to Paul, her client, to thank him for the information about the key safe code – six eight four four – and to ask him again for the actual address of the place, because the rest of the childcare group seemed to think that she was deliberately keeping it a secret from them.

'Haha, don't you like the thought of a mystery tour?' he'd joked on more than one occasion, each time promising to send over the full details and then forgetting.

But she didn't like to be too pushy, as he'd done her a massive favour in letting them have the place for free. At least he'd emailed her the photographs of it and it looked fantastic. Five double bedrooms – one for each parent and child – and a huge sitting room and modern open-plan dining kitchen with sliding doors that looked out onto the beach.

Although Nina would never admit it to the rest of the group, it had been Kim who had come up with the idea of a weekend away for the team and their children. She'd mentioned to Nina about a month ago that she'd seen an online article about another childcare circle who had arranged such a break together and had had a fabulous time, even attracting the attention of *Parent* magazine for a big paid feature.

'Really?' Nina had said, intrigued and challenged by Kim's suggestion. And the thought of getting into print had appealed enormously: she remembered that a friend knew someone who worked for one of the Sunday magazines. It wasn't quite *Hello!* but it would give her an element of kudos, nonetheless.

Kim had laughed. 'Well, I just thought... seeing as you're so brilliant at organising things, it might be worth considering.'

So, Nina, a sucker for such flattery, *had* considered Kim's idea, because she'd literally just been booking hotel conference facilities for a prestigious new client who could be very helpful. Paul Eyrie, a property investor, had a portfolio that included renovated houses by the coast. Maybe a little flirting and a promise to do a good deal on his event hosting would be beneficial, she'd thought.

She'd set to work.

And, despite only communicating with him via email and telephone – even though she'd vainly spent ages on her make-up in anticipation of a video call – her method had worked.

Paul had been taken in by her charm, loving the idea of the childcare circle and what they were doing. And then when Nina mentioned that they might be able to get a tabloid newspaper interested, which would obviously be great publicity for his business, he had almost been falling over himself to offer the place.

An old Victorian house on the Holderness coast in east Yorkshire, it was a holiday home that Paul had personally been involved in renovating. The location was perfect for families, with a stunning beach right on the doorstep. Nina had done some googling and guessed that it was probably in Bridlington.

It would be ideal for their group.

She checked the weather forecast again, even though she

couldn't accurately pinpoint the address and had to rely on a vague map. Luckily, the rain could hold off for the Friday and most of Saturday, but a storm was predicted to hit the coast in the early hours of Sunday morning. She made a mental note to keep an eye on the changing predictions and had packed plenty of suitable clothing.

Surely, it would be good fun, whatever the weather. There were places to take the kids –rock pools on the beach were always great even if you had to wrap up warm – and the house itself had a fabulous entertaining space that would make trips to bars and eateries unnecessary.

Flicking through the photographs of the holiday home again – she intended to be the first to get to the property in order to claim the biggest en suite bedroom – she was filled with self-righteousness at being able to blag such an impressive opportunity.

OK, she told herself. Work to do. There was the task of packing up the breakfast items and the wine.

Suddenly, her phone rang on the worktop, the vibrations shuffling it to nudge up to a waiting case of Prosecco.

It was Paul, her client.

'Hey, how are you? We're looking forward to the weekend away.'

'Oh, Nina. You're not going to believe what I've done.' His voice was soft, low, absorbing. His website profile photograph had showed her that he was pretty hot with stunning bone structure and a flop of dark hair, and he wore quality fitted suits. She imagined him then, with his tie off and two – no, three – buttons undone on his shirt. He would be swinging back in a big leather office chair, right foot up on his left knee.

'This sounds a bit ominous.' Nina laughed in a sassy way.

'I have seriously cocked up and I am ringing to apologise. It's about the house.'

The smile fell from Nina's face. 'Don't tell me you've

double-booked and we can't go. Everyone is looking forward
to it.'

'No, no, nothing like that.'

'Oh, thank goodness. You had me worried.' Nina held a
relieved hand to her chest.

'No, I've just realised... I sent you some info, didn't I? And
the number for the key safe?'

'Yes, I've got all that. Thank you.'

'So, a couple of weeks ago I sent you some photographs,
didn't I?'

'They look great,' said Nina. 'We're all really excited.'

'Well, that's the thing,' Paul replied. 'Oh God, this sounds
so stupid, but I sent you the wrong pictures. They're for a
different property, not the one you're going to be staying in. I've
only just realised.'

'Ohhh.' Disappointment spilled out of her. 'Well, could you
send the correct ones over instead?'

'Hmm, so, that's the other thing. I think I've accidentally
deleted them. I can't actually find them on any of my
devices.'

Nina gave a nervous giggle. This guy was supposed to be a
professional. High-powered, wealthy, managing multiple property renovations.

'I know, I'm a complete disaster sometimes,' he said with a
bewitching lilt in his voice. 'But you don't need to worry. All the
rest of the info is correct. Bedrooms, bathrooms, the outlook
onto the sea and everything. And the beach is a stone's throw
from the back door.'

'Isn't it on *Booking.com* though? Surely the photographs are
on there?'

'No, I haven't got round to sorting that out yet. I wanted to
get feedback from visitors first and that's why it's ideal for a big
party like yours. But, as I said, it's all good – just not *quite* as
impressive as the one whose photos I sent – and there is plenty

of room for the ten of you. There's minor stuff that needs dealing with but nothing that would ruin your holiday.'

'OK,' said Nina warmly. 'Well, don't worry about the pictures. With the price we're getting it for, I can hardly complain, can I?'

'Ahh, bless you. Thanks for being understanding. We'll catch up soon, OK?'

Nina hung up and scrolled enviously through all the property pictures that had been sent in error, before deleting them.

Oh shit, she remembered. She meant to ask him for the address and postcode.

She tried to call back but his phone was engaged. She sighed and checked the weather forecast again. The storm looked to be making an entrance from around eight o'clock on the Saturday night. Fleecy onesies, she was thinking, rather than silk pyjamas. And she wouldn't mention anything about the photo situation to the others. They hadn't seen the pictures so they didn't need to know.

Secrets, secrets, she thought. You have to keep them all the time, don't you?

A shudder rippled involuntarily through her body.

Nina, sensibly, had stopped herself from dwelling on the matter of the stupid letter and text that arrived earlier in the week, telling herself that she wasn't the sort of person who worried about pranks like that. She was measured, logical, level-headed.

But the thought of someone finding out about the thing that had been sitting in the darkest part of her memory for all these years, the thing that she refused to remember...

Because how could anyone know about *that*? And why would they bring it up again, after all this time?

No, it was irrational to assume that the messages were connected to *that*. They were just part of a ridiculous joke. They had to be.

Didn't they?

TWELVE

NINA

Thursday – the day before the weekend away

The next phone call was from Jarvis to say that his ex, Helena, was insisting on picking up Hayden from the holiday property on the Saturday evening as she was having him for half-term week.

'That's fine,' said Nina. 'Will you be planning on leaving, too, or staying with us for the Saturday night?'

'Well, if things are OK with everyone, I'll probably have a drink and stay over. But the reason I'm ringing though, is that I need to let Helena know the postcode so that she can plan her journey.'

'Ahh,' said Nina. 'Everyone is trying to get the mystery post-code by whatever means.' She couldn't possibly tell him that Paul still hadn't given her the information; it would risk making her seem incompetent.

'No, really. She's getting quite irritated with me not telling her what it is. And I can't blame her because what if it's some-where like five hours away?'

'I can assure you that the location is not five hours away. Look, text me Helena's number and I will get in touch with her to put her mind at rest. Is that OK? And you and the rest of the group will get the information on Friday at six.'

Jarvis exhaled. 'Yeah, I suppose. I'll send you her number now.'

The holdall was packed. Long-sleeved T-shirts and warm jumpers and socks for Bobby, plus jeans for playing on the beach. Waterproof coats for both of them. Towels and spare trainers. For herself she'd got a trendy-but-casual wardrobe so that her selfies would look good – windswept but sexy – adding in a black clingy dress and strappy shoes to wear if the evenings took on a more formal vibe.

Next, she turned her attention to the food and alcohol for their Saturday bottomless brunch. Bacon, sausages, eggs, mushrooms, condiments, bread, milk, coffee. She checked her list and reorganised the boxes. Cereals, fruit juices, yogurt. Muesli for Rhiannon. Croissants that could be baked in the oven. Bubbly for the Bucks Fizz; vodka for the Bloody Marys.

She checked the weather forecast again. The Friday evening looked a little bit warmer than originally predicted, but the storm on Saturday night looked much worse with amber weather warnings. Torrential rain. Gale force winds with gusts of between fifty to sixty miles an hour. Risk of flooding and damage to property.

Bloody weather. Trying to prevent them from having fun when she'd lined up a great weekend for everyone. Well, it wouldn't stop them!

She popped a bigger umbrella into the holdall and strode out to pick up the children.

* * *

Outside the school gates, with only five minutes to spare, Nina chatted to a mother from one of the other childcare circles, telling her about their celebratory weekend away.

'Oh, that is such a lovely thing to do,' said the woman. 'I wish our group would be more willing to get together socially, but everyone just sees each other as childminders rather than friends. And you say that you've managed to get a beachside property for free?'

'Well, I have contacts. It's the sort of thing I do all the time.'

'It's amazing. Our circle could really do with your skills and your contacts.'

Nina soaked up the praise. Then Tess, the childcare circle co-ordinator, was suddenly standing beside her. She'd probably heard all the good things about the weekend away and had come to congratulate Nina for arranging it.

'Hi.' Nina gave her an expansive smile. 'You've heard about our weekend away, too?'

There was a frown between Tess's eyebrows. 'Weekend? No, I'm trying to track down Kim. I couldn't remember if it was her day for picking up the children.'

'Kim's day is Tuesday. Is there a problem?'

'Well, hopefully not. It's just that her police check application was rejected and I'm trying to chase up some information so that it can be sorted.'

'Police check rejected? Oh my God, has she got a criminal record?' Nina's imagination was immediately flooded with a picture of Kim pulling a rope around Bobby's neck.

'No, no.' Tess reached a calming hand out to Nina. 'She filled in something wrong regarding an address or past address, and we just need to clarify how long she lived there.'

Nina clasped her fist to her heart. 'Gosh, you had me panicking there. You need to know that you can trust people with your kids, don't you? I could never live with myself if anything happened.'

'Well, if you see her later, can you tell her to give me a call?'

Their conversation was interrupted as the end of school bell rang. Then, the doors were open and children surged through the playground. Coralie and Hayden appeared first, squealing with excitement about the impending trip, and when the others eventually joined them, Nina was swamped with a flurry of book bags and PE kits.

'Come on you lot.' She rounded them up with their belongings and shepherded them along the pavement towards her house.

* * *

Back home, she put *Encanto* on the media screen because it was the kids' favourite Disney film, and brought through a tray of snacks for them all to share. Apple slices, carrot sticks and hummus, cubed cheddar and yogurt-coated mini rice cakes. Nina prided herself on feeding them healthy food.

When they were settled and engrossed in the film and nibbles, Nina took out her phone and typed a message into the WhatsApp group:

> *Kim, there's an issue with your DBS application. Tess collared me outside school to say you've given the wrong address or something. Can you sort it asap?*

Nina knew that she could have dealt with this privately, but thought that the issue should be made transparent with the rest of the group.

Only two minutes later, her phone was ringing.

'This address thing with Kim? I've been meaning to tell you,' Rhiannon was breathless with excitement. 'I found out: she lives in one of those massive houses on The Elms.'

'No!' Nina was unable to believe this version of Kim, who always looked like she wore second-hand clothing from the charity shops. 'Who told you?'

'I saw her on Wednesday as I was passing. She was going up the drive. And then I actually got to speak to the next-door neighbour who confirmed that she lived there, so I had a little chat with Dulcie too, and yes... it all makes sense now.'

'Really? We all assumed she lived in a flat somewhere, didn't we?'

'Yes, but we've never been to it, have we? There's just the routine of collecting our kids from outside a burger bar which, to be honest, should have rung alarm bells from the start.'

'I'm sure someone said they'd seen her working there, taking orders. Wasn't that you?'

Rhiannon's voice went up a tone to show how affronted she was. 'No. We've never bought food from *there*. We don't eat *that* sort of stuff in our house. And anyway, I was saying... Stacey saw her withdrawing a load of money from the cash machine earlier this week, on Monday I think. Hundreds. What's all that about?'

'That is so weird. Why would you put down a fake address on a police check application? Why would you have a massive house and loads of money but not want to tell anyone about it unless you were hiding something? And why would you ever think about working in a burger bar unless you were absolutely desperate?'

'Hey, maybe we should google her name. See what we can dig up about her.'

Nina was shaking her head. 'Already done it. There's not a trace. And I'm pretty good at tracking people down.'

'No social media at all?' Rhiannon couldn't believe that someone could go through life without making a ripple on the internet. 'Still, I suppose it's a fairly common name, though.'

'But there's nothing. I've trawled through every Kim Taylor. She's either been very careful not to be found, or she's changed her name.'

'This is what I mean. Something doesn't add up with her. She's definitely hiding something. I wondered if she was being blackmailed...' Rhiannon paused to see if Nina would mention the anonymous letters and texts.

'What?'

'That letter on Monday? Tell me honestly: was it you playing a prank on us all?'

'Me? Why do you think I'd do anything like that?'

'I don't know, I just wanted it to be a joke rather than anything sinister. Do *you* think it's a joke?'

'I bloody hope so.' Nina gave an empty laugh. 'I wouldn't want anybody getting the skeletons out of *my* cupboard.'

'Me too,' Rhiannon guffawed. 'God, it's sounding like we've all got some dubious stuff in the past, isn't it?'

'It *is* a joke though, don't you think?'

'It's got to be. Someone is winding us up.'

'Could it be Stacey?'

'It's definitely not Stacey. She's as spooked by the messages as we are. And Jarvis got them, and he says that Kim did, too. Everyone in our childcare circle has been targeted.'

'Weird. It must be someone outside of the group then. But why?'

'I don't know. Perhaps they're trying to break up our group? Perhaps they're just jealous and spiteful? I really can't think of any reason why anyone would do this.'

'Well, maybe we should just laugh it off over drinks this weekend,' suggested Nina. 'I've literally packed gallons of booze.'

'Oh, goody,' said Rhiannon. 'I'm looking forward to letting my hair down.'

'Let's not let all this shit get to us. We've got the weekend to enjoy.' Nina was suddenly startled by the presence of a child behind her.

'You just said "shit",' said Hayden with hummus all over his face.

THIRTEEN
THE WEEKEND AWAY

Friday – the first night of the weekend away

Disco music is blaring and a rampant fire crackles heartily in the fireplace. Candles and table lamps light up the shoddy surroundings in a sympathetic manner. The dining room has a long mahogany table with ten chairs around it and a candelabra in the centre. The wood is dull and tired, stained with rings and old spillages, but has been laid out with wine glasses, bowls of crisps, platters of party food and a range of alcohol.

'I know it's not quite what we expected,' says Nina, 'but we might as well have some fun. I've settled the kids down with board games and snacks in the lounge and they've already had pizza at Jarvis's house, so now *we* can have some grown-up time.'

'Done up properly, this place could be quite impressive,' says Rhiannon, looking around the room. 'Did you say it's owned by a businessman you work with?'

Nina nods, her mouth full of crackers and cheese. 'Mmm. A guy called Paul Eyrie.' She pronounces the surname 'ay-ree'.

Kim corrects her. 'It's "eerie", you know, as in eerie-spooky.'

'How do you know?'

'I knew someone with that name and that's how it was pronounced.'

'Well, thanks for your input, Kim, but I have been dealing with *this* Paul *Ay-ree* for a while now and that's how you say his name.' Nina's haughty tone is accompanied by a disdainful look. 'And yes, Rhiannon, he's a bit of a property mogul that is planning on working with me at Van Ryan's for some special events and conferences.'

'So, the hotel doesn't mind that you get freebies from him? Because a lot of employers wouldn't allow it,' says Stacey.

'Well, he's more of a friend rather than just a client. And I haven't actually told Van Ryan's.' She puts a finger over her lips as she pulls an impish face.

'Well, I must say, looking at this place from the outside it was a bit like the set of a horror movie. But now... it doesn't actually seem too bad, does it?' says Rhiannon. 'Open fires add a special vibe to a place, don't they? And it's warming up the room quite nicely. You'll even be able to take that hat off soon, Jarvis.'

He touches his head carefully. Perspiration is beading on his brow. 'Do we have any beers? I don't really drink wine.'

Nina goes to check the boxes. Rhiannon and Stacey sit down at the side of the table that is closest to the fire and pop a bottle of Prosecco. Kim takes a seat next to Jarvis opposite the two women, and gathers up a handful of crisps to pick at.

'Wow. There's been an attack on a woman in her home in Wingfield. It says she's in a serious condition.' Rhiannon's attention is fixed on her phone. 'Did you see all the emergency vehicles as we left town earlier? Looked like they were heading up towards The Elms.'

'Oh, we heard all the sirens, didn't we?' Stacey says to Kim. 'There was definitely something going off.'

Nina returns and hands a four-pack of lager to Jarvis who is scrolling urgently on his phone. 'You're in luck. Although I can't find any pint glasses. You'll have to manage with the tins.' She pulls out the chair at the head of the table and swigs the glass that Rhiannon has poured for her. 'You said something about sirens?'

Rhiannon nods. 'Yeah, police or something around the posh end of town. Did you see anything, Jarvis?'

Jarvis's hands are shaking as he pops his can of lager. 'No. Nothing.' He tips his head and gulps back his drink. Droplets of sweat trickle down to his jawline. He turns his phone screen-down on the table and presses the cold can to his forehead.

'Maybe it was something to do with the attack. Gosh, I wonder who it was? They haven't named anyone yet.' Rhiannon puts down her phone. 'It must be domestic violence if it was in her house. Husband, lover: that's who it usually is. Still...'

'Is it OK if I open a red?' Kim lifts a bottle.

'Yeah, whatever.'

She pours a drink and chinks it against the others' wine glasses before taking a mouthful. 'Well. Here's to us. Childcare and all that.'

'Great job done so far,' says Rhiannon. 'We've kept the kids alive.'

'Well, I must say thanks for trusting me with your children.' Nina stops and stares at the glass in her hand, realising the words she has just uttered.

Everyone stares.

'The letters and texts.' Stacey is the one that says what they are all thinking. 'It's time to own up. Which one of you sent them?'

'You're assuming one of us did. It could have been someone completely out of our circle.'

'Why would they?'

There's a break, where the only sound is the snarl of the fire and the rain at the window. Kim takes a mini-quiche and a spring roll to nibble in turn. Jarvis crunches in his fist the lager can that he has already emptied.

'This thing about the secrets and having to confess them. It doesn't make sense, really. Who are we supposed to confess them to? And then the text that was like a blackmailing "how much will you pay me to keep quiet" kind of message. Did any of you do anything about it? I mean, did anyone actually go as far as to hand money over?' Rhiannon swigs back her glass and pours herself another.

Stacey throws a knowing look at Kim. 'Would *you* pay someone to keep a secret for you?'

'Me? No, I'm skint. As per usual.'

'So, what did everyone do about the texts? Because they wanted us to reply, didn't they? Did anyone actually respond? Come on, be honest now.'

Nina shivers. 'I just ignored everything. Assumed it was a scam and hoped it would go away.'

'Me, too,' says Stacey. 'Although I did start wondering about how much money I could get out of the bank account without Xander noticing. You know, for if things got out of hand.'

'I texted back,' says Rhiannon, flatly. 'Not to offer to pay, but – I don't know – to try and find out what they wanted, or what they already knew, because, well, I suppose we've all got stuff in the past that we'd rather keep a lid on.'

'You texted back? And what happened then?'

'Well, nothing. I've had no further messages.'

'What did you say to them?'

Rhiannon glances nervously around. 'I can't remember. Just, like, that they should leave me alone.'

'Did anyone else respond?' Nina looks towards Kim and Jarvis.

'I deleted the text,' Kim says quickly.

Jarvis's jaw is clenched. He blinks and rubs his nose. His hand is still trembling.

'I've still got mine. It's here somewhere.' Stacey scrolls through her texts to find the offending message.

'Jarvis?' Nina prompts again.

'Oh God, I feel so bad about this.' Jarvis is suddenly gripped by a spasm of guilt. 'I'll hold my hands up and admit it.'

'*You* sent the letters?'

'No! No, I sent the texts, and I feel bad about that now. But it was only for a laugh, to try and root out who had sent the letters. I wasn't going to blackmail anyone. I just thought it would provoke someone to own up. Please, trust me.'

Rhiannon jumps up from the table. 'What?' Her volume increases significantly. 'You? Are you an absolute idiot or what? So, I sent a response and it was to *you*?'

Jarvis covers his head with his hands. 'Look, I'm sorry. Please. Just forget about it all.'

'I can't believe it.' Rhiannon looks around the room at everyone. 'I gave him information.'

Kim sits there, taking long, deep breaths. 'Thank goodness it was you,' she says to Jarvis. 'I didn't know if it was something more sinister because it felt so... oh I don't know, *knowing*. The stress I've gone through this week. But I'm glad you've owned up.'

'So, it's *not* that you know our secrets then?' Nina asks him. 'You were just fishing?'

'I'm sorry. Truly. And no, I don't know your secrets. At all. So let's move on.' He exhales into cupped hands.

The clock ticks. A sense of relief settles around the table; tensions sag out; the fire dances busily beside them.

Stacey picks up her glass and gulps the wine greedily. 'So, who is going to own up to the letters then?'

'Anyone?' says Nina.

Kim sits forward in her chair. 'The most logical thing would be to confess our secrets now, to each other. Then we wouldn't need to worry about the letters either.'

'God, you must be kidding,' says Stacey.

Rhiannon gawks, shaking her head. Then she demonstrates zipping up her mouth.

Jarvis is running his fingers broodingly around his swollen cheekbone, his face wet with sweat. The pain in his head is excruciating. He crushes his second empty can before hunching over and pinching the bridge of his nose.

'Well, if you want to go first, Kim.' Nina's sarcastic tone says that she's not going to join in with this ridiculous exercise.

'Don't you think though, that it does feel better to say something, sometimes? Keeping secrets in can be a burden.' Kim picks up a cocktail sausage. 'There's something that I've been wanting to get off my chest for a while and this kind of seems like the right time.'

There's a pause, and they all listen to the sound of laughter coming from the lounge, where the kids are making up the rules to Pictionary.

Jarvis grimaces as he re-sticks the Elastoplast around his fingers.

Kim's phone buzzes suddenly with a text, and she snatches it up to stop everyone seeing the name of the sender. She'll read it and respond later.

'Feel free to tell us *your* secret, Kim, if it helps.' Stacey's curiosity for new gossip is bubbling over.

'OK. I do feel like I want to say this.' Kim picks up her wine glass with a shaky hand and knocks back a sizeable mouthful. Then she looks at each person around the table in turn before speaking.

'Years ago, I did something that I can never forgive myself for. I killed my little brother.'

FOURTEEN

JARVIS

Friday – the morning of the weekend away

'Fuck. Fuck, fuck, fuck.' Jarvis slapped a hand to his head in defeat. He switched off his phone and tossed it onto the table. 'Not my fucking lucky day. Again.'

He thought about going out for a run to burn off some of his stress and clear his head, but he really needed to go and get some food in for the kids that he was minding later – frozen pizza and oven chips would do – before he made a start on dealing with all the financial admin that he'd been unable to face.

Divorces take their toll, he thought, particularly on the bank account.

After three times he'd learned the hard way. The house had been up for sale for seven months and all he'd had were two viewings. Both unsuccessful. He was three months behind on the mortgage, and Helena, his ex, was getting ever more threatening as she waited for her share. Half of this, half of that. The house, the savings pot (which was emptied long ago), his pension. He couldn't keep up with it all and each demand for payment ate a bit further into his soul.

It was nearly ten o'clock. He didn't need to pick the kids up until three so he'd got plenty of time to try and sort some of this mess out.

OK. So, what were his options? Keep your head calm, make a list of the priorities and the urgent stuff that needed dealing with. That was what the debt advisors told you, wasn't it?

He switched on the kettle and heaped two spoons of instant coffee into a mug. Pulled open the kitchen drawer that was stuffed with bills and final demands among a load of other detritus, and emptied everything onto the table. He'd get it sorted. He could do this.

Rubbish. Rubbish. Didn't know about that. Rubbish. Hmm, was that worth keeping?

He rummaged through the heap, separating the items. Electrical tape, assorted screws, a broken Fitbit. Random plugs and wires. A tube of superglue. Leaky pens, sticky with blue gunk. Some of the stuff went into the bin, some of it back into the drawer.

Hey. Hey, what's that? He saw the glint of silver and reached for it: a lottery scratch card that hadn't been scratched yet. How had that happened? He pulled a coin from his pocket and scratched off one of the panels.

Yes. He brushed away the little mound of grey fragments before scratching the next one.

Yes! Come on baby, we can do this!

And... Fuck yes!

It wasn't the big top prize, but he'd just won fifty pounds. Despite the thousands that he owed amid all the bills on the table, this was a nugget of hope. He tucked the card into his pocket with the lucky coin and sat down to sort through the letters.

Car tax, due at the end of the month. Well, that could wait. An urgent letter from the bank, requesting that he made an appointment with an advisor about non-payment of his mortgage. Hmm, that probably needed to go at the top of the pile. And then...

It was that weird one that came in the post on Monday. He recalled Rhiannon saying that she thought it might be a murder mystery game, something that Nina was setting up for the weekend but... No. He still wasn't sure what it was about. Some kind of chain letter thing? It felt a bit ominous, but there was nothing specific in it, apart from giving him five days to confess. Who was he supposed to confess to? It didn't say. It was a load of bollocks.

He read it again.

He'd thought at first that it was the sort of thing that Helena would do. Something cryptically aggressive to fuck with his mind. She'd have got a buzz from doing that. But would Helena have gone as far as to find everyone else's addresses and send them the same thing? Maybe not.

And was it a hoax or did someone really *know* something about him? He shivered. This childcare circle set-up really got to him sometimes. What you could do and what you couldn't do, and how everyone pretended to be a *team*. They were all a strange lot with their own agendas and he wished that he had the money for proper childcare so that Hayden could go to an after-school club, like his colleague's kid who got picked up by a minibus and transported to a centre where they did sports and arts and games. It cost a fortune though, so unfortunately he was stuck with this option.

The rest of them didn't want a man in the circle. It was pretty obvious at that first meeting: the looks of horror, like if you'd got a dick between your legs it made you incapable of looking after kids. That was how it seemed at the time. That feeling of smugness he got, though, when they all had their police checks done and his was the first to come back, totally clear.

Rhiannon was probably the best one of the bunch even though she did that irritating thing of clapping when she laughed. It had been good of her to help him out when he was in dire need of cash. OK, it wasn't quite kneecapping time for him, but it had been a relief when she'd returned at lunchtime and put the notes in his hand. God knows how or where he would get the money to pay her back though.

Nina was the power-crazy one. Confident, assertive, motivated: not the type of woman he'd want as a partner. Just her dress sense terrified him. Those crisp suits, harsh pointy shoes that shone too much, massive handbags that she swung onto her shoulder with the control of an Olympic hammer thrower.

He was wary of Kim. She was a sly one, dressing down and looking like a victim all the time. There was depth and mystery to her. On quite a few occasions he'd seen her strolling around the posh area of town. Yet when the parents collected their kids from her, they all had to meet up outside a crappy takeaway. Why didn't she take the children to play at her house; why did they always have to go to the park? There was definitely something sneaky going on.

And Stacey. Well, they barely made eye contact. She must be so embarrassed about the time she literally threw herself at him in that wine bar. OK, so it was what, eight years ago? Maybe longer than that. He was still married to Helena then, happily or so he'd thought at the time. Yeah, it was just before they'd had Hayden, the romantic years. He sniggered to himself. Anyway. Perhaps when they all went away this weekend he should mention the wine bar thing to Stacey so that they could just have a laugh about it and clear the air.

God only knew what it would be like being in the company of four women. They'd probably end up killing him and dumping his body in the sea.

He rang the bank and arranged an appointment to talk to someone about his mortgage next week. It felt good getting it sorted, and he crossed the task off his list.

The council tax issue was the next thing he needed to deal with, but he was put on hold and had to listen to an infuriating sequence of messages as he waited for forty minutes to speak to an advisor. By then his temper was raging and he was unable to get the sympathy he was hoping for. If the arrears were not settled by the end of the month then legal action would be taken to recover the debt.

He wondered if he could increase his credit card limit, knowing he'd already done that four times and couldn't keep up with the payments. Or perhaps he could return his leased car and get a cheaper model. Everything was just getting unbearable, unmanageable. He really needed his luck to change.

He pulled the weird letter out of the pile and read it again. It had to be some kind of game, didn't it? Because, really, what secret did he have that had the potential to bring him down?

Truly, he couldn't think of *anything*.

He'd gone through crap times, like a lot of people. Marriage break-ups that'd been messy. Affairs and one-night stands, some of which caused trouble and lost him friendships, some of which he'd forgotten about. Some were regrettable only in the sense that they were a bit awkward. That woman who told him she loved him after he'd bedded her just the one time. He couldn't even remember her name. And there was that three-some once, with the girls, nothing dodgy though, mind. They definitely weren't underage. So that didn't count. None of these things were *dark secrets*. They weren't events that he ever worried about.

So, what else was there?

He'd done a fair bit of shoplifting at one point: it was an easy enough thing to get away with. Bottles of spirits. Sports shirts. Printer cartridges. Why queue and pay for the damn things when you could just walk in and take them? He'd only been caught once – a four-pack of burgers and a bar of chocolate of all things – and got away with a caution and a ban from the supermarket.

What else? He'd had a fight with a guy in a pub once. Just a drunken argument that had got out of hand, something to do with football. But no one had been killed or hospitalised. The police hadn't even been involved.

Surely, none of these things could be classed as *dark secrets*? It was all really peculiar. He raked through his mind again. Nope. Nothing. Was the letter some kind of scam, a bit like a phishing email? But no one had asked for his bank details, had they? He laughed cynically. Not that there was anything they'd be able to steal anyway.

Weird. Totally odd. He picked up his spare mobile, the old Nokia pay-as-you-go one that he'd sent the texts from, and looked in his incoming messages. Nothing new. He'd been expecting more but nothing else had turned up and he didn't know if that was a good thing or a bad thing.

When that first reply had come back from Rhiannon, he'd been hopeful that it would bring a financial benefit to him. Not so. All she'd done was try to sidetrack him with some dirt on Kim. He looked through the text again:

> *Whoever you are that keeps hassling us with these stupid messages, maybe you should just check out Kim Taylor and leave the rest of us alone. She is the one with all the secrets. And the one with all the money.* SHE IS HIDING SOME-THING. *There's been an issue with her police check about her address – she lives at 4, The Elms, which is a substantial property,* GO AND SEE IT FOR YOURSELF. *She was also seen a few days ago withdrawing a large amount of cash.*

Jarvis distracted himself by gathering up a few things for the weekend: clothes, toiletries, Hayden's football from the garage. He packed a separate holdall for Hayden to take to Helena's house for half term.

He tidied up the kitchen and emptied the dishwasher, put out the recycling. He stacked up the pile of bills and slotted them back in the drawer, mulling over the situation with the letter and the text, pondering his worsening economic situation and his next move.

'Ahhgh.' He rubbed furiously at his head, berating himself for being such a procrastinator. He needed to take action; he couldn't just wait and hope for a lucky source of money to turn up on a scratch card or a lottery ticket or an online roulette win. The gambling was seriously affecting his finances and his mental health.

He checked for any new texts again – still nothing – and then turned his mind to that information about Kim. It could be put to good use if he handled it correctly, and he'd already put out a few feelers. Like this morning in the school playground where he'd tried to chat with her, be a bit more friendly.

'Don't worry about the situation in the park the other night,' he'd said, reassuringly. 'I won't let the cat out of the bag.' He'd tried to be smiley, approachable, a bit flirty.

She was quite good-looking if you could see beyond the dowdy coat and jeans: it was something that he'd only recently recognised. Olive skin and brown eyes; full natural lips that could look so carnal with a practised flick of the tongue. Having a decent man in tow might encourage her to make more effort with her appearance. She'd got a sexy smile if you could get one out of her. And a nice arse and legs. He'd snapped a couple of discreet photographs of her as she'd left through the school gates.

Where had she come from? Jarvis was certain that Dulcie hadn't been at the primary school for long, maybe only a year.

Where had they lived before? What other people did she have in her life? Friends? Partners?

He wanted to know much more. Because if Kim had money...

He needed it. He was desperate.

He'd thought about how he could play this. It had to be something subtle. Maybe he could strike up a friendship, and before too long, an intimate relationship. He'd certainly give that a go and could think of no reason why she would reject him. There were actually two good reasons why it would work well: he got on with Dulcie and she trusted him; and Hayden liked Kim. It seemed like a no-brainer.

They could get drunk together at the weekend away, he could make a move... By the time the kids were back at school after the half term they would be a few dates down the line and probably even getting it on in bed.

Yeah.

Two coffees later, and he'd decided that it was his best option.

He nodded and smiled to himself. Well, well, well. A house on The Elms: number four to be exact. She'd kept that little secret under her hat. He checked the time and found that he'd got over two hours to spare before school finished.

Seize the moment, he told himself. He would take Rhiannon's advice; he would go and see it for himself.

FIFTEEN

JARVIS

Friday – the first day of the weekend away

Jarvis threw a neutral green hoodie over his tracksuit and put on his walking boots. A brisk stroll to the edge of town would pique his curiosity, and then he could call at the Tesco Express to pick up food for the kids on his way home.

The Friday afternoon traffic madness hadn't hit full throttle as Jarvis made his way out of town and through the leafy avenues. A moody sky foreshadowed the start of an early dusk. As he reached the perimeter of The Elms and saw from a walker's perspective the grandeur of the properties and the prestige vehicles parked in the driveways, he couldn't believe that Rhiannon had got her information correct. This surely couldn't be where Kim lived, could it? It was baffling to think that Kim had been residing in some luxury abode – the type of residence where you'd find millionaire bankers and company executives, no less – while hiding behind the shabby façade of budget clothing and free childcare and menial jobs.

Jarvis crossed the road to get to the even-numbered houses. By his judgement, number four was the next one along, just past where an Aston Martin slouched on the wide, grassy verge. He stepped up his pace in anticipation.

Ahh. Number four. There it was. A lichen-covered sign hanging on the open sagging gate displayed the name Carmel.

He stood at the end of the drive, taking it in. Yes, it was a massive period residence, almost on the scale of a small stately home. But there was no denying its poor condition, its dilapidation. The window frames had shed their paint and opened their grain to the elements. Fallen roof slates lay broken on the path, and a section of guttering hung precariously from one remaining rusty bracket. There were acres of greenery swathed around the place: wild and rambling lengths of bramble and ivy had mauled the render off the west wall and were within easy reach of the crumbling chimney stack. Bold, deviant trees stalked the borders: a liability waiting to happen.

There were no lights visible inside the place. Perhaps Kim was out, at work. Surreptitiously, Jarvis edged along the sprawling shrubbery on the drive to take a closer look at the house. The path was breached with thistles and there were algae-ridden steps up to a covered porch area. The front door was huge, a rectangular oak slab rough with age that displayed a creepy-looking cast iron door knocker. He stepped between the pillars, underneath the canopy, and saw that the door knocker was in the shape of a severed hand. It was like something out of a horror film. Beside the door there was a stone bench with a pile of logs on it and a pair of muddy boots underneath that he immediately recognised as Kim's. Hanging on a nail above the bench was a navy waterproof coat, flecked with dirt. He'd seen Kim wearing that very garment: the hood low over her eyes, collar zipped up to the rain when she picked up Dulcie last week.

So, Rhiannon's information *was* correct.

But how did someone get to live in a place like this? He remembered that at the first childcare circle meeting Kim introduced herself as a single parent, so there was obviously no rich husband around, but maybe she was gifted the place as part of a divorce settlement.

Suddenly, the front window was lit up and the glow spilled out onto the path. Jarvis flattened himself against the frame of the door. He couldn't leave yet; Kim might see him. But what if she opened the door? What if she was on her way outside? He needed to construct a convincing story to explain his presence on her porch. Maybe something to do with the weekend away and that he'd tried to call her but his phone was dodgy so he'd been passing and had decided to drop in instead.

But how did he know where she lived?

Hmm. His story had fallen apart. He needed something better.

Perhaps he could say that someone had left a wallet at the gym with a driving licence in it and he'd come to bring it back to number *fourteen* The Elms. Then she would say that this house was actually number four, and he could pretend to be a bit of an idiot and they would have a laugh about it without him having to show her the wallet or the licence.

Yes, that could work. In fact, he should just knock on the door and use the story anyway. He didn't need to wait for her to come out and catch him.

The heavy iron door knocker was cold and freaked him out as he lifted it. It felt like a dead child's hand. He rapped it three times and waited. Behind the door he heard scraping, a creak, some kind of movement in the hallway, then the click of another light switch.

'Just a moment,' a frail voice said. It wasn't Kim; maybe it was her mother?

He smoothed a hand through his hair in readiness.

The door groaned open eventually and Jarvis was confronted by a grizzled old lady, harshly made up with stark, white face powder and blue eyeshadow. Her crimson lipstick had bled into the wrinkles around her mouth and smudged onto her teeth. She leaned heavily on a walking frame, panting at her effort but holding a hand up to prevent him from speaking first.

'Ahh, you've finally arrived to do the trees,' she said, after her breathing had settled. 'I thought you might have come yesterday but I expect the rain must have kept you away. Kim clarified with you the branches that need to come off, didn't she?'

'Kim?' said Jarvis. 'Is she around?'

'I'm afraid she's not at the present time, but no matter. I have the money and, yes, in fact I will pay you now because it will save me having to do it later. I like to get comfortable for the afternoon instead of running up and down answering the door.'

Her version of running up and down was different to his, thought Jarvis. He had no idea what she was talking about, but she had obviously confused him with someone else.

'Please do come in a moment.' The old lady pulled the door out wider and shambled slowly along the hall to a walnut table where she slid open a drawer.

Jarvis hesitated, not knowing what to do.

'Come inside. You're letting all the warmth out.'

The lady had authority in her voice and Jarvis could do nothing else but step inside and push the door closed behind him. Immediately, his nostrils were inflamed by the smell of something unpleasant, like decomposing vermin. He'd put rat poison in his loft once, to deal with some nocturnal scratching, and the resultant stench of dead animal that leached out through his walls over the next fortnight was something that he would never forget.

He gazed around, flitting his eyes over the walls at gold-framed oil paintings whose canvases had warped with damp; the crystal chandelier thick with dust that hung from the high ceiling; the intricate silver vases on the table that had blackened with disregard.

'So, are you Kim's... mother? Grandmother?' Jarvis had clearly triggered the old lady with his question, because she turned sharply and glared at him.

'I am certainly not Kim's mother or grandmother. I don't have children, and that is by choice. Kim is my employee, my maid and personal companion.'

'Ahh, it makes sense now. I thought she lived here.' Jarvis had solved the puzzle but was disappointed by the news that Kim was unfortunately not as rich as he'd hoped.

'Kim works for me and was delegated to deal with you regarding the trees that need to be cut back, but it is I who will be paying for your services. If you need to speak to Kim again, I'm afraid she won't be back here until Monday. As I said, we *were* expecting you yesterday.' The old lady had her hands full of cash and was shuffling through a stack of twenty-pound notes.

Jarvis watched, his body beginning to buzz at the sight of the money.

'I understand that Kim agreed six hundred with you?' She held out the notes. 'You might want to check it yourself as my eyes are not what they used to be.'

Jarvis stiffened. What should he do? It was like the perfect crime even though it didn't even feel like a crime: he hadn't broken in; he hadn't tried to con her deliberately. It was just a mistake on her part. And she was loaded anyway; it was unlikely that she would miss the money. It was an opportunity being offered up; his lucky break.

Needs must, he thought, as he reached out and took the cash from her hands.

She stood there, as if expecting something from him.

'Thanks,' he said.

But she wanted him to count through it, and so he flipped his thumb through each note – two, four, six, eight, one hundred – while she watched him. Five-twenty, five-forty, five-sixty.

It was forty pounds short. Should he tell her?

'It's wrong, isn't it?' she said. 'That's why I wanted you to check for yourself. How much?'

'I need another forty,' he replied, unable to believe his good fortune.

She opened the drawer again, and he saw that there was even more cash inside – a whole *lot* more – just stuffed loosely among takeaway menus and window cleaning flyers.

'Here you are.' She handed over the forty pounds. 'I'll just go and lock that front door behind you. You can get through the kitchen to the garden. I'll leave the back door unlocked in case you need to come in and use the lavatory while you're working – it's just through that door opposite the scullery – but please try to be quiet as I'll be having my afternoon nap shortly.'

She pointed the way along the hall, and Jarvis tucked the cash into his pocket as he went through to the huge, cold kitchen that smelled like blocked drains. There was an unlit range – a four-oven beast, its chrome lids pitted with rust – which dominated the far wall, and a variety of battered saucepans sat on a shelf above it. A wooden dresser was adorned with dangling teacups, and a loud bluebottle pestered three wizened apples that rested wearily in a cut glass fruit bowl. Everything looked unloved, neglected.

'Excuse me?' the old lady called after him.

Jarvis turned guiltily. Had she realised her mistake?

'Your tools? Ladders? You haven't left them on the porch, have you?'

He had to think quickly. 'No. No, they're in my van. I've parked out on the road. I'll just go out the back to remind myself what needs doing and then I'll get everything from the van.'

'There's a path by the side of the house. I'd rather you used that than bring everything through the hall.'

'Yep, that's all good. I can do that.'

'And you'll keep the noise down while I have my sleep?'

'Absolutely.' Jarvis did a mock salute before he let himself out of the back door, his left hand curled comfortably around the six hundred pounds in his pocket.

* * *

Outside, he strolled furtively around the trees. Glancing back towards the house, Jarvis wondered if the woman was watching him from one of the windows. He needed to give the impression of authenticity because if she had the slightest suspicion that he wasn't the tree surgeon then she might call the police. Approaching the imposing trunks along the border of the property, he took out his phone and photographed them from different angles. Then he inspected the hefty, rough bark of one of them with a rub and a slap as if it were the rump of a prize bull. He looked again at the house, examining the corners and roofline for signs of CCTV – who wouldn't want at least an alarm installed in a place like this? – but there were no security cameras, no wires; the place was practically inviting criminals around to help themselves.

The rest of the expansive garden was wild with rampant shrubbery. Nettle patches, elder, blousy roses on the verge of releasing their last petals, and an aggressive prickly bush that had pushed in the glass of a wind-buckled greenhouse. He could see at least three rabbits hopping around the distant orchard. There were rat holes in the soil by the fence. Nature had reclaimed the land.

With some proper TLC this place could be worth a packet, he thought. Surely, if the woman can afford six hundred quid to have some trees pruned, she could put money into having the rest of the place tidied up a bit.

He wondered how much Kim got paid to work for her. What tasks she did: cleaning, cooking? Maybe admin and financial stuff too? Rhiannon had told him that she was seen withdrawing money from a cash machine, so it was likely that she had access to the old lady's bank account. He thought back to how the woman pulled out the drawer, revealing all the twenty-pound notes that were stuffed in. He was sure he saw flashes of red fifties, too. It was obvious that she didn't have a clue how much was stashed away in there.

How long did he need to hang around for? He checked the time and found that he'd spent nearly fifteen minutes in the garden. There was no sign of the woman at any of the windows; perhaps she was asleep already. He crept down the path at the side of the house, ready to make his getaway. But then...

What if she'd already looked out of the front window and spotted that he hadn't got a van on the street? What if she was already suspecting him of foul play? If she saw him leaving down the drive she'd be straight on the phone to the police if she hadn't already done so.

Jarvis didn't know what to do. He was suddenly struck by pangs of guilt. Maybe he should return indoors and hand the money back. Oh God, he didn't want a criminal record: he could end up losing his joint custody of Hayden. Why did he ever consider it a good idea to take the cash? No, he needed to do the right thing. He'd be haunted to think that he had stolen money from an old lady.

He slipped back into the house by the kitchen door. Down the hallway he could hear a gentle snoring, and he put his head around the door of what he assumed to be the living room to discover the woman fast asleep in an armchair, head tipped back and her mouth open. Smiling with relief that she wasn't on the phone to the police, he reviewed his options. So. He could either put the money back in the drawer and let his conscience be clear, or he could leave quietly and get away with the perfect crime. Use it to pay the outstanding amount on his council tax bill.

Which course of action would benefit Hayden the most? he

asked himself, knowing that it was a loaded question. Because, of course, his mounting debts would inevitably bring the bailiffs to his door, would get his house repossessed, would leave him and Hayden homeless. And then, what would happen?

He hovered by the walnut table in the hallway. His hand brushed against the handle of the drawer. And before he realised what he was doing – because he certainly didn't want to knowingly steal anything – the drawer had been slid open and he was gazing at the hundreds, maybe even *thousands*, of pounds that filled the space.

Just think what good he could do with that money. What it would mean for Hayden. What it would mean for himself, to not have to worry about the final demands, the threats of court action, the online gambling debts that were accruing daily. It seemed like this was the answer to his problem, his leg up to getting his finances properly sorted out. His late mother used to speak of *blessings in disguise* and this really did feel like such a thing. He needed money – he needed it urgently – and here it was, almost as if it was being offered to him.

There was no other option, really. To refuse it would be like spitting in the face of fate.

He put his hands into the drawer and began to gather up the notes, quietly collating them into a tidy wad. The drawer was deeper than he first realised and as he tried to pull it out a little further the damp wood jarred on its sliding mechanism. The silver vases on the table rocked and clattered, and Jarvis held his breath and grabbed out too late as one of them fell and crashed onto the tiles below. The metallic sound rang out in the hall for far too long.

Fuck, fuck, fuck!

He rammed the stack of cash into his pocket but in his haste dropped a flutter of notes onto the floor. He bent to pick up the vase and set it back on the table. Quickly, he had to get out of here before the woman woke up. But, hang on... He remembered that the front door had been locked. There was no key in the door. He would have to exit through the kitchen, through the back door and down the path at the side of the house. Panicked, he turned to make his getaway without closing the drawer, then suddenly...

What the fuck?

There was an unexpected whack, a flame of blinding pain in his head, and she was here, beside him. The old lady, minus her walking frame, had appeared silently without warning. She had a fireside poker in her hand, raised above her head and ready to hit him again.

'Hey!' Jarvis slammed a hand to the top of his head and felt a warm gush of blood. He stumbled back with the shock, as a swathe of blackness threatened to sink him into unconsciousness.

'You've picked on the wrong person if you think you are going to rob me!' Her splodgy scarlet lips twisted with anger, and she struck him again, catching his cheekbone and the hand that he was holding up to protect his face.

The hall table was knocked and another of the vases tumbled to the floor as Jarvis overbalanced and dropped onto one knee. He willed himself to stay with it; to keep his eyes open, keep his brain and body functioning as he felt the blood from his head wound running down his neck.

'No, no, please.' He cowered with his hands over his head as the woman lurched towards him again, lashing at his arms and fingers with the heavy poker.

How could this be happening? A frail old lady, so deranged with anger that she could possibly even kill him right here. He couldn't let it happen. Hayden was his life: he needed him; he had to think of Hayden; he had to *survive* for him.

Scuffling around on the floor, Jarvis dodged the vicious swipes and managed to get himself upright again. He knew he had to get out, but the woman was blocking his route and the door behind him was locked. He had to do more than just defend himself. He had to act immediately or he could die here. There was nothing else for it.

With a burst of energy, he sprang up and kicked her in the chest as hard as he could.

Thump!

She reeled backwards and her head smashed against the door frame. Air groaned from her lungs as her body crumpled heavily onto the floor. With a clatter, the poker skimmed across the cracked marble tiles and stopped at his feet.

'Shut the bloody door!' There was a shriek from inside the living room. 'Shut the bloody door!'

Jarvis froze. He hadn't realised there was anyone else at home; he'd been sure the old lady was alone when he'd looked in on her sleeping only a few minutes earlier.

He had to get out before anyone saw him. He didn't have time to check that the woman still had a pulse, or to return the money to the drawer, or to wipe away any fingerprints from the handle. With his mind frantic and his body wrapped in a cold sweat, he blundered over her motionless form, trying not to look down at her head and that gruesome gash of a mouth, as the rivulets of blood crept along the outlines of the tiles. In a final moment of madness, he bobbed down and swept up another handful of cash to stuff into his pocket.

Running to the end of the hall, he fiddled with the kitchen door handle, shaking and breathless, eventually breaking outside.

'Shut the bloody door!' The words still screamed after him as he dragged his hood up around his bleeding head and sprinted around the side of the house, down the drive and out onto the road.

SIXTEEN

JARVIS

Friday – the first day of the weekend away

Jarvis set the shower as hot as it would go and stepped in, stripping off his bloody clothes and kicking them into the corner of the tray. The water burned his skin but it didn't stop him shaking uncontrollably, and the steamy receptacle filled with a scalding pink puddle. His head was throbbing with pain and his cheek was so badly swollen that he couldn't properly open his left eye. There were tender weals on his knuckles and fingers, ingrained black with the poker's soot.

What had he done? Oh God, what had he done?

He had surely killed the woman. The way her body was twisted in a heap on the floor. The amount of dark blood that leached away from her head. If he went to prison what would happen to Hayden?

He couldn't bear to think about it.

He couldn't let himself get caught. Oh God, no.

Still trembling, shivering, he switched off the shower and got out, to look at himself in the mirror. Oh fuck, what a sight! The bleeding from a deep cut on his head wouldn't stop; he applied pressure from a towel as hard as he could. His face looked like he'd been in a boxing ring, and he wondered if his cheekbone might be fractured.

Self-defence.

Yes. That was what it was. If she hadn't done *this* to him, he wouldn't have kicked her. He would have given the money back and left quietly. But she attacked him and then stood in his way. She basically got what she deserved.

He removed the balled-up bloody towel and checked his head wound again. It was still bleeding. What could he do? In forty minutes' time he had to go and collect five kids, bring them back home, feed and entertain them for two and a half hours and then drive to Christ-knows-where for a mystery weekend break with a load of women that he didn't particularly like. Add into that the whole bizarre complication of the anonymous letters and secrets and confessions and then the possibility of the police coming to arrest him and who knew what might happen...

Fuck.

Suddenly, the thought of the woman lying on the floor came back to him and the enormity of what he had done hit him straight in the gut. The room reeled and he gripped the bathroom sink with two hands before he was retching, spewing up sour strands of bile, his stomach contracting and pulling him over and over to groan and spit and wipe the dripping sweat from his face. His eyes watered so much that he couldn't see. He vomited again and again, whimpering like a child.

Eventually, when his body felt totally wrung out, he took some deep breaths and gulped cold water straight from the tap. All he wanted to do was lie down and sleep but he knew that he couldn't be weak: if he was going to survive then he needed to motivate himself. He needed sugar, energy. He had to make a plan.

There was a can of Red Bull in the back of the fridge and he swigged it down as he listed his priorities.

First aid first. He couldn't possibly go to A&E, and he knew no one with medical knowledge that he could call in a favour from.

With a vague but inspirational scene from *Rambo* in his mind, Jarvis knew that he needed to deal with his injuries. He remembered that there was superglue in the kitchen drawer, and he was sure that there was something on the internet about using it instead of stitching up cuts. Whatever, it would have to do, because he was no good at sewing.

He collected what he needed, then parted his hair around the cut, drying up as much blood as he could with a clean towel.

This is it, he told himself. Come on, you can do it.

He pierced the end of the glue tube and squirted the whole lot along the seam of his head wound before pressing the edges together. Fuck, that stung! Five seconds. Ten seconds. Fifteen seconds. He carefully removed his fingers and watched for bleeding. There was nothing seeping out. It appeared to have worked.

Next, his swollen eye and cheekbone. He got a pack of garden peas from the freezer and held them onto the side of his face. It felt better immediately. He found Elastoplast strips for his fingers and knuckles, and taped them up neatly.

The wet, bloody clothing in the shower tray was removed and bagged up for the bin. He dressed in a clean tracksuit and squirted a liberal amount of cologne around his neck. He gathered up all the money – ten, twenty and fifty-pound notes that he'd thrown onto the bed before showering – and shoved most of it in a sock to secrete at the back of his underwear drawer, stuffing a handful into his pocket.

Time check: he'd got fifteen minutes before he had to be on his way to school.

Face check: the swelling around his eye had reduced but it

looked like his cheekbone was showing signs of bruising. He put the peas back in the freezer because they'd started to defrost.

He mopped all traces of blood from the bathroom and shower, and treated some red droplets on the landing carpet with stain remover. Tidied away the wet towels and first aid stuff. Wiped around the sink and mirror.

Story time, he told himself as he looked again at his busted face in the mirror. Everyone would ask how he did it, wouldn't they? He couldn't say that he did it at the gym because then employer liability would be brought up and he'd have to fill in loads of forms. No. It had to be something quite random but accidental. A trip while out jogging. Face plant against the kerb. That would explain his cheek and fingers. He wouldn't mention the injury on the top of his head because it would be difficult to sustain something like that from a fall on the pavement. A hat was required. He would cover up his head, and then no one would even see the damage.

He took his favourite beanie from a bedroom drawer. One last look at his superglued wound – the bleeding had stopped completely now – and he pulled it on, down over his ears, before setting off to get the kids from school.

SEVENTEEN

THE WEEKEND AWAY

Friday – the first night of the weekend away

Bated silence crams the room. It's like after a bomb goes off where there's that surreal, vacant period before people start screaming.

'Shit,' says Stacey eventually, quietly, as she puts a hand up to her mouth. 'You killed your brother?'

'How?' Jarvis twitches.

'Don't tell me, I don't want to know.' Rhiannon shudders and gives Kim a look of disgust.

Nina gets up and shuts the dining room door so that the noise from the children is muffled. She goes and stands by the window, looking out at nothing but the vehement sea spray that flings itself sporadically at the glass.

'You've been looking after our children for the past seven weeks,' says Nina. 'We have put them in your care and trusted you to keep them safe. Why weren't we told about this? Is this why you've evaded your police check?'

'I didn't evade the police check, it was just a mistake,' says Kim. Her shamed face glows in the candlelight. 'I didn't go back far enough with my previous addresses. But I've redone the form and sent it back.'

'How old was he?' says Stacey. 'What was his name?'

Kim's head is in her hands, hanging over the table. A tear drips onto the mahogany. 'He was eight.' She sniffs and wipes a hand across her face. 'He—'

The door suddenly bursts open.

'Mum, Hayden is being silly and keeps trying to pull my trousers down.' Freya's crumpled face tugs Rhiannon away from the table to go and check on the children.

There's a commotion through the open door with protestations and arguments, and the running through of Coralie to hurl herself into Stacey's arms where she begins to cry.

'OK, I think it's probably time for the kids to go to bed.' Nina stands up and marches into the middle of the turmoil. 'Bobby! Bedtime. Go and put your pyjamas on and get into bed. I'll bring you up a drink and a biscuit.'

Kim composes herself before disappearing discreetly to collect Dulcie and take her up to the chilly attic room.

Jarvis looks across at Stacey who is still comforting her daughter. 'Well, what do you make of all that then? Do you think we'll be safe tonight? Or had we better lock our doors?'

'Shh.' Stacey puts a finger over her lips, a repulsed frown in her brow. It ought to be obvious that the subject of Kim killing her brother shouldn't be spoken about in front of the children.

'So, you're happy with her being here, are you? Under the same roof as us and our kids, knowing what she's done?'

'Of course not.' Stacey shivers and shakes her head. 'I'm just as shocked as you. But we don't know the facts, do we, and until we do, maybe we shouldn't speculate.'

Jarvis pulls a face and holds out his hands. 'Whatever. But I'm just thinking of child safety. Come on then, dude.' Hayden is waiting to be taken to bed, still claiming that he hasn't touched Freya's trousers.

. . .

An hour later, the children are asleep and all the adults apart
from Kim have returned to the dining room to continue with the
drinks and food, this time with the addition of urgent discussion. Music plays at a lower volume and they keep their voices
suppressed so as not to wake their sleeping offspring or let Kim
hear their gossip.

'So. What did you make of her *confession*?' Nina draws
inverted commas in the air. 'Do you think it was actually
genuine?'

Rhiannon sits forward. 'What, you mean it might just be
her... I don't know... attention-seeking?'

'Christ, you wouldn't make up that sort of thing, would
you?' says Jarvis.

'How dangerous do you think she is, though? What are we
supposed to do now?'

'Really, we ought to leave. Just take our kids out of bed and
go home. How can we stay, knowing what we know?'

Rhiannon closes her eyes and presses her fingers on her
eyelids. 'We're stuck here. The road is flooded and we can't get
out.'

'It might have cleared now.' Jarvis picks up his phone to
check their situation.

Nina is already scrolling. 'No, the road is still closed. It
looks like we're staying.'

'Well... to be fair... what can she actually do to us? We could
easily overpower her. And she's been childminding our kids for
the past seven weeks, so why are we panicking now, just
because she's told us *that*? I think she's making stuff up to get
attention. She likes to tell stories.' Rhiannon is insistent. 'We
don't really know much about her, do we?'

'I found out a few things on the way here. She told me that
she was brought up in care,' says Stacey. 'She's moved house so

many times – she was listing all the places where she lived in children's homes and foster care – because her mum died when she was young. She came to the town a year ago because she wanted Dulcie to go to a nice school.'

Rhiannon appears not to accept Stacey's information. 'Do you really believe that? When she actually lives on The Elms?'

'She doesn't,' says Jarvis, instantly regretting his words.

'How do *you* know?' Nina stares at him. She looks menacing in candlelight: sunken cheeks; lips twisted in a scowl; stencilled eyebrows guarding her dark eyes that are like portals to a haunted place.

'Well, I mean...' Jarvis pulls at the neck of his shirt and looks away from her. 'She can't *possibly* live there. I can't believe for a second that she does.'

'Yeah, we all found it hard to believe, too. But it's true. Her secret home.'

'She never mentioned a younger brother to me,' says Stacey. 'It's like she has two versions of herself.'

Nina's eyes widen. 'Perhaps she's been in prison? That would explain the issue with the police check and the addresses.'

'Hmm, you could be right. Or it could have been a young offenders' institution if she was under eighteen.'

'But, how does someone go from being locked up for murder to living on The Elms? It's quite a step up, isn't it? I just can't get my head round it.'

'And she also said earlier that she wouldn't pay blackmail money to anyone because she was broke, yet I – one hundred per cent true – saw her taking out a massive amount of money from the Sainsbury's cash machine.'

'Compulsive liar. That's what she is.'

'I have the horrible, deep-down gut feeling that she *did* kill her brother, though. I just do. She had such an authenticity about her when she said it. Didn't you notice?'

'I really don't know how she can be up there sleeping after telling us what she's just told us.'

'And to think that she's been looking after our kids all this time... If only we'd known what she'd done. Well, we just wouldn't have had her in the circle, would we?'

They resign themselves to spending the night in the house, finishing off the stack of profiteroles and opening another bottle of Prosecco. Jarvis has got through the four cans of lager and switched to the bottle of red wine that Kim started earlier. Rhiannon rises to tend to the fire, tossing on more logs. The room is warm, and the alcohol combined with Kim's revelation has put everyone in a strange juxtaposition of mellow-minded-ness and vigilance.

'So, what do we do about her?' Nina asks. 'She's upstairs, actually in the same house with us and our children. I mean, should we assume that we might be in danger?'

'Better lock the knives up,' Jarvis says.

Rhiannon is tapping a finger against her chin pensively. 'We should go upstairs and question her about it. Wake her up.'

'Like interrogators do when they're torturing people?' Stacey looks appalled.

'But it's not as if we're going to hurt her, though, is it? We just want answers, because this affects all of us.'

'And then what? If we find out she's a cold-blooded killer, what do we do? Send her back to bed with a cup of cocoa?'

'Well, we'll insist that she leaves. We can't have her around the children.'

'She hasn't got a car,' says Stacey. 'I gave her a lift here. And Dulcie is with her. We can't just kick them out in this weather in the middle of the night, with the road blocked and nowhere for them to go.'

'So, are you happy for her to stay? Whatever her story is?'

'I've had enough of this discussion. Come on,' says Nina, decisively pushing back her chair and indicating to Jarvis that he should accompany her. 'The fairest thing to do is go and wake her up and bring her back down here. Dulcie doesn't need to be involved in the questioning, so if we can try not to disturb her.'

The door clunks suddenly and swings open.

Everyone jolts and turns; Rhiannon gives a gasp of surprise; Stacey knocks over her glass.

Kim stands there in the doorway.

'Let me tell you something else, too,' she says. '*I* sent the letters.'

PART TWO

EIGHTEEN
KIM

Before the childcare circle

Secrets.

I have lots of them. When you've been around as many places as I have you collect them like souvenirs. It seems that the fewer friends you have, the more secrets you store up, because you don't have anyone you can trust enough to unload onto.

There have only really been two people that I have ever been close to.

One was my little brother, Dylan.

And the other is Paul Eyrie.

Dylan was the funniest, loveliest little brother. If only we could have had a normal, less tragic upbringing... My mind often drifts to how things might be now if our mother hadn't died when she did. Christmases would be fabulous affairs of laughter and family and meals: gatherings with me, Dulcie, Mum, and Dylan and the partner and children he never got to have. A table heaving with food and crackers and chinking glasses and cousins enjoying each other's company. Presents and cooking smells and the type of chaos that can be seen in Christmas adverts when a household throws a party, where it's not quite perfect but everyone loves each other nevertheless.

What if it could have just been like that?

It wasn't, though.

Our mother died of ovarian cancer when I was seven and Dylan was two. I don't remember much about our father, who left before Dylan was born, apart from brief scenes of tension and fear and feeling the need to keep out of his way. My last memory of him was a major argument between him and my mother about a lost passport that he needed, which resulted in him ripping off my bedroom door in anger before leaving the house and razzing up the road on his motorbike.

After he had gone, our mother told me in a drunken confession that he had emigrated with a slag of a woman to Spain. She'd tried her best to stop him, she said, taking me into the kitchen and heaving out the cooker from between the greasy units. There on the floor was our father's missing passport: Mum had secretly dropped it down the back of the appliance in an effort to prevent his departure. I looked at the photograph that seemed to bear no relation to what he looked like; I traced my finger under the name *Jeremy*.

We never saw or heard from him again. He never got to set eyes on his son, Dylan, who was born only a few weeks later.

When our mother died and we were in our early days of foster care, the social services claimed to be trying to get in touch with him, and I speculated that the warm Spanish climate would have nourished him, bringing out his previously hidden paternal feelings to burgeon like a flowering shrub. Maybe he would come to claim us, and it would be like the sort of bitter-sweet ending that all the best films had: we would run to each other in an airport and then he would take us away to live in a place that was gloriously sunny and every meal was a barbeque by a pool.

Of course, nothing of the sort happened. Our elusive father could not be traced. We were put into care and this was with foster families who had their own children that hated us, and it was also in children's homes where the staff changed constantly and we struggled to attach ourselves to either places or people.

The only bond we had was with each other. I would have done anything for Dylan. Anything. I would have fought to the death to protect him.

Despite our chaotic lives where we were moved from home to home, we vowed to each other that we would never be separated, and thankfully the social workers always ensured that we were kept together in every placement. We craved and lived for the time when a prosperous and doting couple would adopt us and give us the happiness and security of a normal family.

But by the time I was twelve and Dylan was seven, we were stuck in yet another children's home and hope had almost gone that we would land the parents we so desired.

We had been at Summerbone House in north Lincolnshire for around eight months when Paul Eyrie arrived there. He was eleven years old, a scrawny kid with colourless skin, close-cropped dark hair, and bulging eyes that always looked sore and itchy. One of his arms dangled, loose and ineffective, inside the sleeve of his mock-leather jacket, the result of an injury at birth that had left it partially paralysed. Yet, although his appearance initially screamed out *victim* and *easy prey*, we were soon surprised. Paul ranged the home with an admirable authority, quickly gaining the respect of staff and children. A gift of the gab; a good sense of humour; a flair for diffusing difficult situations with some quirky form of entertainment like tap dancing or balancing spoons on his nose. Like us, he had been in the system for many years, having been removed from his family who had severely neglected him. Unlike me and Dylan, though, he had actually flourished under the state's care.

'You have to embrace life,' he told us, when we asked him why he had such positivity. How could he not recognise how bleak our lives were? 'Our hearts are beating, we have air in our lungs, a bed to sleep in and food to eat.'

We tried to point out to him that it would be so much better to be with a family; we would be able to do stuff that was normal.

He laughed. 'Normal? Who wants to be normal? Families aren't always the best option: I'm proof of that. We're in an exceptional position here where we have our basic requirements met and our futures in front of us. All we need is an open mind. And because we don't have families, we have to believe in *ourselves*.' He tapped his forehead with his good hand. 'We can do anything, change anything. Being happy is like a way of getting revenge on the bad stuff that's happened before.'

He was like a preacher. Convincing, charismatic, infectious. He spoke with a wisdom that belied his age. And so we actually started to believe that adopting his mindset would help us, too.

A level of contentment settled in me that calmed my inner dissatisfaction. I started to see how optimism and hope could take me from one week to the next without any risk of a crying fit or trashing my room or yelling abuse at the staff who were only trying to do their jobs.

I was even persuaded to consider that life was pretty good on the whole.

But then the unthinkable happened.

I sent Dylan to his death.

NINETEEN

KIM

Before the childcare circle

Summerbone House teamed up with other children's residential establishments in the county for a Christmas party in a centrally located community centre. A gathering of unwanted misfits with emotional and behavioural issues between the ages of five and sixteen years was organised in the hope that it would bring some seasonal cheer and good publicity in the local newspapers.

There was music and games and an excessive buffet. A mayor from somewhere turned up dressed as Santa Claus and gave away a stack of selection boxes while avoiding physical contact with any of the children. Someone was sick. Someone kicked off and had to be taken outside. Someone was made an example of for trying to steal a youth worker's phone. A couple of teenagers that we didn't know were caught groping each other in the toilets. We were cajoled into doing the Macarena. All the tinsel on the Christmas tree was stolen to be worn as decorative scarves as we yelled our hearts out to 'I Wish It Could Be Christmas Every Day'. This was the extent of the fun.

At the end of the event there was a special announcement. There would be a seaside holiday at the end of May, in a specially donated cottage on the east Yorkshire coast, accommodating four staff and six children. Obviously, this meant that not everyone would be able to go, so it would be decided upon in the style of a lottery.

'Well, not a lottery. More like a Wonka type of golden ticket,' said one of the youth workers who was trying to get everyone excited about the prospect.

We all had to pick an envelope out of a sack.

'You can either open them now if you want to find out, or you can save your envelopes until Christmas and then it will be a nice surprise,' we were told. I thought at the time that it would only be a nice surprise for the people who got the golden tickets, and the majority of us would end up being disappointed.

The children who were either impatient or who hadn't understood the instructions opened their envelopes right there and then: most of them contained a slip of paper wishing them 'Season's Greetings'; a lucky girl called Tegan squealed as she revealed the shiny corner of her winning place on the coveted holiday.

Paul thought that we should save ours. The anticipation would make Christmas Day more of an event, he said, which immediately convinced Dylan to follow suit. Someone on the bus back to Summerbone House opened theirs and found a golden ticket, and after all the thrill and jealousy of their good luck, I messed about for the rest of the journey pretending to tear my envelope open to the switching hilarity and protestations of Dylan and Paul.

We returned to our rooms and put our envelopes underneath our pillows, making a serious vow to each other not to touch them until Christmas morning.

But I was the one that gave in first, the one that broke our vow.

Temptation taunted me until I came up with a plan that would validate my secret curiosity. I should have left things alone though and not interfered with fate. Because if it hadn't been for my weakness, Dylan might still be alive.

* * *

The door to the office was open as it often was, and Andrea, one of the youth workers, tip-tapped on the computer. I noticed a box of envelopes on her desk and sidled up to stand beside her. She clicked out of her screen and turned to see what I wanted as my fingers reached out to touch the envelopes.

'Everything OK?' she asked me.

'Yeah. Fine. Can I have one of these?' I asked innocently. 'I thought about making a card for someone but I need something to put it in.'

'Help yourself,' she replied without even questioning my lie.

I took three just because I could.

Upstairs, I found that the envelopes were exactly the same as the one under my pillow. I pulled out the sealed one, locked myself in the toilet and opened it.

I had already made a promise to myself: if I got a 'Season's Greetings' slip I would put it in a new envelope and return it back under my pillow to open on Christmas morning; if I got a golden ticket I would put it in a new envelope and swap it with the one under Dylan's pillow. I would give him the holiday at the seaside that he'd never had before.

My heart was thudding as I ripped the flap open. With my eyes closed, I slid my fingers in to feel the glossy exterior of a winning ticket.

Yes. Yes. Yes!

Triumphantly, I pulled it out and pressed the gold surface to my lips. I wanted to cry with bliss, imagining Dylan's delight as he unwrapped his amazing prize. My hands were shaking as I slotted the ticket into one of the new envelopes and sealed it up. Oh God, this was going to be so good! My chest was filled with emotion: pride, altruism, intoxication at the thought of my random act of kindness.

I swapped the envelopes while Dylan was in the shower and waited with butterflies flitting in my belly until Christmas morning.

There were only five of us in the home for Christmas; the other children had been sent out on temporary foster placements. Me, Dylan, and Paul were downstairs by eight thirty, but the twin sisters Rosie and Roxy, who were fifteen and had little to do with us, were still in bed.

The place was staffed reluctantly by three youth workers who would rather have been at home with their own families. Attired in Christmas jumpers and fake smiles, they watched us drag out our presents from under the plastic tree. We unwrapped the usual toiletries, hats, puzzle books and sweets that had inevitably been donated by a local charity. And then it was the moment of truth, the unveiling of the special envelopes.

We held them out in front of us.

Paul laughed and said, 'Does anyone want to swap?'

'Me!' shouted Dylan, and I felt myself go faint as I jumped up to try and grab the prize that I had carefully set up for him to win.

'No, don't do it,' I yelled, unable to stop the envelopes being switched.

Paul shrieked and Dylan threw himself back onto the sofa, and there was a moment where the three of us wrestled and two of the envelopes were dropped before one of the youth workers split us up and tried to restore order in the situation.

'OK, which is which?' Andrea held them up. Mine was still secure in my fist.

Andrea did a shuffling thing and held them out for Paul and Dylan to choose. They took one each and Dylan waited while Paul opened his first.

'I've got one!' He fluttered the ticket high in the air with his good arm and it felt like all the bones in my body went floppy with distress. I couldn't believe that my plan had gone so horribly wrong. In that instant, I hated Paul. I didn't want to be happy anymore.

'Go on, Kim,' Dylan said to me. 'Open yours.'

I made a show of opening my losing envelope and tried to hide the wobble in my bottom lip. 'Ahh, that's a shame.' I screwed up the 'Season's Greetings' message and threw it on the floor.

Dylan's face was a scene of worry and concentration as he carefully worked open the glued seam. I couldn't physically pull my lips into a smile, and looked through my pile of gifts to see what I could give him that would compensate for his disappointment. He could have my big bag of Haribo, I decided.

Suddenly, there was a scream.

'It's a gold one!' He scrambled off the sofa and ran three laps around the room before jumping on top of Paul and yelling with glee.

They started up a chant. 'We're going to the seaside, we're going to the seaside,' and I felt my open-mouthed grin start to make my face ache as I joined in with their celebration. There was a rising sensation, hot and bubbly inside me, that this was the most remarkable thing I had ever done.

Paul pulled himself out of Dylan's grip. 'It's a shame you're not coming, Kim,' he said.

'I'm OK. I'm just so pleased that Dylan got a place.' I winked at him and he winked back at me.

'So am I,' he said.

'You'd better look after him,' I said to Paul, and he assured me that he would.

But he didn't.

He came back without him.

TWENTY

KIM

Before the childcare circle

They told me it was an accident. A storm and high tide had brought down the cliff edge onto the beach. Dylan had become trapped under the detritus, drowning as the water rose. Residents of the resort had been experiencing the coastal erosion for years, but this was a particularly bad landslip, claiming part of a caravan site, and half a bungalow whose remains tottered on the edge, its missing side wall exposing the gaudy pink décor and matching corner suite. Photographs of the devastation appeared on the front page of the *East Riding Gazette* alongside a grainy black and white picture of Dylan. The thick headline shouted:

ORPHAN BOY DROWNS IN WORST STORM FOR SIX YEARS

I was supposed to be shielded from all media but I stole the newspaper from Andrea's handbag on the Monday morning while the children's home was in a subsequent state of chaos.

His death battered me.

How would I live without him?

How would I ever forgive myself for sending him there? It was my ticket. *I* should have gone. I would have been strong enough to survive; I would have returned to be with him again.

'But what was he doing there, on his own?' I screamed at everyone, when the golden-ticket holiday was cut short and they all came home without Dylan.

A social worker that I didn't know and a rigid-faced police officer sat me down with a glass of Coke and explained that he had gone missing at some point late in the afternoon of the Saturday, just before the storm started to break. He had apparently made friends with some older girls: he had been seen playing with them on the beach the day before, and it was assumed that he had gone to find them. Youth workers on the residential went out to look for him around the town after some confusing information from another child about an incident in the penny arcade, but the alarm was not raised about his disappearance until around eight o'clock in the evening when the lifeboats were sent out. There was no sign of him, though. The weather was worsening and the high tide was ferociously scooping out chunks of terrain; already the holidaymakers at the Crag Point Caravan Park had been evacuated to bed and breakfast accommodation as the cliff edge began to fall into the sea. It became too dangerous for the search team that had been out on the rocks; they had to wait until morning, until the storm had subsided and the tide had gone out. An inspection of the beach began at first light, and volunteers combed through the layer of crumbled cliff and bungalow debris and trashed caravan panels.

In the middle of it all, Dylan's body was found, buried deep in the sand with only his head and neck exposed.

My hysterical tears were enraged, burning my face, as adrenaline dealt with the news. I howled and kicked over the coffee table, drenching the social worker with my untouched Coke.

'Why was he on his own? Why was no one looking after

him? He was only eight years old!' I ran for the door, to find
Paul, to inflict some grievous punishment on him: rip off his
limbs, gouge out his eyes, anything that would transfer my pain
onto him. But the staff caught me before I could reach him; they
pinned me down, held me in a safe position where I couldn't
harm myself or anyone else, and waited for a doctor to come and
administer something to suppress my flaming emotions.

* * *

No one ever gave a proper reason why a member of staff wasn't
with Dylan at the beach that afternoon. Of course, there was
some kind of inquiry that found failings in the care procedures;
of course there were sackings; of course someone higher up
resigned at the end of it. But no one properly got arrested or
punished. No one *paid* for it in the way that I wanted them to.

No one hurt like I did.

* * *

Only a couple of weeks after the tragic holiday, Paul Eyrie was
moved to a different children's home. It was probably for his
own safety since I had made so many threats against him,
blaming him above everyone else for Dylan's death. In those
initial days of my grief, I was given constant one-on-one supervi-
sion and watched Paul through an adjoining glass door as he
resumed his life nervously with the others in the common room.
His filo-pastry skin was even paler than before, a veil of bluey-
white translucence over his web of veins; his bad arm seemed
more withered and lifeless, shrunk inside his left sleeve. There
was no longer a smiling enthusiasm about him: he jittered
awkwardly around the place, acting clingy with the staff and
being watchful, occasionally glancing ashen-faced through the
toughened glass panel that retained my fury from him.

The mood in Summerbone House changed. Staff were careful with everything – hot drinks, locks on doors, sharp objects – and whispered endlessly about risk assessments and culpability.

I lost track of time because without my brother I could never see beyond the end of each day, but at some point after Paul had been transferred, on a dour and misty morning, there was an obligatory funeral service for Dylan, and his body was cremated in a small, simple coffin. I don't remember what I wore for the service – medication was my best garment at that point – but I recall that the event took place in some kind of official building a bit like a church, and I had to stand sandwiched between two social workers throughout the service. I wasn't allowed to speak publicly, but someone read out a poem that I had written for the occasion. It didn't rhyme though, and I always regretted that and wished that I could have done better. Later, Dylan's ashes were given to me in a cardboard cube which I decorated with felt-tip hearts and flowers, and I kept them beside my bed for a while. Months, almost half a year, I think. Ultimately, until Christmas crept towards us again and reminded me of what I had done the previous time with the golden ticket – how I had killed my own little brother – which inevitably caused my mental health and behaviour to go on another downward spree.

I did stupid stuff without properly thinking about the consequences.

Just as the weather turned properly cold, everyone from Summerbone House went out to a Christmas Lights Switch-On in a nearby town, and I was insistent that I took Dylan with me, too. But on the way home, just before the food ordering point in the queue of a McDonald's Drive-Thru, I decided on the spur of the moment to cast the box of ashes out of the minibus window. No reason. Numbly, I watched through the back window as we moved up the queue to collect our order and the tyres of the car behind us rolled over the patch of grey dust that was Dylan.

Afterwards, I realised that there were much nicer places where I could have sprinkled his ashes – the glorious park where we once spent a day catching frogs, or the Alton Towers Air ride which was his favourite, or the BMX track near Doncaster where he had learned to ride a bike – but I console myself nowadays with the fact that Dylan always liked Happy Meals.

* * *

I never expected to cross paths with Paul Eyrie again. He was more dead to me than Dylan was. But as my nineteenth birthday loomed, I was on the verge of being shoved out of the care system and into the world. The sheltered hostel accommodation that had been my home for the past two years would no longer be mine; already a claim had been put on my room for the next care leaver.

It was the end of summer: for weeks a stifling August heat had made the hostel bins linger with a smell of fruity putrefaction. No one ever emptied them apart from the supervising staff; a sense of responsibility from independent living had yet to emerge from any of us that resided there. I was in the communal kitchen swishing a teabag around in a cup that said *Keep Calm and Stroke Cats*, which was a bit ironic because pets weren't allowed in the place. Behind me, the door creaked open and I felt the presence of someone standing there, maybe waiting to use the kettle, and I thought, *good luck with that, you'll have to wash one of the dirty mugs in the sink if you want a cuppa*. But then there was an intake of breath, a sense of someone shifting weight from one foot to another and then a voice said,

'Oh God, it's Kim Taylor.'

I spun around.

Paul Eyrie had grown up.

He was taller than me and had beefy shoulders, although one was noticeably bigger than the other. His skin was plump and honey-tanned and his chin was dotted with dark stubble that matched the thick flop of hair on his head. I looked into his eyes, which were a deeper blue than I remembered, and worked out that he would be seventeen years old.

It was discomfiting because he had caught me unprepared for that moment. If I had expected to see him again I would have had my rage ready to be unleashed. But I didn't know what to do as I stood there with the spoon held out, the teabag dripping onto the floor.

He postured his good arm as if to brace himself for an attack; his back was against the wall.

'Don't be mad at me,' he said, in a voice that had clearly broken during the years we had not seen each other.

In that moment there was a surge of emotion. My feelings for Dylan and how I blamed myself for giving him the ticket that took him to the place where he died. My regret at trusting Paul to look after him. My memories of the time in Summerbone House where it seemed like Paul had changed our lives for the better and we'd all had such an unbreakable bond. Me, seeing Paul again and realising how much I'd missed him.

'I don't want to be mad with you anymore.' I dropped the spoon and teabag out of my hand and covered my face as I burst into tears.

He moved forward and held me, pressed against my body as my long-imprisoned sobs of grief erupted and were absorbed by him. We stood like that until my tea had gone cold, until we eventually worked out that throughout all this time of separation there had still been a tiny spark of friendship barely glowing. That day, we had breathed on it so that it could be a burning ember again.

It could be a blazing fire.

TWENTY-ONE

KIM

Before the childcare circle

Paul moved into the hostel, into the room next to mine. I only had three months left to secure new accommodation and my way in the world. But having Paul back gave me a new hope and that place of ethereal positivity which I had inhabited just before Dylan died.

He was like a new brother.

He got a grip of everything, just the way he used to. As soon as his stuff was neatly unpacked into his room, he got the bins emptied and rinsed out, the windows opened to air the place and alleviate the smell. He washed all the dirty pots and cleaned the kitchen; vacuumed the lounge carpet and cleared out all the empty takeaway cartons.

I watched as the place was revitalised, as he put his special stamp on it. Over the past two years there had been hostel staff on hand who would take measures in an emergency and bring in cleaners to deal with our disorder, before we gradually allowed it to return to its usual state of squalor. This wasn't like a token deep-clean, though. This was Paul, the motivator, who devised and pinned up a rota in the kitchen and gave us pep talks and challenged every pizza box that was left on the floor. He hadn't arrived there to be the hostel cleaner; he wasn't going to do it every time. Instead, he inspired and persuaded us to do it for ourselves, for the benefit of each other.

It wasn't just me who was turned by him. He could do it with everyone: he just had that way of convincing people that they could be involved in a better way of doing things. Leadership qualities. That's what he had.

And having him back in my life was fantastic. It was just what I needed at the right time.

By November, though, our residence in adjoining rooms came to an end. I had to prepare for independent living outside of the hostel where I would have to survive on my own.

Being away from Paul in a different town was unthinkable, so with the help of a support worker I found a bedsit in a basement flat only ten minutes' walk away. And, despite leaving school and college with only the most basic qualifications, I got my first job.

Paul fell about laughing when I told him. 'No way! That's just amazing.'

'It's only temporary,' I said. 'But it's better than nothing. And I get a uniform.'

The job was at a garden centre, being a Christmas elf. My duties were to welcome people and take the children through to Santa's Grotto and wait happily before showing them the way out. At the end of the day I had to clean up the grotto and wipe down Santa's armchair, then wrap all the presents ready for the next morning.

I took my job seriously, being polite and punctual and doing every task properly. Paul told me that I would have the chance to make a good impression on my employer which could pay off in other ways. And he was right. By Christmas Eve, when my elf role was terminated, I was offered part-time work as a cleaner. It felt like I had just stepped onto a long, long ladder. But each rung took me to a better life than the one I'd had before.

* * *

I met up with Paul at least three times a week. He was at college, doing business studies which he loved. He talked about investments and profits and how to make a lot of money, as if it was the easiest thing for someone in care to do. But that was him all over: he didn't acknowledge barriers and thought he had the same opportunities as privileged people.

'But we've been in the care system for most of our lives and now we're stuck with this label which means that it's harder for us to get on in the world than it is for normal people. You can't just say you're going to make a lot of money; you need support to get started.' I always doubted his fanciful ideas because I could never see beyond the obstacles.

'I have a plan,' said Paul. 'I'm going to go into property. You can make a lot of money from investing in property.'

I snorted out loud. 'There are people with good jobs who can't afford to buy a home. How can you just say that you'll make money from investing in property? You need *loads* of money for a deposit and then you have to keep up with mortgage payments.'

'Let me tell you a secret.' He was pensive. He massaged the length of his bad arm with his good one, before arranging it in his lap. 'I have money in a trust fund. When I'm eighteen I get access to it. It's nearly two hundred thousand pounds. So, I'm going to buy a house and do it up and sell it and make more money, and then I'm going to keep doing that until I'm rich.'

'A trust fund? How did you get that? I thought your parents neglected you.'

'You see my bad arm?' He poked at the futile limb. 'This is due to something called Erb's Palsy, which was caused by hospital negligence. I was a breech birth and my mother had a long and difficult labour, and the surgeon should have done an emergency caesarean but instead chose to pull me out. It ripped the nerves in my shoulder and left me with a permanent disability. My parents sued, thinking that they would get the money, but instead it was put in a trust fund for me.'

'Wow,' I said. 'Two hundred thousand for an arm. It's a lot of money.'

'I'm going to put it to use as soon as I can withdraw it.'

'So, you'll never have to do a cleaning job for minimum wage,' I said, somewhat bitterly.

He did a half-shrug. 'I could help you as soon as I get access to it. You know I would.'

'I don't need your money. I can earn my own.' I was poor but proud, having recently been contracted to work extra hours at the garden centre, not just cleaning but helping out with shelf stocking, watering plants and marshalling the car park on busy weekends. Stubborn, resilient, I was determined to make my own way in the world without the help of anyone.

* * *

We celebrated Paul's eighteenth birthday with scampi and chips and pints of cider in a pub, and I asked him what it felt like to be a rich adult and if he would still want to associate with me.

He laughed and told me that no amount of money would ever break our friendship. Not even when he became a millionaire.

'You wish,' I said.

'You wait,' he replied. 'I've already been doing some research. There are bargains on the property auction websites and it won't be long before I get a place of my own.'

Just like me, he would have to leave the care system and learn how to live independently. But this was Paul, and obviously he would be brilliant at it because he always had the right attitude to everything.

* * *

He ended up in Rotherham, in a grotty little terrace that he bought cheap due to flood damage. Upstairs, he lived in one of the bedrooms with a kettle and microwave while he painstakingly learned the business of renovating houses. He made mistakes with contractors: plumbers let him down and electricians ripped him off, and his own left arm was often a barrier to some of the tasks that most people would be able to do for themselves, but despite this he struggled on and kept a smile on his face.

I visited occasionally, but it took two buses to get there and I was often faced with cold and dirty conditions: a ceiling in the process of being pulled down, or the absence of a bathroom with a bucket being used for a toilet. So, for what seemed like a long time, we saw a lot less of each other.

And with only the threads of our shared past connecting us, we drifted apart; we made separate lives.

I fell in love with a thirty-year-old horticulturalist called Willis who breezed into a job at the garden centre, completely reorganising the shrubs and trees section in order to create a polytunnel area where he could propagate indigenous heritage plants. His passion for his work rubbed off on me and soon I was part of a guerilla gardening group, planting pumpkins and beans on waste ground, and sowing wildflower seeds on verges and roundabouts. We got our hands dirty together, and he introduced me to new things: kimchi and sourdough bread; bamboo toothbrushes; soap nuts; the songs of Roy Harper and Martha Wainwright and Nick Drake. We sat in a corner and French-kissed like our lives depended on it at the end-of-summer work's barbeque, not giving a toss about what any of our colleagues thought.

I would have given everything to spend the rest of my life with him and I assumed he felt the same. But it wasn't to be. He was a free spirit and by the following February he had gone. Someone told me that he'd got a job in New Zealand; someone else said he'd gone travelling in Thailand. Willis himself, despite writing me a long and beautiful letter urging me to carry on with the radical planting, didn't say where he had gone or why.

* * *

By the time my broken heart had mended, Paul had sold his house and bought another one that was just as dilapidated as the first. This time though, and with lessons learned from his initial effort, he used contractors that he could trust and only did the work that he knew he was capable of. Within three months it was completed and sold, and yet another one bought, and it seemed that Paul had firmly established himself as a property developer. His most recent house was only a short bus ride away and – partly to distance myself from the whole Willis situation – it felt like the right time to resume our friendship.

We went out and ate pizza – I paid for my share – and the special spark was still there. His eyes shone as he told me about his work; he hugged me and said 'well done' when I told him I was finally over Willis.

'It's great to have you back,' he said. 'I've missed you so much.'

We clinked glasses.

'Best friends forever,' said Paul.

TWENTY-TWO

THE WEEKEND AWAY

Friday – the first night of the weekend away

'You sent the letters?' Stacey is horrified. 'Why? Why would you put us through a week of absolute torment, wondering if we're being blackmailed?'

Kim returns to the chair she was sitting in earlier. 'It wasn't blackmail. I never asked for money. It just seemed like a good method—'

'Look, Kim – I don't know if you were listening outside the door just then – you may have realised that we've got concerns about you being here now that you've admitted to murdering your brother.'

'I didn't *murder* my brother.' Kim's chin is set hard as she turns to answer Nina. 'I came to get a glass of water and heard you all talking about me and realised that you've made some wrong assumptions, thinking that I'm some kind of mad and dangerous child killer. So, I want to tell you everything, I want to tell you *my* darkest secret. Right now. Then you'll be able to sleep without worrying that I'm going to kill your kids during the night.'

There's an expectant pause, where everyone waits, and the only sound is of Stacey, dabbing at the spilt water on the table.

'Ready when you are,' says Nina.

'I don't know why you thought I murdered my brother. I didn't. But I've lived with this dark secret for years, thinking that I caused his death by sending him somewhere he shouldn't have gone. I won a prize – a trip to the seaside – but I gave it to him so that he could go in my place because he'd never been to the seaside before. And while he was away he drowned; he never came back. I felt like it was all my fault.' Kim's eyes are brimming with tears. 'It broke my heart. The guilt has plagued me for years but I have never told anyone about it.'

'But why the letters...?'

'This group has been the closest thing I've had to friendship in my life. I wanted a reason to open up to everyone, and I thought it would be good for us all to share our secrets. The letters were just a tool to facilitate that. I'm sure I read about it somewhere as, like, a method of therapy.'

'A method of therapy?' Rhiannon is clearly angry. 'Surely you understand that people have secrets for a reason? They don't want to share them because... well, because...'

'Because we're ashamed of what we've done and we just want to bury that shame and forget about it. Not dig it up again.' Stacey speaks quietly, a contrast to Rhiannon's outburst.

'It seemed as if the letters were accusing us of being criminals, didn't it?' Nina says to Jarvis. 'As if someone *already knew* what our secrets were and they would expose them if we didn't tell. It certainly didn't feel like *therapy*.'

'Well, I'm sorry if you were worried by the letters. But, as I said, I just wanted to be able to talk about my little brother because I've never properly got over him.'

'You could have told us any time. We would have listened.' Stacey tries to sound kind and sincere. 'Some of us have experienced grief, too. You don't need to go through it alone.'

'So, we don't need to worry about you being upstairs tonight? We're all safe then?' Jarvis seems breathless as he wipes his sweaty brow.

Kim looks at the table and puts her finger over a pastry crumb. Tears are dripping down her face. 'You're all safe tonight. I promise you.'

'I think maybe we should get some sleep,' Rhiannon suggests. 'The kids will probably be up sooner than we'd like.'

Everyone rises from the table, shifting plates and glasses to the kitchen. Their moods are more subdued; their earlier fears calmed.

'Thanks for letting me tell you,' says Kim. 'I'm not good at all the people stuff, but it feels better now that you know about Dylan.' She wipes her eyes, takes a glass of water and leaves the room. 'Goodnight, everyone.'

The rest of them stand and survey each other, listening to Kim climbing the stairs.

'Bit weird,' says Nina in a low voice.

Stacey shrugs. 'Well, it's like she said: she's not really a people person.'

'Hmm. It feels like there's more to it than that,' says Rhiannon.

'Well, at least we're safe.' Jarvis looks through the window at the end of the room, out towards the street. No flashing blue lights, no officers on the drive. His head throbs in agony; sleep won't come easy tonight.

* * *

The attic is freezing, but Dulcie is fast asleep underneath a pile of blankets on the bed. Kim keeps her socks on and slips quietly in beside her, setting her alarm for seven thirty in the morning.

Below her, she listens as the others make their way upstairs to their rooms. She sends a text to Paul:

All going as planned. See you tomorrow.

* * *

Saturday – the second day of the weekend away

It is still dark when Kim wakes up. She dresses quickly without putting the light on, feeling her breath cloud around her face.

Downstairs, she makes a start on breakfast, cooking all the bacon and sausages and leaving them on a low oven setting to keep warm. She butters bread, grills the tomatoes and mushrooms, and Dulcie helps her to lay the table. When everything is prepared, Kim washes all the glasses and crockery from the previous evening and puts them away.

It's not long before there is movement from upstairs. Hayden and Bobby make an appearance first, and are eating cereals at the table by the time Freya and Coralie turn up.

Stacey follows in a fluffy dressing gown. 'What's going on? It feels like it's still early.'

'I thought I would take the kids out onto the beach for a run around,' says Kim. 'I'm always an early riser and I don't mind if everyone else wants to lie-in.'

'I'm not sure about...' Stacey peers out of the window to the grey coast.

'The tide is out and we can go and make sandcastles.' Kim points to the buckets and spades that she's already lined up by the door.

'Yes! We want to go on the beach!' Coralie jumps about excitedly and starts a loud chain reaction in the other children.

'Will you be OK on your own with them?' says Stacey. 'I mean, it won't take long for me to get dressed: I could come with you.'

'It's fine,' says Kim. 'You chill out here. Help yourself to breakfast, it's all in the oven.'

Stacey opens the oven door and smells the bacon. 'Oh gosh, you're a saint. What a lovely thing to do.' She reaches out and touches Kim on the arm. 'Last night. It was a bit, you know. I think some of us just misunderstood you initially. I'm sure people didn't mean what they said. But I hope we can all make it work this weekend.'

'I'm sure we can.' Kim pulls a tight smile and indicates for the children to put their shoes on because she's ready to take them out.

Stacey helps Coralie zip up her coat before planting a kiss on the top of her head. 'Be careful, sweetie. Don't go near the edge of the sea or the rocks. Beaches can be dangerous places.'

'Morning, campers.' Rhiannon skips barefoot down the stairs in a Lycra bodysuit.

Nina and Stacey are wrapped in cosy bathrobes over their nightwear, hungrily tucking into the breakfast that Kim has left for them. Jarvis – still wearing his beanie hat – is leaning his head into his hands and taking deep, measured breaths.

'You don't look well,' Rhiannon tells him. 'That swelling on your face seems to have got worse. And the bruising has come out more.'

'I feel like crap,' he says. 'Really hot and sweaty, like I'm going down with a fever.'

'Maybe you need to take that hat off.' She swipes towards him as he dodges out of her way.

'Leave it alone. I'm just...'

'...dealing with a monstrous hangover.' Nina laughs.

'No. I didn't drink much. This feels more like flu.' Jarvis shivers and wraps his arms around his body. 'Does anyone have any painkillers?'

Rhiannon collects a pack from her handbag and tosses them

across the table. 'How come it's so quiet? Where's everyone else?'

'Kids are at the beach.' Stacey wags a thumb towards the window. 'Kim took them out to play earlier.'

Rhiannon stares out of the window, trying to spot where the children are. 'Can't see them anywhere. The beach looks deserted. Should we go out and check?'

'Don't worry about them; they'll be fine,' says Jarvis, popping pills out of the blister pack and pouring himself a glass of orange juice.

'That's not what you were saying last night when you thought Kim was going to kill us all in our beds.' Rhiannon turns to him. 'Hey, did you get your bank card sorted out? I meant to ask you yesterday.'

'Ahh, yes.' Jarvis gives an embarrassed laugh. He rummages around in the pocket of his hoodie. 'I need to sort out my debts, don't I?'

'You do indeed.' Rhiannon winks at Nina and Stacey as she takes a seat beside Jarvis.

'Yep, er, so that's fifty, sixty, eighty, hundred...' He shoves a crumpled fist of cash towards Rhiannon, who goes to deposit it into the zipped pocket of her handbag hanging on the coat stand.

'So,' says Nina, brightly, after the money has been sorted out, 'I thought that when the children return, we could give them an early lunch and then take them out to the Playland event. There's supposed to be some kind of burger meal provided later, so we probably only need to give them a few bits. Hummus, crackers, carrot sticks, that sort of thing.'

'Are you sure we don't need to pay for anything?' Stacey asks. 'It seems too good to be true that your client, Paul, is providing this holiday home *and* entertainment for the kids.'

'It's all on him. Everything included.' Nina scrolls through the texts on her phone and flashes her screen towards the others, to show them the communication where Paul has said that he's organised a full, supervised afternoon for the children to have fun in the arcade. She smiles and wiggles her little finger. 'I've got him wrapped around this.'

Suddenly, there's a ping on everyone's phones. A Whats-App message.

Jarvis opens it first. 'It's from Kim. She's sent us a picture of the kids playing on the beach. Although...' He turns his phone around and zooms in on the picture.

'What the hell are they doing?' Rhiannon's brows have knitted together as she stares at her own phone.

Nina opens the picture. 'Oh my God.' Her face turns white.

Stacey stares at the photograph. 'Is this supposed to be a joke?'

The picture shows the children's heads in a line on the beach, eyes closed, their bodies buried up to their necks in sand.

Nina shoves her chair back and runs from the table towards the damp cloakroom at the end of the corridor, where she throws up into the sink.

TWENTY-THREE

KIM

Before the childcare circle

It was just before my twenty-second birthday when Paul told me that he had done something crazy. He needed to show me, he said. I had to trust him.

So, I met him at the railway station and we travelled to east Yorkshire, to the Holderness coast where a damp wind slapped us in the face when we got off the train. Something felt significant, weighty.

'This is the place,' said Paul.

A lump filled my throat as I realised where we were.

It was the first time that I had visited the location where Dylan had died. I sat with Paul in a beachside café, looking out at the fractious grey sea that had filled my little brother's lungs and killed him.

'Are you all right?' said Paul. He'd finished his coffee and was waiting for me to start mine.

My gullet felt closed; my neck ached. Perhaps it was my body trying to keep the tears at bay. I nodded. I was sombre but

OK, wondering why I had never thought to come here before and see the place for myself.

'I thought it might give you some closure to see it,' said Paul.

Something spun round in my head. A tremor grabbed at my legs. My heart started racing, ready to get angry or upset. Things inside me weren't closing, they were waking up. 'You know what? Seeing it feels like it's stirring up a load of stress inside me. Because there were so many lies told about his death and the police never got to the bottom of it, did they? People were there; people saw things, didn't they?' My voice came out loaded with acrimony; my eyes glared at Paul only because he was the one sitting in my line of vision.

He stared at me with an open mouth, a twitch in his shoulder. 'What do you mean?'

'Dylan didn't just drown. It *wasn't* an accident. Someone killed him.'

'What makes you say that?'

'Over the years I've read all the police reports, all the articles in the media and on the internet. The accounts don't fit with an accidental death. And being here has just triggered something. I want to find out what really happened to him: I mean, maybe there's more that *you* remember. Because I feel like I have to get to the bottom of it all, for his sake.' I glugged a mouthful of coffee. Someone behind the counter dropped a handful of cutlery and everyone turned at the clatter to watch the waitress's embarrassment for a few seconds. 'Tell me about that trip, everything that you can. I want to know it all: everything that Dylan did. I want to imagine him here, being happy. But I also want your version of the timeline so I can align it with what I already know.'

Paul looked at the ceiling and jiggled his foot as I waited for him to talk. He pulled in a deep breath. 'I feel like I haven't been totally straight with you. There *were* people around, people who might have seen things. Or – like you say – people who might have been involved. I never wanted to bring the subject up before because it seemed like you'd reached a point in your grieving where you were dealing with it and I didn't want to open up your wounds again.'

'Go on.' There was a churning in my stomach. 'Tell me *everything*.'

'Well. This is what I remember. We went to the beach on that Friday. The youth workers were supervising from a distance. Obviously, we weren't allowed to swim in the sea; we could only paddle. But there was a group of girls we didn't know – three of them – who ended up talking to Dylan, helping him to make a sandcastle. I tried to get involved because, you know, I wanted to look after him, but they took the piss out of me and called me Quasimodo and stuff like that, making fun of my arm. They were older – maybe fifteen? – and were asking Dylan about what it was like to live in a children's home, that sort of thing. I didn't get a good feeling from them...'

'Well, you wouldn't if they were calling you names. Teenage girls can be such bitches.'

'So I didn't hang around them for long. I suppose I was envious in a way that they liked him and not me, and Dylan had clearly taken a shine to them. They had been in some kind of competition and won medals. One of the girls had even let Dylan wear hers, and he came back to the cottage with it around his neck saying that he'd borrowed it. Then he was asking the staff if he could go back to the beach the next day, because he wanted to go and find those girls again.'

'Were they locals?' I asked, wondering why the police hadn't interviewed them.

'Probably not. There were a lot of people in the town that weekend,' Paul said. 'I mean children, like on a school trip. There were a lot of girls, teenage girls, all dressed up fancy as if they were going somewhere special. Maybe a big party or some kind of celebration. It could have been something to do with the competition that they'd won.'

'So, these girls could have killed him?'

Paul shivered. 'Hmm, maybe. Listen... A couple of years after I'd been moved from Summerbone House, I was sent to another place where there was a red-haired girl who had been on that seaside trip with us. Tegan? Can you remember her winning a golden ticket at the Christmas party? Well, anyway, we got talking about Dylan and what had happened, and she said she'd seen him on the beach: she must have been one of the last people to see him alive. He'd been with a teenage girl and they'd been messing around, wrestling and digging a big hole and she was shoving him into it. Tegan said she'd tried to explain to the police at the time but they didn't listen. Well, she was just a kid, wasn't she? What did she know?'

'So that teenage girl: she could have killed him.' My heart was thumping with rage as I imagined my little brother being forced into a hole, being buried in sand, being left to be smothered by that grey, briny tide.

'Yes.' Paul nodded solemnly.

'You see, the police should have looked into this. Their explanation for Dylan's death doesn't make sense. I've spent so much time thinking about it. So, here's the thing. The autopsy said that he died from drowning. He was supposedly trapped under fallen rubble and stuff and then the tide came in and killed him. But that's the wrong way round. The tide came in first and took out a chunk of the cliff and the caravan park. The rubble only fell on the beach *after* the tide came in. So, he couldn't have been trapped under it *before* the water rose. If you read the reports you can see that the caravans were evacuated in the middle of the night and didn't fall down onto the beach and onto Dylan until the early hours of the morning. He would have been dead a long time before then.'

'Yeah. I see what you mean. But the police did say they found his body buried in sand underneath the rubble.'

'But I'm thinking that he could have been buried in the sand first. Trapped. There's a weird thing in the reports about when he was found. It says that his body was deep in the sand, feet first, as if he was standing. With just his head sticking out. Don't you think that's strange? Imagine if someone put him there deliberately. And then the tide came in. That's why he drowned: because he couldn't get away. And *then* the cliff and the caravans fell on top of him, when he was already dead.'

'Hmm.' Paul raised his coffee cup to his lips even though there was nothing left.

'So, this teenage girl then. Messing around and shoving Dylan into a hole. She never came forward, did she? But surely, if she was innocent, she would have given the police information, she would have helped.'

'Are you wanting the police to open the case again?' Paul asked. 'Surely they wouldn't...'

'No, I don't think they would. But I could do my own investigation, couldn't I? I could find that girl who was with him and get to the truth.'

'I could help you,' said Paul. 'You know that I'd do everything I could.'

A laugh bubbled out of me because it felt like my chest was bursting with everything that I was trying to hold in. His words had fed my hypothesis, had given me the sustenance that could dispel the insurmountable sadness and anger and remorse and self-blame that had plagued me for years. And when I had the truth, I would be able to settle and properly get on with my life.

We stopped talking and gazed out of the window at the sea. It hypnotised us with each wave that advanced along the sand, breaking frothy and foamy before pulling back to slop over the rocks, swelling boldly in readiness for its next incursion towards the cliffs.

'There was another reason I brought you here,' said Paul.

'What?' I watched as his face flushed for a moment, and had the ridiculous and fearful thought that he might spring a ring from his pocket and propose to me.

I was wrong, though.

'I've got something to show you.' He scraped back his chair and zipped up his coat, even though I'd hardly touched my drink.

'Hang on.' I gulped a mouthful of tepid coffee before following him out onto the street.

We walked for a few minutes towards the beach until Paul stopped and turned, scanning the side of the cliff.

'Look, up there.' He pointed to a large, detached property, orphaned on the edge of the rock. It looked as if a chunk of its garden had slid into the sea, so for safety measures a flimsy orange barrier had been erected along the perimeter.

'What?'

'That house,' he said. 'I've bought it.'

TWENTY-FOUR

KIM

Before the childcare circle

Kittiwake House. That was the name painted in a gothic font on a board over the front door. The place wasn't a complete wreck. Inside, it was habitable, more so than the last three derelict terraces that Paul had purchased. Some furniture remained: a huge dining table with ten chairs, two chesterfield-style sofas in cracked green leather, assorted Persian rugs that covered the draughty floorboards, and bedsteads and wardrobes in most of the upstairs rooms.

'No one has lived here for eight years,' said Paul, swinging the bunch of keys as we walked from room to room. 'It was part of a will. And because it had been on the market for such a long time I went in and made an outrageous cash offer – basically most of my spare money – which they accepted.'

There were swathes of cobwebs trembling from the ceiling and a thick layer of dust over all the surfaces. I pulled open the doors of the imposing kitchen dresser to discover saucepans, a gold-edged dinner service and crystal sherry glasses.

'This is incredible.' I laughed, and we ran through each echoing room, checking the cupboards and finding goose feather eiderdowns, old gramophone records, and a fusty leather Bible that was the size of a small coffee table.

'We could live here,' said Paul as we stood in the bay window of the master bedroom, looking out at the heaving and rolling of the North Sea. 'There's plenty of room for both of us.'

I didn't really know what he was suggesting. An arrangement where we just shared the house as friends? Or something more, like a relationship?

'It's a bit too far from my job, though,' I said weakly.

Paul made a spluttering noise in his throat and I couldn't tell if it was a laugh. 'You don't need to do that job for ever,' he said. 'There will be other stuff. You could help me with the renovations.'

I could work for Paul?

But something in me rejected this idea. I was afraid of getting too close to him. All the people I had loved before had either died or left me.

'Well...' I began carefully. 'Maybe I could come over occasionally and help you paint the rooms. I'd be happy to do that. You could let it out to holidaymakers when it's done up. It could bring in some decent rent during the summer.'

'I know,' said Paul. 'I'd already thought of that. But I just wondered if you might want to be here, you know, to be near Dylan.'

'He's not here, though.' I remembered the patch of ash outside the McDonald's Drive-Thru. 'He's not really anywhere.'

We watched the sea again; watched a man tugging a reluctant dog along the edge of the shoreline.

Paul shrugged. 'OK. I just thought. But yes, it would be good as a holiday let. And I could still keep doing up the small terraces on the side, to boost my profits and have somewhere to live.'

I could tell that he was disappointed. We surveyed the rooms again and I tried to make comments about what colours the walls could be painted – 'what about a blue and white seaside theme in here?' – but the mood had dipped.

Paul locked the place up and we walked into town. A light mizzle was sending people into doorways, so we took shelter in an amusement arcade, feeding two pence pieces into the coin pushers and watching the focused expressions of the old ladies on the bingo machines. I wondered if Dylan had been in here, if he'd felt the joy of knocking down a stack of coppers into the metal cash tray. The carpet was sticky. There was an overriding smell of body odour and cooking oil. Desperate vibes from a suited man slotting pound after pound into a fruit machine and winning nothing started to make my skin itch.

We bought a bag of candy floss and ate it on the train home.

'But did you think buying the house was a good idea?' said Paul. He seemed keen to get my approval. 'I haven't done something stupid, have I? It just seemed like such a bargain. And so... kind of *appropriate*.'

'It's your money. You can buy what you want with it. And I'm sure you could make a profit with the house, whether you sell it or not.'

'But you really don't want to live there?'

'Sorry. I think the whole town just somehow gives me the creeps.' I turned and looked out of the window, and we didn't say much for the rest of the journey.

* * *

The trip seemed to trigger something in me that took me back to a state of grief. And then I knew with absolute certainty that I had to search for Dylan's killer. I had to find her. It was the main thing that would put the whole trauma to rest.

What did I want to gain? Revenge? I didn't know at that point. All I knew then was that I had to find the truth.

TWENTY-FIVE
THE WEEKEND AWAY

Saturday – the second day of the weekend away

'Ring her!' Nina screams from behind the cloakroom door. 'Find out what the hell is going on.'

Rhiannon dials but gets no response. 'She's not answering.'

'Hey, calm down.' Jarvis's face is beaded with sweat. 'It's just a photo. They're only playing in the sand.'

Stacey pushes past his chair and hurtles upstairs. 'I'm going to get dressed and go out and find them.'

Rhiannon keeps redialling but it goes to answerphone every time.

'Look, I'll go down to the beach. I'm sure it's nothing and I could do with some fresh air.' Jarvis, gasping wearily, disappears out of the back door.

Nina returns to the table with her hands over her face. 'That bitch is up to something. I know she is.'

Rhiannon puts an arm around her shoulder. 'I know the photo looks weird, but, well, *she's* weird, isn't she? They're probably just messing about...'

'It's all to do with her brother, isn't it? I've got a horrible feeling that I know who he is.'

'Really?'

Stacey appears, in jeans and a chunky red sweater. 'What's happening now?'

'Jarvis has gone to see what they're doing.' Rhiannon runs a hand through her hair and turns to the window, even though the only visible part of the beach is empty.

'Are you thinking what I'm thinking?' Stacey says to Nina.

'That boy on the beach when we won the dance championship?'

'I'm sure he said his name was Dylan.'

'Oh Christ,' says Rhiannon. 'That was *him*?'

Nina nods. 'I think it was. And I think Kim knows that we were with him.'

* * *

They hear the squeals and laughter of the children before the kitchen door bursts open. Plastic spades with a covering of wet sand are dropped onto the floor; boots are kicked off; gusts of cold air slip inside like thieves between them all.

'That was so fun,' says Bobby. 'I wish we could've stayed longer.'

Kim and Jarvis are in conversation as the children take off their coats. Relaxed, light-hearted: casually laughing about how Hayden almost got his finger nipped by a crab in one of the rock pools.

'Everything OK?' Nina says to Jarvis in a loaded tone.

'Yeah. Fine.' He shrugs dismissively.

Stacey and Rhiannon are quiet, waiting for Nina to mention the photograph.

'Did you enjoy breakfast?' says Kim. 'I hope you saved some

bacon for me. I'm famished now.' She ignores the atmosphere, which is clumsy, unbalanced, like a tower ready to topple.

Nina discreetly pulls Jarvis out of the room. 'What did she say?'

He shakes his head. 'What do you mean? She was just playing with them on the sand and they were burying each other and taking photographs. The kids loved it apparently.'

'No, no. She has an agenda. There's a lot more to it than you think. She was putting our children in danger and taunting us.'

Jarvis laughs nervously. 'Don't be silly. Why would she do that? She just wants to be part of the clique. She's just trying to get us to *like* her. Making breakfast for us, taking the kids out so that we can all have a lie-in. What makes you think it's malicious?'

'I've got a sixth sense.' Nina takes a deep breath. 'All this thing about her brother, this thing about the letters and secrets. She's playing a game. And I really don't like the way it could go.'

'Well, I'm not seeing what you're seeing. To be fair, she's gone up in my estimation and I feel guilty for judging her so badly before.' He reaches out and pats Nina on the shoulder. 'Come on. Give her a chance.'

Nina bristles and backs away from his touch. 'All I'm saying is...' She does the pointy thing with two fingers at her eyes. 'I'm being careful.'

'Whatever.' Jarvis holds up his hands and walks back into the kitchen to receive the mug of coffee that Kim has just made for him.

Kim and Stacey push the dining table back to the wall to create some extra floor space, and Rhiannon leads the children in a performance of the dance that they have been working on for the past seven weeks.

'Wow, that is so impressive!' Nina applauds loudly, and the children beam with pride.

'Remember when we were actually here in this town and won the championship? We got medals and everything.' Stacey reminds Rhiannon of their unforgettable experience. 'It seems so long ago now, doesn't it?'

'I know. But it was the thing that essentially gave me my big break.'

'And we weren't even tipped to win the contest, were we? There was that other group, remember? Everyone, literally everyone, said they were guaranteed to get first place, but then they just dropped out of the final without performing.'

'It was because one of them got ill,' Nina interjects. 'She was taken to hospital. I heard she was vomiting blood.'

'Oh God.' Jarvis grimaces and touches at the burning patch that is spreading on his face.

Rhiannon purses her mouth tightly and makes no comment. She busies herself dragging the rugs back into place and moving the chairs around. The children have all disappeared into the lounge to watch television.

Kim listens as Nina and Stacey reminisce about their achievements, before asking, 'How old were you at the time? Fourteen?'

Nina shoots a glance at Stacey.

'Yes, fourteen.'

'Hmm.' Kim absorbs the information, and Nina looks at Stacey again, subtly putting a finger over her lips. Rhiannon watches them, trying to interpret the signals. The undercurrent feels thick and edgy.

Jarvis checks the time. 'We ought to sort out lunch if we need to get the kids to the Playland place by one o'clock. Who's taking them?'

'I know where it is,' says Kim. 'I don't mind going.'

'I'll come with you,' Stacey says suddenly. 'I wouldn't mind some exercise.'

Nina casts her eyes around everyone again before getting up to prepare snacks for the children.

* * *

'Sorry to be a pain,' says Rhiannon, 'but if you're passing a shop would you be able to pick up some paracetamol, please? I gave the last of mine to Jarvis.'

'Sure,' Kim replies.

Rhiannon takes her handbag from the coat stand and unzips the front pocket where she has stashed the cash that Jarvis repaid her. She grabs a ten-pound note and hands it over to Kim. 'Doesn't matter what brand.'

Kim is just about to stuff the money in the back pocket of her jeans when she stops and looks at it. Something dark red and sticky – blood? – has attached a thin white receipt to the note. She peels it off and looks at it.

> *Thank you for your kind donation. One hundred pounds to the World Parrot Trust received on the fourth of October.*

'Is this yours?' she asks Rhiannon, rubbing at the gluey red patch.

'What?' Rhiannon looks at the receipt, puzzled, turning it over. 'World Parrot Trust? I don't know anything about that.'

'That's strange,' says Kim. 'Because I *do* know someone who donates to them.' She takes the receipt back and scrutinises it again.

Rhiannon clicks her fingers. 'Jarvis. He gave me the money.' She lowers her voice to a whisper. 'I lent him some money a few days ago – and strangely enough, that was for a hundred pounds – and he paid me back this morning. I just shoved it in my bag without looking. It must have come from him. He doesn't seem the type to donate money to parrots, though.'

'No.' Kim has a furrow between her brows. 'No, he doesn't.'

'But, hey, who are we to make judgements?'

Stacey is standing by the door with the kids, who are waiting patiently. 'Are we ready to go?'

'As ready as we'll ever be.' Kim drops the receipt in the bin.

They file out of the door, and Nina closes it behind them. 'Is it too early for a drink? I've got a growing sense of impending doom and I think the only thing that can cure it is booze.' She lets out a long sigh as she opens a bottle of Chardonnay and pours herself a large glass.

TWENTY-SIX

KIM

Before the childcare circle

The internet is a fabulous thing.

It was incredible how the information was right there, at the ends of our fingertips. Local news archives told us that on the weekend of Dylan's death there had been a national dancing competition at the theatre, the Street Dance Championships. The finals of a prestigious event with schools from all over the country taking part. The town had been overflowing with teenage girls and their families that had brought them to compete.

We started to build up a file of information. It was an agonisingly slow process, but we made progress when new stuff turned up online as people put photographs of their achievements on social media, or discussed previous school life on reunion sites.

Then, one day, I tried a new search engine. I followed the link to a website for a choreographer and dance teacher that had the phrase 'National Street Dance Championship' flagged on one of her pages. I clicked through the impressive, professional photographs in black and white: of her humourless portrait; of her on stage mid-dance showing off her wiry frame in various contorted poses; of her gratefully receiving a number of awards. It seemed like she was some kind of celebrity who had even been on television. I read her lengthy and heartfelt account of how, from the age of ten, she had devoted her whole life to dancing, even excusing herself from friends' birthday parties in favour of working on her moves until her feet were bruised and she was crying in pain.

Christ, my heart bleeds, I thought sarcastically. Yet I couldn't help but carry on reading.

Her sliding-door moment came when she was part of a dance trio at Wingfield High School which got through to the finals for the National Street Dance Championships, held in the Pavilion Theatre in a resort on the east Yorkshire coast.

My senses pricked, and I sat up straighter, moving into my laptop screen. It was the correct year. And there was a *trio* of them.

I continued reading her biography...

One of the girls' fathers took them there for the weekend and they stayed in a guest house in town. They performed their dance on the Friday morning to rapturous applause and top marks from the judges, and then collected their winning medals at the two o'clock ceremony which was covered by the local press and a number of industry talent scouts. She was tearful with pride. It was her big break...

I sat back as I processed the information.

Then I put her name through the different social media channels, working out that she would have been fourteen at the time. It was the closest match that had turned up so far.

I had to let Paul know what I'd found. He answered on the second ring, just like he always did.

'Hey.'

'I think I've struck gold on the street dance thing. I have a name.' My heart was thudding in my ears as I told him.

'Go on then.'

'Rhiannon Ford.'

Paul checked out Rhiannon Ford's photographs. She was a person who loved seeing herself on a screen, that much was obvious. As well as recent pictures, her fourteen-year-old self was displayed all over the internet for Paul to identify. There were so many photographs: a pictorial timeline of her achievements and career.

He rang me back ten minutes later. The waiting had almost driven me crazy.

'I've been through loads of stuff. And it's her, there's no doubt about it. She was definitely one of the girls on the beach that was with Dylan on the Friday afternoon. She might even have been the one that was being unkind about me.'

I trembled with fulfilment. 'What do we do now?'

There was a pause. Neither of us was sure.

'Well, we can't just email her and make accusations,' Paul said. 'I think we have to find the others. But they should be easier to find now that we have more information. Looking through her profiles we've got the name of her secondary school and the town she was brought up in.'

'She might still be living there.'

'And the others could be, too.'

'We should check through her friends' list. You might recognise photographs of the others,' I said. 'Then we'd have the three of them.'

*　*　*

Over the next weeks we examined every picture we found of Rhiannon Ford: where and when it was taken. We tried to identify other people that were photographed with her and kept a record of these names, too. We filed and organised everything.

I set up a profile on Facebook using a fake name and sent a friend request to Rhiannon, in the hope of gaining access to her list of friends. After some time, when she clearly hadn't responded, I joined the Facebook group of the Wingfield Area History Society who I assumed might have information about past students of the high school. I engaged with the page positively, commenting things like 'beautiful picture' on snowy scenes of the church, and 'I'm sure I can see myself in the back row!' on an old infants class photograph so that people would think I was genuine.

Although Rhiannon didn't use the group, it eventually felt like the right time to enlist the help of the members. I wrote a post:

Hi, I am looking for information about the girls who represented Wingfield High School in 2006 at the National Street Dance Championship – can anyone remember who they were please?

Within minutes a comment came in:

One them was called Rhiannon.

Then another:

Rhiannon Ford. She's actually a bit of a celebrity now.

I waited. Hours passed. Two days passed without further information, but when I woke up on the third morning there was a notification that someone else had commented on my post. Hopeful of another name, I held my breath and clicked.

I think one of the others was Stacey who's married to Xander McCrell, but I can't remember what her maiden name was. And the other was Nina, but again, don't know the surname.

I clicked a heart on the comment: the person had actually done me a favour by giving me a current name anyway. I searched for *Stacey McCrell* on social media. Her Facebook profile was private but at least displayed a picture of herself. She was blonde and pretty with flawless skin and sparkling azure eyes, a butter-wouldn't-melt look in her smile.

I sent the profile link to Paul.

Does this one ring any bells?

He messaged me back:

I'll do some more delving but 99% sure it's her. There was definitely a blonde girl at the beach.

It felt like we were getting somewhere. We knew that we would eventually catch up with them.

Our patience and persistence were paying off.

And then the girls would pay for what *they* did.

TWENTY-SEVEN

KIM

Before the childcare circle

A point of frustration had blocked our efforts. We had the names of the girls but we didn't know where to find them, despite trying all the people-finder websites and electoral roll searches. And we really needed to locate them so that we could get into their lives.

Paul and I had both set up Facebook profiles with fake names – I even used a photograph of my next-door neighbour's cat as my picture – and sent friend requests to Rhiannon, Stacey and even Xander McCrell in the slim hope that they would accept. But none of them would take the bait. We pondered how we could get them interested in *us*.

There were times when we thought we could track down Rhiannon as, on her website, she often advertised shows where she had done the choreography. We travelled to two of these – in Sheffield and Leicester – where we spoke to box office staff, checked out the programmes and waited around after the show had finished to try and identify her in the crowd of theatre goers streaming out of the front doors. But everything led to a dead end.

They were all so elusive.

I returned to the Wingfield History Society's Facebook group again. Maybe someone there could help.

> Hi, I am organising a reunion of the high school street dance teams. Looking for Rhiannon Ford, Stacey McCrell and Nina something. Does anyone know if they still live locally?

It was worth a try.

Within a couple of days I had answers. The members of Facebook groups can be so beneficial, so willing to give out the personal information of others. Stacey was still living in the same town. Rhiannon had moved to London. Nina was abroad, thought to be in Berlin. And did I know that her married name was Ronson?

Despite finding out Nina's surname, the knowledge of their whereabouts depressed me. How could I get into their lives with them dispersed across such an area? I had never been out of the country. I had never been to London. The thought of having to visit these places was daunting. I had hoped that they would all be together, socialising together in the local cafés and bars where it would be easy to hang around and befriend them.

'Don't be disheartened, because we could look Stacey up, though,' said Paul. 'She shouldn't be difficult to find. Wingfield isn't that big a place, and we have to start somewhere. In fact, she could turn out to be the guilty one, which means that we wouldn't need to track down the others.'

'Yeah, maybe.' I didn't have Paul's optimism; it couldn't possibly be as easy as that. 'Will you come with me?'

'If you want me to,' he replied, with some caution.

I knew that he was still a bit prickly about the whole Kitti-

wake House situation. We hadn't been back there since he
showed me around the property, despite my offer to help him
with the decorating. He was currently living in one of his renovated terraces while trying to sell it, and had nothing much to do
apart from look for potential new projects. A couple of weeks
back he had suggested putting in a big order of paint and decorating essentials so that we could go and have a long weekend at
the seaside at the same time as making a start on the necessary
improvements. I'd turned him down, citing a sore throat and
also having to feed the neighbour's cat. Both of the excuses were
lies and afterwards I'd felt guilty, remembering all the times he'd
dropped everything to go off on an internet tangent for me.

It was time I gave something back, I decided. I couldn't just
continue to be a taker.

'How about we go for a trip to Wingfield this weekend?' I
suggested. 'Then the following weekend I'm on rota at the
garden centre, but the weekend after that we could go and do
some painting at Kittiwake House. Does that sound like a plan?'

Paul was already nodding. 'That would be brilliant.'

He started talking about neutral colours and feature walls,
but in my mind I was already walking along Wingfield High
Street, seeking out a blonde-haired woman through all the shop
fronts.

It was a charming little town. Clean, with a compact market
square that had flapping bunting and some colourful planters
displaying herbs and aromatic shrubs. These were the types of
things that – as a former radical gardener – I took note of. We
spent a couple of hours pacing out the streets to get a vibe for
the place, before going to see where the schools were. Nothing
gave us a clue about Dylan's killer, though; I didn't know why
I'd thought a visit would achieve anything.

'We should ask if anyone knows Xander McCrell,' said

Paul. 'An unusual name like that could throw up some surprises.'

So, we went in a pub and ordered drinks, and Paul asked the barman and a man on a stool if they knew him, and it took only five minutes of asking around some of the regulars in the pub to learn that he lived out towards the new Burlow Dale development.

'Not in one of those actual properties, because they were only built last year and cost a bomb, but on one of the roads just before you reach it,' said a beardy bloke. He was sitting at a table with a woman who wore false eyelashes and pale pink lipstick. 'He used to go to the Cross Keys on a Sunday afternoon with all the rugby lot, but I've not seen him there for a while now. Although he got married not that long ago, didn't he? Is her name Sharon or something?'

The woman squinted at the ceiling and picked distractedly at a beer mat. 'Stacey, not Sharon. And it was at least two years since they got married. Although I heard she's pregnant now.'

My teeth were clamped together, and my insides were crying out, 'Oh my God, we're getting so close,' and I realised that my head was nodding excitedly as I devoured the facts offered by these strangers.

'Are they mates of yours?' Paul asked.

'Not really,' the bloke replied. 'But he was in the same school year my younger brother and it's a smallish place so everybody gets to know everything.'

'What do you want him for?' said the woman. 'Is he in trouble?'

'No, nothing like that.' I was quick to invent a story, keeping things vague. 'We're trying to organise a bit of a reunion with some long-lost friends but struggling to find some of them. Actually, you might know the others, too. Rhiannon Ford and Nina Ronson?'

'That name rings a bell. Rhiannon Ford.' The man tapped a finger against his lips.

'Dancer,' said the woman. 'She's been on telly but she was originally from here. I've not heard of the other one, though.'

'They all won a dancing award together, years ago.'

'Really? Oh God, I love *Strictly*, don't you? I'd love to learn how to do the Charleston properly.' The woman started to talk about the last series, and the man pulled out a stool from under the table, indicating for me and Paul to join them. I was reluctant, but Paul was there already because he's the sort of person who thinks that making friends with anyone will always be beneficial.

We chatted for over an hour with Ally and Glenn about the town – where the posh areas were and which streets should be avoided – and the best takeaways from which to get a meat feast pizza. They assumed we were a couple and asked if we were thinking about moving there, so we played along with them and pretended that it was a place we were interested in, and Glenn even showed us on his phone a smart little town house that was available to rent just two doors down from where they lived.

'Let me add you on Facebook,' said Glenn. 'Then if any news crops up about your mates for the reunion I can get in touch.'

'That would be great!' Paul got his phone out and made friends with Glenn. 'Although, don't tell them we've been asking around because it's like, for a surprise thing.'

Glenn tapped his nose. 'Your secret's safe with me.'

* * *

'That was an enjoyable afternoon, wasn't it?' Paul said later, as we strolled in the direction of the new Burlow Dale development. 'They were really nice people.'

I had always eschewed making small talk with strangers, but

I was encouraged by my efforts, even though our intentions had been devious. 'It wouldn't be such a bad place to live, would it?' I said to Paul. 'If all three of the girls were here I could move in and stalk them.'

He gave a hollow laugh. 'You wouldn't want to leave your job though, would you?'

Kittiwake House was obviously still a thorny issue, a topic we skirted around so that we wouldn't risk an argument. Paul wasn't usually as bitter as this and something inside me clenched to think that he had been hurt by my rejection.

'Hey.' I grabbed his hand, the curled-back one like a waiter taking a tip, the one that was on his bad arm, and swung it a little as we walked. It used to embarrass him when I touched this arm, but then he seemed happy that I didn't find it offensive like other people often did. 'Don't be in a mood. We've had a fun day so far. Who knows what else we might find out?'

'You're still up for helping me with renovations in a couple of weeks?' he reminded me.

'Of course I am.' I smiled but I didn't want to think about that view, that beach, that stark and gusting place of death. Paul didn't need me there. He could easily have booked tradesmen to do the job much better than I would. But it wasn't really about that. It was about some kind of healing process that I still didn't understand. 'It will be good to get on with the work so that you can start taking bookings for summer.'

We walked for another hour, around tree-lined roads of neat terraces and semi-detached properties, waiting for something that would jump out at us and point to Stacey's house, but of course it didn't happen.

When the rain spits started as the light faded, we decided to call it a day. We were closer to the truth, that's what we told each other. Inch by inch, we would find it.

However long it took, we could wait.

TWENTY-EIGHT

THE WEEKEND AWAY

Saturday – the second day of the weekend away

'Is everything all right with you?' Stacey asks Kim as they walk back from the Playland Arcade.

'Everything is great. Why wouldn't it be?'

'Well, you know. After all the thing about the secrets last night. Nina seemed to think there was more to it.'

'In what way?'

'Well, we just got the impression... Your brother who died. Dylan, wasn't it? Do you mind me asking about him? Because I just wondered if – you know you said that he drowned – well, where that happened, and like, if it was actually *here* that it happened?'

Stacey waits awkwardly for an answer as Kim seems to go into a trance, her eyes staring blankly at the road.

'...because if it *was* here, then I'm sure it was a complete accident about Nina bringing us to this place and it all being a mystery location, and then I can understand if it's a shock for you to return to somewhere where your brother died...' Stacey blunders on with the conversation because the silence is too uncomfortable to bear.

Finally, Kim stops outside a corner shop and pulls cash out of her pocket. 'I need to get some paracetamol for Rhiannon. And yes, it *was* here where Dylan died. On that beach that we can all see from the kitchen window.'

Stacey reaches out to touch Kim's arm. 'Well, I'm so sorry that we ended up coming back here and raking up bad memories for you. But as I said about Nina, it was a complete accident.'

'No,' says Kim. 'It was no accident. Neither Dylan's death nor this holiday was accidental.'

'Oh.' Stacey's face blushes at Kim's abrupt tone. 'Do you want to go home? I mean, if you want to leave early, with me giving you a lift here, I could cut things short because the road might be open now, and I totally understand if that's what you'd prefer.'

'Cut things short? No, no. I'm here for the full weekend. I've been looking forward to it for ages. For years, actually.'

Kim leaves Stacey somewhat bewildered, outside, as she slips into the shop to buy the painkillers.

The walk back to Kittiwake House is uncomfortable, and Stacey sticks to small talk: the lack of tourists; the noise of the sea; the rain that has fortunately held off. Suddenly there's a buzz, and Kim takes her phone out of her pocket to check an incoming text.

Hi, it's Neil, the tree surgeon. Tried to call you but got no answer. Just trying to find out what the situation is after Friday.

'Everything all right?' Stacey asks.

Kim shakes her head in frustration. 'Oh, just unreliable workmen. It's not urgent though; I'll deal with it later.'

When they reach the house, there is a car parked a little way further up the street. Kim smiles as she sees the sleek, black Audi, with the back of the driver's head visible in the front seat. She checks her watch. It is quarter past one.

Time to start the party.

* * *

Nina is wearing a red cocktail dress and a face full of make-up as she pours glasses of wine. Rhiannon is still in her Lycra; Jarvis in the same loose tracksuit with his beanie hat on.

'Do you think Helena will want to come in and have a drink with us when she arrives to collect Hayden?' Nina says to Jarvis.

'I bloody hope not,' he replies. 'No. She'll just pick him up and get going. She's not really one for socialising and particularly not if it involves me.'

'Ahh, that's a shame. But anyway, I've taken the liberty of writing out some charades and forfeits, because it could be fun to have a few drinks and play some party games,' says Nina, handing out glasses.

'Do we have to?' Stacey groans. 'Can't we just have a laugh some other way?'

'Tell us a few jokes then,' Jarvis suggests, still scrolling through the news app on his phone.

'Are you going to make an effort and get changed?' Nina looks Kim up and down as she passes a glass of chilled wine to her. 'Your jeans look a bit damp and sandy.'

'I don't have anything posh to wear.'

'Well, maybe just some dry trousers then?'

'I'm sure it doesn't matter,' Stacey says. 'It's not as if we're going out anywhere.'

'I'll see what I can find,' replies Kim as she traipses upstairs.

* * *

In the attic room she changes into a different pair of jeans and a clean T-shirt. She straightens the duvet on the bed and then packs all hers and Dulcie's belongings back into her rucksack before taking it down to the first floor and putting it in a cupboard. From the landing window she looks out towards the Audi on the street and checks the time again. Her heart races. There's a gurgle and a flip in the pit of her stomach. She's waited a long time for this moment.

Enjoy it, she tells herself. She gropes the back pockets of her jeans: phone in the left one and key in the right one.

OK, here we go, she thinks. I'm ready.

TWENTY-NINE

KIM

Before the childcare circle

It turned out that painting and decorating was a kind of therapy for me. I loved being able to transform a wall, a room, with the power of a colour. We put music on – bouncy ska tunes – that motivated us as we worked late into that Saturday evening, brushing away the old flaking surfaces to replace them with clean, vibrant ones. Paul ordered a curry to be delivered and we finally lit a fire and sat down to evaluate our efforts in the downstairs rooms.

'A few of the walls need another coat which we can do tomorrow,' he said. 'And then there's the woodwork to paint which is a bit more tricky.'

'It's looking good, though.'

'Well, we've worked hard. You're a better grafter than most of the contractors I hire.'

'Thanks. I was feeling like I owed you, but then I started to enjoy doing it anyway.' I smiled. It was true. There was a welcome glow in my muscles. The core of my belly radiated joy.

Even the smell of the paint seemed like it had something whole-some about it.

Amiably, we discussed our plans for the next day, the roller techniques we'd discovered for a better finish, how we needed to repair some crumbling plaster around one of the windows.

'Which room do you want tonight?' he asked. We had retrieved the bedding and eiderdowns to air in front of the fire as we'd forgotten to bring sleeping bags.

I shrugged. 'Don't mind. Although not that grotty attic room. It feels cold and creepy.'

'It might be haunted.' Paul laughed.

'Don't.' I shivered. 'I'll take the big one on the first floor with the en suite. You have the one next door.' I'd never been the sort of person easily frightened by bumps in the night, but it suddenly felt like I needed him closer than I thought.

A hammering noise jolted us, and the warm contentment inside my body was gone. I held my breath, tense and alert to the sounds of outside.

'Oh crikey, it must be the food. I'd completely forgotten.' Paul jumped up and ran to the door to receive the cartons of chicken balti and rice and popadums.

I slept fitfully under the fusty duvet. Scratchy feather quills poked through the silky lining and in the end I got out of bed and put my hoodie back on to protect my arms. A crick in my neck from vigorous use of the paint roller meant that I had to sleep on the wrong side of the bed and continually adjust the pillows. Outside, the weather was quiet, the sea calm, but the thought of the waves lapping the beach had set my brain into some kind of rocking motion and by dawn I was convinced it had made me nauseous.

We worked until mid-afternoon, when we had to clear away our materials so that we could get the train back home. The downstairs rooms were looking much better and we arranged to return for another weekend of work at the beginning of the next month.

Paul radiated happiness in a way that I had never seen before. The Kittiwake House project had captivated him, but it was something that he wanted *us* to do rather than bring in tradespeople. He believed that it would heal me, bring me peace because the spirit of Dylan was nearby. He believed that eventually the house would make everything right. These sort of new age beliefs were something that he'd been increasingly expressing recently, and although I'd initially scorned them, they did seem to ease my mind the more I considered them.

So, for a time, I abandoned all thoughts of getting revenge on the dancing girls and put my heart and energy into transforming these old and shabby rooms. Over the next six months we spent weekends at the place, tidying it up, making small repairs, scrubbing the floorboards and tiles, and painting every room. Obviously, it didn't change the fact that the property required some major renovations: new kitchen cupboards, new bathrooms, new central heating boiler, new glazing in many of the windows. The roof and guttering needed some serious attention. And the garden was a problem. Each time we returned we would find that another sliver of the coastal perimeter had slipped into the sea.

I voiced my worries about this to Paul, to no avail. 'There's plenty to go at before it reaches the house,' he would tell me every time. 'It will be literally years and years away and I'll probably be dead when that happens.'

'Well, maybe you need to get a more secure fence in place if you're thinking about having guests here. Because that temporary plastic netting has just about disintegrated and it looks crap. It's useless.'

Paul rolled his eyes. 'Yes, yes, I know. It's on my list so don't worry about it.'

But I did worry about the way that the climate was changing. I kept track with photographs and sticks in the ground as
the area shrank further back with each lashing storm. It would
only take a few more extreme events like the one that had
brought the cliff down on top of Dylan, and the sea would be at
the door.

By the end of the summer, we had finished redecorating the
interior. It wasn't a show house by any standard, but it was
clean and functional, even though the rooms were still only
furnished with what had already been in the place when Paul
bought it. He got some quotes for all the other work that needed
doing including the external stuff like re-rendering and resur-
facing the drive, but it was going to cost a fortune.

'Why don't you let it out at a cheaper rate and get each job
done as you can afford it?' I suggested, even though I knew
nothing about property development. 'Guests might not be
bothered about the old bathrooms if it means they can have a
bargain holiday.'

Paul was dubious. 'But if I do that and get a load of bad
reviews on Tripadvisor it won't help with future bookings.' He
rubbed a hand through his hair and sighed. 'I don't know, I
really don't.'

In the end, he locked the door and we left it alone to brace
itself against the wind and the sea and the weather over a
ghastly winter. It grieved me that the house wasn't being used or
loved when we had put in so much work to bring it back to life.
But Paul's finances were struggling – his money was tied up in
two renovated terraces that stubbornly refused to sell – and
until the housing market picked up and restored his cash flow,
then Kittiwake House would have to be left to fend for itself.

I retreated to my laptop to search out Rhiannon and Nina,
but found no satisfaction there either. Christmas came and

went again, with all the memories and associations of guilt, and I continued to meet up with Paul a couple of times a month at a pub where there was a special deal on Thursdays for a burger and a drink. My life was so boring. I needed to do something different, to break out of this chronic monotony on my journey to middle age.

'Why don't we just go to Kittiwake for a weekend?' I suggested to Paul. 'Just for fun, for a change. It would probably be good to check the place over, light the fires, give it an airing.'

Paul seemed invigorated by my proposal. We picked a date at the end of February and booked train tickets.

The house waited, gloomy and forlorn. Inside, damp had crept its grey fingers up the walls again, and spiders had made their homes in the corners of the ceiling. Dust smothered every surface.

'You can't just let it go to rack and ruin,' I said, sweeping down the cobwebs. 'Why don't you just sell it again rather than leave it to rot?'

Paul shrugged, pacing around and looking out of the windows towards the North Sea. 'I might make some enquiries and see what my options are. Anyway, let's not get disheartened. We're here for a holiday this time, aren't we? At least *we're* getting some use out of it.'

Around the town it was quiet. The arcades were locked up; the pubs kicked out early due to lack of customers. We found a bar that had eighties music videos playing on a big screen and got a seat next to a radiator. It seemed appropriate to order a bottle of red wine, and we chugged our way through it, enjoying the flush it brought to our cheeks, enjoying how it brought out our thoughts into the space between us so that we could share memories of the times, all those years ago, when we'd lived together in Summerbone House.

'It's like you're my extra brother,' I told Paul, my voice starting to slur. 'My living one.'

He had a weird look on his face, as if he might suddenly cry.

'Aren't you pleased?' I said, throwing a coaster at him.

'Hmm. Yeah.' He was looking at the table, digging his thumbnail into the grain of the wood. ''Course I am.'

'Let's do shots,' I said. Impulsive was out of character for me but the red wine had bashed my guard down.

I went to the bar and ordered six shots of tequila, which were served on a board in tiny glasses, with wedges of lime and a small bowl of what looked like sugar. The girl who served me didn't mention what I was supposed to do; I had no experience of drinking this concoction but had seen it experienced on television.

'What's all this?' said Paul, licking his finger to dip in the bowl. 'It's salt!'

For a while, we argued about the method of using it until Paul googled the instructions and we sprinkled the salt onto our fists. Then we licked, knocked back the alcohol and squeezed the wedge of lime into our teeth.

I winced and laughed, and Paul's eyes watered. We looked at each other without speaking and there was some kind of connection, some fleeting moment where I saw him differently, as if he were new.

'Last orders,' shouted the girl behind the bar. 'We're closing at nine.'

The music on the big screen was muted, and we were the only people remaining.

'Let's buy something and take it back with us.' It wasn't like me at all, but I was in the mood for drinking.

So, we bought another bottle of red wine and got a pizza from a greasy takeaway as we teetered up the hill. It was only when we got inside the house that we remembered there were no logs or sticks with which to make a fire.

'I'm not scouting around out there,' said Paul, after I suggested that there might be something in the garden we could burn.

'But it's freezing in here!'

Our breath made clouds in front of us as we looked in dismay at the empty fireplace. There was only one solution.

* * *

We snuggled up in the bed that I had slept in last time. There was a pair of old lamps with stained-glass shades that lit the room in a cosy, subdued way. The easterly wind sang to us through a gap in the window frame. We drank the wine out of crystal glasses and ate the pizza carelessly, dripping oil onto the eiderdown.

'Put some music on your phone,' I begged Paul, wanting ambience so that it would drown out the noise of the sea. 'Please. Put Roy Harper on.' I hadn't listened to the songs since Willis left me – they would only keep the cracks of my heart open – but the alcohol made me feel ready to be stirred into remembering him.

I rested my head on the cold bolster pillows, and the room spun as the songs dug into my soul and made me crave Willis's love all over again. Paul stroked my hair, and I let a tear slip down my cheek.

'Shh,' he said, kissing it away. 'Don't cry. Everything will be all right.'

I reached for him, turning my lips to his, and then we were suddenly hungry for each other. The pizza box slid to the floor. I unbuttoned my jeans and kicked down the legs under the covers until they were off. I wriggled out of my knickers. Paul's hands were hot on my skin; mine were cold on his as we gripped and held and snaked our fingers under each other's clothing.

'Are you OK with this?' Paul was breathless against my neck. 'Is this what you want?'

My eyes closed and the room tilted again. I swigged a breath of the chilly air. 'Yes. It's what I want. I need it.'

I reached out a hand and switched off the lamp beside me; Paul left his on to cast long shadows on the ceiling as we drunkenly devoured each other.

I forgot what I'd said earlier about him being my brother.

THIRTY

KIM

Before the childcare circle

Regrets. Throwing up. Banging headache that scraped the inside of my skull. I couldn't bear to look at Paul the next day. Everything was wrong; it felt like our friendship was ruined. I would have cried but my head hurt too much.

I pressed my face into the crook of my elbow to block out the light and told Paul that what we had done had been a mistake. He ran his fingertips up and down my neck for a while before he silently arose and went out for a walk on the beach while I wallowed in bed, hating myself.

We shouldn't have done what we did, I said to myself, over and over. I'd heard people at work talk about *friends with benefits*. Now it seemed that I *was* one. And I *had* one. When really, all I'd wanted was Willis.

It was late afternoon when Paul returned, with a pre-packed egg-and-cress sandwich for me.

'How are you feeling now?' he asked as I shuffled into a sitting position and broke off tiny morsels of the bread to roll carefully around in my mouth.

'I don't think alcohol is good for me.' My headache had subsided somewhat, but I had ventured into a phase of sudden shivering bouts.

Paul watched me with an expression of sympathy. 'About last night... I hope you don't think I took advantage of you. I just thought at the time it was what you wanted.'

My eyes couldn't meet his. I pushed a clump of mashed egg between my lips and forced myself to chew it.

'If I thought that you'd be so upset, I never would have...'

'Look,' I said. 'Maybe we should have some time apart. Make other friends or something. I've been getting too reliant on you.'

'But what's wrong with that?'

I shrugged, before feeling another shiver take hold from the shoulders down. 'I don't know. People think we're a couple when we're not. There are just too many expectations and it's all getting too intense.'

There was a pause, and I realised that Paul was crying.

'Don't.' I reached out and joggled his knee.

'I love you,' he said to my hand. 'You don't realise how much I've loved you all these years, waiting and hoping that you would love me back.'

My remorse was like a stone in my belly; I couldn't bear the pain I was causing him. I shoved the sandwich into its packet and slid back under the eiderdown to close my eyes on my stupidity.

* * *

It was glorious; blindingly bright the next day when we went to catch the train. We said very little on the journey as the sun strobed through the window, and I had a sour, metallic taste in my mouth even though I had scrubbed my teeth numerous times after the previous morning's vomiting.

At the station we hugged loosely, awkwardly, before taking different buses home.

Six weeks later, I realised that I was pregnant.

THIRTY-ONE

KIM

Before the childcare circle

I couldn't tell Paul. How could I? He would want to be involved; he would want to be with me. I'd thought that I was over Willis, but it seemed that my break-up with him was still eating away at my heart and I had been living with the irrational hope that he would return.

It was three months later when I arranged to meet up with Paul in our usual pint-and-a-burger pub, where I wore a baggy jumper over my jeans even though I hadn't even started showing. It was the first time we had seen each other since that drunken night together. Casually, I dropped into the conversation that I was in a relationship with a guy called Gavin, someone who worked at the garden centre, a specialist in grafting roses. Looking at Paul's dejected face, I think he believed my lies.

'Anyway, enough about me,' I said, putting on a jolly smile. 'What's happening with things at your end? Have you sold any houses lately?'

'I've had an offer on one of the terraces. A bit lower than I would have liked but I'm just going to take it. Then maybe I can spend some money getting the roof fixed on Kittiwake House.

'Well, holiday season has started. You could be making an income.'

'Yeah, I know. Although there's a bit of admin to do before I can take bookings. Insurance and all that.'

'It's not insured?'

Paul shook his head, a crazy look in his eyes. 'It was a spontaneous cash purchase. The solicitor did say that some insurers would be reluctant to take it on what with it being in an area of coastal erosion. And then I never got round to sorting it out.'

'God, Paul, you must be mad. It could be falling into the sea as we speak.'

He nodded and gave a constrained laugh. 'Well, we all take a chance on things, don't we?'

It felt like he was having a dig at me about something, but I ignored it and we changed the subject. Underneath my jumper, I thought I felt a squirm in my belly and wondered if the baby could hear us, could hear the voice of the father that I would never let it know.

* * *

I didn't see Paul for another two months. By then I'd had scans at the hospital and had given up eating soft cheese. I tweaked my due date and told Paul that the baby was Gavin's, and when he asked if he could meet Gavin at some point, I suggested that we get together for a barbeque because Gavin had a great recipe for char siu ribs that I knew Paul would absolutely love.

We agreed a date. Paul said we could use his current house because it was almost renovated and had a small back yard where we could have the barbeque.

'I'll bring the food if you get the charcoal,' I said with a smile. There would have to be another elaborate story to construct: I wasn't sure at that point whether to claim that Gavin was working abroad or if our relationship was over. My knowledge of char sui recipes was zilch, but I had to be one step in front of Paul and give him no reason to ever consider that the baby might be his.

* * *

Dulcie was a tiny bundle of delight: I fell in love with her the moment that I saw her pink face scrunched in annoyance, limbs pedalling frantically as the midwife raised her like a trophy. I shed tears of bliss and release as she slotted perfectly into my arms, and tears of regret that she would never know her uncle or grandmother.

And Paul...

Looking into her big, trusting eyes, I knew that Paul would want to play a part in her life – I thought that maybe he could be her godfather and we could have some kind of ceremony even though neither of us was religious – but I wasn't ready to tell him the truth.

I didn't know if I ever would be.

THIRTY-TWO

KIM

Before the childcare circle

During Dulcie's first years, life was a mixture of peaks and troughs. I loved being a mother, but I was unemployed. I couldn't return to work at the garden centre because childcare was unaffordable. We moved to a different town, to a cheaper bedsit on a busy road, and most days I walked miles with Dulcie in her pushchair, through the park, around the charity shops in the shopping precinct, then to the library where we would sit on the floor and look at pictures in the children's books. I hung around the market at closing time so that I could buy reduced-price vegetables, and sustained us with homemade soup. Being too proud to go to Paul for help, I was trapped in a poverty routine, unable to see beyond it.

Meanwhile, his property development business boomed, and he was buying and selling houses until he was managing five renovations at once. He passed his driving test and bought himself a brand-new car. He wore tailored suits and went to a salon to have his hair styled and his eyebrows tamed. His expensive phone was never out of his hand, and he juggled his

projects and his contractors with competence and profession-
alism without ever making enemies.

I veered between feeling huge admiration and intense jealousy for his skills; when I thought of how he'd had a leg-up with
his trust fund I had to remember that the money wasn't a privi-
lege: it was compensation for a disability that should never have
happened. But still, I continued to imagine what his bank
balance could do for me and Dulcie. A proper home, with
carpets, where we could put on the heating with impunity.
Nicer clothes. A more exciting and varied diet that included
treats. All I had to do was open my heart a little and be honest
with him; maybe get a DNA test to show him.

I could never let myself do it, though, and after all the times
of Paul begging me to let him help, he stopped offering. He was
still my best friend but there had been some hardening of our
shells, some protective layer that we both wore to keep us from
accidentally hurting the other. To outsiders, we were the most
mismatched pair of allies imaginable.

Kittiwake House was a sad and separate matter that we
avoided mentioning. It had been left entirely abandoned to the
elements. Paul had got the roof fixed and the en suite bathroom
replaced, but all the insurance companies had refused to cover
the house because of the risk and its proximity to the cliffs. This
also meant that he wasn't allowed to let out the house to paying
tenants or holidaymakers, and so the place stood friendlessly
guarding the sea, feeling the full force of every storm, a white
elephant that I never returned to.

* * *

It was quite remarkable how we found the other girls.

'It just shows how being friendly with people can pay off,'
said Paul. He was on a bit of a high about it all.

Glenn, the guy in the pub that we'd chatted to on our visit

years ago to Wingfield, had, out of the blue, messaged Paul to say that the celebrity dancer and choreographer, Rhiannon Ford, had been featured in a local magazine because she had just bought a plot of land in the town on which to build a modern, architecturally designed house. She and her partner had decided that Wingfield was the ideal place to settle and bring up her four-year-old daughter. Having great memories of her schooling and teenage years in the town, she was looking forward to being part of the community again.

Paul forwarded the message to me, with an attached link to the magazine article.

How incredible, I thought, after I read through everything, trying to hold down the excitement that had vainly bubbled up so many times before.

But that wasn't the only thing.

Because of Paul showing the perfect amount of gratitude to Glenn for getting in touch after all that time, he was delivered *only six days later* with another jewel of information. Glenn's sister, who worked on reception at Van Ryan's, a swanky hotel on the edge of town, had mentioned that a new events organiser, Nina, had been employed after name-dropping Rhiannon Ford at her interview. *You might not believe it, but it was me who choreographed the routine for our championship dance in 2006, the event that propelled her to fame. She owes me big time.* Nina had stood and pirouetted, kicking out her legs right then and there, charming the MD of the hotel chain and immediately landing the job.

'Wow,' I said to Paul. 'Any more info about her?'

Further gossip confirmed that Nina had a young son, a husband that often worked overseas and a house on the coveted Burlow Dale development.

Bingo.

There they were, all three of them together.

All in the same town.

And after all this time, all this searching and waiting for this magical alignment to happen, I knew it was absolutely the right moment to take things up a gear.

It was time for *me* to make a move.

THIRTY-THREE

THE WEEKEND AWAY

Saturday – the second day of the weekend away

'Hey, there's a boat on fire out in the sea!' Kim's excited tone makes everyone turn and take notice. 'Have you seen it?'

They all leave their drinks and phones on the table as they rush to look out of the kitchen window.

'Where?'

'I can't see anything.'

Kim nudges in between them. 'Ahh, you can't see it from here. It's out in the bay. Looks like some kind of cruise ship and there are flames pouring out of the top of it. Listen! I thought I heard a helicopter just then. Maybe there's a rescue operation going on.'

'Which side of the bay?' Jarvis asks.

Kim points over to the right. 'It's probably beyond the rocks over there. You can see it from the attic window quite clearly. Look, there's a big patch of smoke coming from behind that cliff.'

'I can't see any smoke,' says Nina. 'Where are you looking?'

'Just over there. It's definitely smoke. Go and see it from the attic if you don't believe me.'

'Is that OK?' laughs Rhiannon. 'You haven't left your mucky undies on the floor?'

Kim gives her a friendly slap on the arm. 'No, my mucky undies are all packed away. I don't mind if you go and have a look out of the window. It's a much better view from there.'

Jarvis leads the way as they all scramble up the two flights of stairs to the attic room, desperate to see what is happening in the sea. Kim follows behind, pulling the key out of her pocket as she goes.

This is it now.

Her sweet revenge.

She stands in the doorway and watches as they clamour around the tiny, draughty window that looks out not to the sea, but towards the road and the bleak roofs of the town. Quietly, she slips the key into the lock and pulls the door shut.

'Where's the boat?'

'Hey, you can't see anything from here! There's no sea view at all.'

Kim turns the key in the heavy oak door and listens with delight at the solid *clunk* it makes. Their reactions are priceless.

'Wait, what's happening?'

'Kim! What the fuck...?'

'She's locked us in!'

There's a thundering on the other side as they all suddenly realise what has happened. They tug at the handle; they hammer their fists at the door. The slab of wood holds up nicely, though. No amount of knocking and banging and kicking will break it. They are in there for the long game.

They are in there until Kim decides what to do with them.

THIRTY-FOUR

THE WEEKEND AWAY

Saturday – the second day of the weekend away

Kim returns to the dining room and sends a text to Paul.

All sorted. They're locked in.

A minute later and he's at the table with her, pouring himself a drink.

'OK, let me see,' says Paul. He's got his iPad with him, and he switches it on, logging in to the security camera app. 'Yes, it's picking them all up.'

The secret camera that Paul installed in the attic room is working well. On the iPad screen they can see that Rhiannon and Stacey are sitting on the bed, Stacey with her head in her hands. Jarvis is fiddling with the door handle and ramming his shoulder at the door, perhaps unaware that it opens inwards and not outwards. Nina is pacing, tugging at the roots of her hair, her mouth twisted in an enraged rant.

'Should we tell them yet that we can see them?' Kim giggles uncontrollably.

'Let's make them sweat a bit first.' Paul zooms into the scene and switches on the sound.

'*I knew there was something going on with that devious bitch,*' says Nina as she stomps around the room. '*She's out to get us.*'

Kim laughs and slurps a mouthful of wine, holding her glass towards the screen. 'Cheers, Nina!'

Jarvis stands back from the door and attempts a couple of showy karate kicks, to no avail. Obviously, he still hasn't noticed the way it opens. Limping, he retreats and goes to examine the window instead.

Paul and Kim are in hysterics watching him. 'This is better than any comedy film I've seen for a long time.'

'*What about our children?*' Stacey suddenly whines. '*How can we go and collect them if we're stuck in here?*'

'*Surely Kim will go and pick them up?*' Rhiannon's eyes open wide as she realises what has just been said.

'*And then what will she do with them?*' Nina shrieks and tears at her hair again. '*This is all because of that boy on the beach, isn't it? Well, isn't it?*'

'*What boy?*' Jarvis asks.

'*Kim's little brother, the one who died. She thinks we had something to do with it.*'

Kim leans into the screen. 'Turn it up a bit,' she says to Paul, and he adjusts the volume.

'*Well, I had nothing to do with it, so why has she locked me in?*' says Jarvis.

There's a pause in the conversation, and Kim and Paul sip their drinks. An unexpected buzzing on the other side of the table makes them both jump as Nina's phone starts to ring. Kim reaches over and picks it up to see that an unidentifiable number is calling.

'Answer it,' says Paul. 'Pretend you're her.'

Kim swipes the green dot. 'Hi, Nina speaking.'

'Hello, it's Doctor Choudhary calling again from the Royal Hospital. It's about your aunt. I'm afraid she died this morning without regaining consciousness. Obviously, there will have to be an inquest due to the nature of her injuries, and I will let you know about that. The police are now involved and may also want to speak to you, too. I'm so sorry to have to ring you with this bad news. Would you be able to arrange to come in and sort out the legal documents? As soon as possible if you can.'

'Er, I'm sorry, I...' Kim flounders. The news seems shocking even though it is not for her. 'Could you call back later or something? I don't have my diary at the moment.'

Paul gives her a quizzical look, and she shakes her head at him before hanging up abruptly on the call.

'Oh God, I think one of Nina's relatives has just died.'

'Really?'

'Yes, a doctor just rang to let her know. What should I do? Go up there and tell her?'

Paul rubs a hand across his mouth. 'I don't know. You can't say you answered her phone. Can you? It doesn't seem, I don't know, ethical.'

'What, and me locking them up in a room and watching them on a camera *is* ethical?'

'Look, the hospital will probably ring back, and she'll get to find out later, won't she?'

'Or will she?' Kim gives a crafty smile.

Paul reclines in his chair and takes a deep breath. 'Kim. I know you've waited a long time to get to this' – he waves his hand at the iPad screen – 'this stage. But what exactly are you going to *do* with these people upstairs? We never planned beyond this, did we? Because – in my mind – it never really felt like we'd ever get to this point. Even when I was sitting outside in the car earlier... it didn't feel real. All the research and everything: it only ever felt like a game that we were playing, a sort of occupational therapy to help you find closure.'

Kim's heart pumps in her throat as she imbibes his words, thinking about the truth of them. What revenge *does* she want to impose on the three women upstairs? And what should she do with Jarvis who is an unnecessary inconvenience?

She looks at Paul but her mouth is unable to form a sentence, and she can't tell him about all the grotesque things that she has imagined doing to these people in order to avenge the death of Dylan.

He tilts the iPad a little towards her and tries again. 'I mean... are you planning on just scaring them? Or hurting them? Because you don't even know which one of them caused Dylan's death, do you?'

It is as if Paul has suddenly realised that he will be implicated in this action: they are in his house; he arranged for all the suspects to be here; he is now with Kim watching these four people's imprisonment and making no effort to release them.

'I think that we need to get to the bottom of who the killer was. And then just deal with that particular person, in whatever way is appropriate.' Kim's eyes are still on the screen.

'Appropriate would be going to the police and getting them to confess.'

'Is this being recorded?' Kim points to the iPad. 'I mean, if we have a confession on here then that would be something.'

He taps the video icon. 'It is now.'

Kim returns her focus to the scene in the attic, where Nina is hammering on the tiny window and shouting '*help!*' over and over again. Rhiannon has her arms around Stacey who is a blubbering mess, and Jarvis is working his way around the room kicking at the skirting board as if there might be a secret way out behind them.

'Jarvis is the answer,' Kim tells Paul. 'I need to get him to find out what happened to Dylan.'

Paul looks puzzled.

'Trust me,' Kim says as she heads back up the two staircases to the attic door.

* * *

She knocks sharply. There is a sudden silence as all activity stops.

'Let us out, you mad cow!' shouts Jarvis.

'Shush.' Rhiannon speaks in a lower tone. 'She's not going to respond well to that sort of thing.'

'What do you want from us?' Stacey calls out in a voice that is scratchy and thin from crying.

'Remember the letters that you got last Monday? Asking about your darkest secrets. Well, I told you mine, which was about my little brother being killed. And I suspect that some of *your* darkest secrets involve my little brother, too. So, what I want to know is how Dylan was killed, and who it was that killed him. No one comes out of this room until I get the truth.'

'What have I got to do with all this?' Jarvis shouts. 'Your brother is nothing to do with me.'

'You are the mediator in this situation,' Kim replies. 'Talk to the others and coax out the details. Solve the puzzle. And, Jarvis, when you know the answer, then I will let *you* out and decide what to do with the others.'

'You can't do this!' screeches Nina. 'Just let us go!'

'What's going to happen to our children?' Stacey is sobbing again.

'I want the truth,' Kim tells them firmly. 'I will be back up here in fifteen minutes and Jarvis will tell me everything I need to know.'

She closes her ears and her mind to their pleas as she turns and descends the stairs back to Paul.

THIRTY-FIVE

THE WEEKEND AWAY

Saturday – the second day of the weekend away

'So,' says Jarvis. 'You'd better start talking.' He leans his back to the door and indicates for Nina to sit on the bed alongside Stacey and Rhiannon.

'I knew she was up to something with us. It wasn't just about her being open and talking about her brother. The scheming bitch. Trying to pretend that it was all about *therapy*.' Nina looks towards Stacey for support. 'I said to you, didn't I?'

Jarvis points at the three women in turn. 'Which one? I need someone to confess, because I feel like absolute shit and there's no way I'm staying in here a minute longer than I need to. So, start at the beginning and tell me what happened, how you got involved in killing a little kid.'

'It wasn't like that!' Stacey shrieks. 'What do you think we are?'

'Tell me what you are, then. Tell me what happened.'

Stacey presses a hand against her chest to slow her pounding heart. 'OK. This is how I remember everything. We came here, eighteen years ago to compete in a street dance competition, representing our school. The three of us. My dad brought us, and we stayed in a guest house up on that top road. At some point during the weekend, we befriended a kid on the beach – he looked about eight or nine – and then after we'd gone home we heard that he'd drowned. I couldn't even remember that his name was Dylan.'

'I didn't know his name was Dylan,' says Rhiannon. 'He just hung around with us on the beach. It must have been that Friday evening. We dared him to do stuff and he made us laugh and then one of his mates tried to join in but he was older and a bit weird.'

'You were quite nasty to him,' says Nina. 'He had something wrong like he was paralysed down one side and you called him a one arm bandit and stuff like that.'

'It was *you* who said that,' says Stacey. 'You started throwing sand at him, and he got it in his eye and looked like he was going to cry. I think he actually did cry.'

Jarvis throws out a fist and bashes the door. 'Come on! You're not giving me the information. All this crap about some kid getting sand in his eye. It's not what I need to know, is it? How did the other one drown? What did you do to him? That's what you should be telling me.'

'Dylan seemed like such a sweet boy. I let him wear my medal, remember? He loved that.' Nina smiles as she recalls the memory.

'Ah, yes. We'd just had the presentation before we went to the beach, and we were wearing our gold medals,' says Rhiannon. 'I've still got mine.'

'You even put a picture of it on your Instagram recently,' Stacey reminds her. 'I think my mum has probably got mine.'

Jarvis holds his hands up. 'Shut up about the medals. Just shut up.' He goes to look out of the window again. Roofs, chimneys, tops of the balding autumn trees. No cars, no people. Only seagulls, devilishly riding the brink of each easterly gust.

'Oh God, I can't bear to think what's happening with Coralie.' Stacey puts her face into her hands again.

Rhiannon grips her wrist. 'Coralie is fine. As are the other kids. They are at the play centre, remember? They will be there for hours, so there is nothing to worry about yet.'

Jarvis turns to face them again. 'So, let me get this right. I need to know when all this stuff happened. What day you went to the beach. Who was there, who left at what time, that sort of thing. I need to know specific details. Stacey, you said your dad took you there. What day, what time? And what happened when you got there?'

Stacey closes her eyes in thought. 'We arrived on the Friday morning and we danced in the semi-finals, I don't know, about eleven o'clock, it still felt quite early in the day. I think there were about twelve teams or something like that. We got through to the final six and never thought we'd win it. But then in the afternoon it was the finals, and there was some kind of incident where an ambulance was called for one of the girls—'

'Two girls,' says Nina. 'Two were taken to hospital but only one ended up in intensive care is what I heard.'

'...OK, two girls were ill and so their team dropped out. And theirs was actually the best dance – we'd seen them perform earlier in the day and they really wiped the floor with us, so we didn't have a chance of winning – but with them out of the contest we were kind of more motivated and gave it everything and ended up with the gold medals at the presentation in the afternoon. The Friday afternoon. And then we went to the beach afterwards, so maybe about half past four or something.'

'Yeah, I'd say that was about right,' says Rhiannon.

'And that's when you met Dylan?' Jarvis asks.

'And his freaky mate.'

'And you hung around with him, but he got into some kind of trouble and drowned? So, he died that Friday evening?'

'No, no,' says Stacey. 'Because *I* saw him the next day when

I was on my way back to the guest house after the celebration party for all the dancers. Then we left to go home on the Saturday evening just as a massive storm started, and then we found out the next day – the Sunday – that he had drowned, because my mum saw it on the news.'

'Apparently his body was discovered under all the rubble from the storm,' says Rhiannon.

Nina suddenly clicks out of the trance she has been in. 'What I want to know is this: how the fuck did Kim know that *we* were with him?'

'So, you *were* with him when he died?' Jarvis asks.

'No! And we didn't *kill* him,' says Stacey. She looks wildly around at the others. 'Did we?'

'I certainly didn't,' says Rhiannon. 'So you can cross *me* off your suspect's list.'

'Shhh.'

They go quiet and listen to the approaching footsteps on the uncarpeted stairs.

'She's back,' says Jarvis. 'What am I supposed to say?'

A rap on the door makes them all hold their breaths again.

'OK, Jarvis,' says Kim from the other side. 'What do you know?'

'Look, we're getting there. Just give me a bit longer and we'll sort out what happened. I'm trying to put together a timeline and as soon as I've got the info, I guarantee I will tell you.' Jarvis uses a composed, friendly voice to gain Kim's trust.

'Well, time is ticking and there are the children to think about,' says Kim.

'What do you mean?' Stacey screams. 'Don't you dare do anything to harm my daughter! I will rip your fucking skin off if you ever do anything to hurt her!'

'Stacey, hey, listen, we're dealing with this.' Jarvis moves to lay a reassuring hand on her shoulder. 'Don't get stressed.'

'Fifteen minutes,' says Kim. 'I will be back again in fifteen minutes and I want answers. And this time, to focus your minds, I *would* like you to think about what might happen to your children if I don't get those answers. Just remember your darkest secrets. You can't keep them hidden anymore. It's time to talk.'

THIRTY-SIX

THE WEEKEND AWAY

Saturday – the second day of the weekend away

'You sounded quite menacing there,' says Paul when Kim gets back to the dining room. 'I mean, mentioning the children is a bit threatening, don't you think?'

She shrugs. 'I have to do what it takes. Tighten the screws, so to speak.'

The clock on the wall tells them that it is ten past two. They have plenty of time before the children need to be picked up. Plenty of time to play with the captives in the attic. Kim is pleased with how it's going so far, particularly with how Jarvis has taken on the role of interrogator. She can sense that the women won't need much more persuasion before they all start talking.

She settles down again with Paul and the iPad, watching how the women take turns striding across the floor; the way they pull at the collars of their clothing; the way they tug at their hair and chew at their fingernails. These mannerisms of fear and desperation are fascinating to observe. And the sounds they make, too: the keening, the sobbing, the endless 'please please

please please no'. The thing is, they could just confess instead of covering up for each other, instead of having to go through all this.

Suddenly, Kim's phone rings in her pocket and she pulls it out to look at the number. It's Neil, the tree surgeon again.

'I can't be bothered to talk to him,' she tells Paul, indicating that they are too busy dealing with their hostage situation. 'It's only about Mrs Coates's trees. I'll get back to him next week.'

She ignores the ringing and eventually it stops, but a few minutes later there's a ping and a text comes through.

Hi, it's Neil again, about Mrs Coates. Is she OK? She seemed in a pretty bad way when I found her on Friday. Don't worry about rescheduling the tree pruning, that must be the least of your worries now.

'What?' Kim turns her phone to Paul and shows him the text. 'I think maybe I should ring him back. It sounds like Mrs Coates might have had a bad turn yesterday.'

She returns Neil's missed call, and he answers immediately.

'Oh, thanks for getting back to me. I was concerned about what happened to Mrs Coates after they took her in the ambulance, so I hope you don't mind me getting in touch. I did try ringing the hospital this morning but obviously they wouldn't give me any details apart from saying that she was poorly. Have *you* heard how she is?'

'What? I don't know anything about this. I haven't seen Mrs Coates since Thursday. Has she got a virus?' Kim knew that she occasionally suffered with diarrhoea and vomiting – probably picked up from the damn parrot or the ceaseless vermin – but she would never let her even call a doctor, always being insistent that the illness would be gone in twenty-four hours and she didn't need medical intervention.

'Well, no, it was quite a bit more serious than that. I found her on the floor of the hall on Friday afternoon with what looked like a nasty head injury. She was unconscious and I assumed that she'd had a fall and gone back into the door frame, you know, and cracked her skull on the way. There was a fair bit of blood on the floor, so I rang 999 and it was pretty soon, I must say, before the paramedics turned up and then the ambulance.'

'Oh, thank goodness you found her,' says Kim. 'Because I'm not due to go in until Monday, so who knows what could have happened if she'd been left there all that time. She's not great on her feet and she often thinks she can get around without using the walking frame.'

'Well, I think there might have been more to it than that. There was a load of cash on the floor which I thought was a bit strange. You know, twenty-pound notes, and that. I picked it up and put it in the drawer but some of it had been in the blood. I didn't count it or anything. There was no sign of a break-in or anything like that, but it just troubled me that things didn't feel right, so after the ambulance had taken her, I rang the police and they came to have a look around the house. They took a statement from me and were still there when I left but I don't know what the current situation is or how Mrs Coates is doing.'

'Well, I...' Kim gets up and paces the room. 'I'm away at the moment, so... Er, I'll try to ring the hospital and find out how she is and when they might be sending her home. Give me ten minutes and I'll get back to you.'

'Everything OK?' Paul asks.

Kim puts a hand to her forehead; tries to blink away the light strobes behind her eyes. Something seems strange, wrong. She pictures Mrs Coates, crumpled and bleeding on her hall floor amidst a scattering of bank notes.

'Mrs Coates is in hospital,' she tells Paul. 'The tree surgeon found her with a head injury yesterday, in the hall. I need to ring the hospital and find out how she is.'

After googling and trying three different numbers, she

finally gets through to reception where she tries to explain her relationship with Mrs Coates.

'I'm her main carer. She has no family apart from an estranged niece or something, so I'm the person who deals with everything. I have the keys to her house and need to know how she is and when she will be home. It was only just now that I found out she was in hospital, when the tree surgeon rang me. He's the person who found her with the head injury.'

'OK, let me take some contact details and I will get the doctor to ring you back.'

Kim leaves her name and number and turns her attention back to Paul. 'God, my brain is all over the place now. I don't know what to think.'

He is still watching the attic scene on his iPad. 'I turned the sound down while you were on the phone, so I don't know what's been said. Shall I turn it up again?'

She shakes her head. 'Wait till the hospital has called back.' She looks at the screen, at the people she has imprisoned. Silently they stride around and throw out their arms randomly; Stacey's face has a pleading quality about it; Jarvis is looking grey, ill.

Kim's phone rings. She snatches it up. 'Hello?'

'Hello, it's Doctor Choudhary calling from the Royal Hospital. I'm afraid Mrs Coates died this morning. She had quite a serious head injury and never regained consciousness. It's a matter that the police are now involved in. I did inform next of kin a little earlier today, and she will be coming in hopefully next week to deal with the legalities.'

'No! Oh, no. Oh, Mrs Coates. I'm...' Kim is too stunned to form a sentence.

'I'm so sorry.'

Kim puts her phone quietly, carefully, back on the table. 'She died this morning. I didn't even know she was in hospital. Apparently the police are involved.'

Paul slides his good arm around her shoulder and pulls her into him. 'That's such horrible news. You really liked her, didn't you?'

She nods forlornly. 'But... what's also a bit bizarre... That phone call earlier for Nina? I think – well, I'm pretty certain – that it was about Mrs Coates. It was the same doctor I just spoke to. I think that Nina might be her relation, the one who never bothered visiting or anything.'

'Wow. Really? What a turn of events.'

The situation in the attic has suddenly been downgraded as Kim considers the situation with Mrs Coates. She pictures her lying on the hall floor, her caved-in head and the money in the blood, and wonders who will take care of Vincent now that she is gone...

Something jolts inside her like an electric shock.

Money. Blood. Parrot.

She goes to the bin to retrieve the receipt for the donation to the World Parrot Trust. The dark red blot in the corner that had stuck it to the back of the ten-pound note: it's blood, she's sure it is. And there is only one person Kim knows who would have given money to a charity for parrots.

'I think Jarvis had something to do with her death,' she says to Paul. 'He must have been at her house.'

'Jarvis?'

'Look at him.'

They watch Jarvis on the iPad, observing with interest his severe facial injuries and the plasters covering the fingers and knuckles of his left hand.

'He didn't have those injuries on Thursday night when he collected Hayden from Nina's house. And he didn't have them the following morning at the school gates. He got them some-time on Friday before we set off to come here. Just like Mrs Coates, who didn't have injuries when I saw her on Thursday, but was found seriously hurt on Friday afternoon.'

'So, you think Jarvis attacked Mrs Coates but also got *his* injuries from *her*? As in, she tried to fend him off?'

'He must have. And he was quizzing me about being on The Elms the other day, so maybe he went there to find me or something?'

They turn to look at the screen again, where Nina has suddenly taken off her left shoe to bash the heel hysterically at the window.

'This is all getting pretty intense,' says Paul. He points to his iPad. 'Look, she's broken the window now. She's pulling pieces of glass out. It's not like they're just sitting around discussing their secrets anymore, is it? We have four people locked in my attic here and at least two of them are killers. Kim, I think we need to call the police.'

'No. We need to wait.' Kim's face is set, hard and angry. She can't bring herself to let them out, to let them off. There's too much at stake now.

She's not done with them yet.

THIRTY-SEVEN

THE WEEKEND AWAY

Saturday – the second day of the weekend away

Jarvis groans. His head wound is hot and throbbing. Perhaps the superglue is causing an infection. All he wants to do is get into bed and close his eyes on everything. But he knows he can't; he has to manage this crazy situation that they are trapped in; he has to keep trying to find the answers to Kim's questions. 'OK. So establishing a timeline isn't really working. We need to go back to the beginning.'

'I already told you about the dance contest,' says Stacey.

'I don't mean that sort of beginning. I mean the letters. The ones we got on Monday. We need to talk about our secrets. Like, just make a deal with each other that we won't tell anyone else, that everything we confess stays within this room. And it might help you get a story together that Kim will be satisfied with. Then we can all get out of here. I'm sick of this place and desperate to get home now.'

'OK, then, *I'll* talk about that weekend. I'll tell you my version of it as long as it goes no further than us four people,' says Rhiannon.

She stands and walks to the end of the room. Her move-ments are jerky; her breaths quick and shallow. 'You know the girls that dropped out of the contest, the ones that were taken to hospital? I did that. I spiked their drinks with bleach so that they wouldn't be able to dance in the final. There. That's *my* darkest secret. It's nothing to do with Dylan.'

There is a stunned silence. Finally, Stacey speaks.

'So, we *won* because you got them to drink bleach?'

'One of them ended up in intensive care,' says Nina. 'She could have died. How did you do it?'

'Their bottles of orange juice were in the dressing room next to the sink. And a cleaner had been and left a bottle of bleach out – I know, I know it was mad and irresponsible and I shouldn't have done it – but I saw it as an opportunity. For us. So, I tipped out some of the orange and topped the bottles up with bleach. I mean, there was every chance the girls wouldn't drink it. But they did. I just never considered the seriousness of my actions. All I thought about was us, and how we needed to win that contest. And what I did has haunted me for all these years, wondering if I harmed them for the rest of their lives. Even the smell of bleach terrifies me now. I can't use it at home.'

'Well, it's a horrendous confession, but it's nothing to do with the information that Kim wants,' says Jarvis.

'But it *is* my darkest secret,' Rhiannon replies. 'We were asked to confess our darkest secrets and this was mine.'

'I can't do this.' Nina suddenly lurches up from the bed and screams into the palms of her hands. '*She* can't do this to us! We've got to get out of here.' She pulls off her left shoe and begins to smash the heel at the window.

'Nina! Nina, calm down.' Rhiannon tries to pull her away, but the glass has cracked and shards are falling onto the floor.

'I can't stay here. There must be a way out.' She rips at pieces of the glass with her bare hands, pulling it out of the frame until a jagged hole appears.

'We're up on the second floor. It's not as if we can shin down the drainpipe,' says Jarvis. He is leaning his head resignedly against the wall, cupping the swollen side of his face with his hand.

'Nina, please. Come away from the window: if you fell from this height you wouldn't survive. Look, you've cut your hand now.' Rhiannon fumbles in her pockets for a tissue to stem the flow of blood that is dripping from Nina's hand. 'Please, just sit down. We're going to get out. Panicking won't help any of us. We just need to talk about how we can give Kim the information she'll be satisfied with so that she will let us out.'

Dazed, Nina allows Rhiannon to lead her back to sit on the bed with Stacey.

'OK then, Jarvis. We were confessing our darkest secrets, and I've just told you mine. In confidence, obviously. But it's your turn now.' Rhiannon talks evenly, trying to take control of the situation because Jarvis is looking seriously unwell again. 'You tell us yours.'

'What?' Jarvis throws his hands out. 'I'm nothing to do with the kid that got drowned, am I? There's no point in knowing what *my* secret is.'

'It's only fair. If we all tell you ours, then you have to disclose yours, too. So, what is it? No, let me guess. An addiction of some sort. Like heroin. Or sex.'

'Fuck off. I'm not a druggie.'

'So, it's sex then?' Nina taunts him as she balls the blood-soaked tissue into her fist.

Jarvis has had enough. He slams his fist against the door again. 'If anyone is addicted to sex you should be looking at her.' He points his finger towards Stacey. 'She only needs a couple of gins and she'll open her legs for any bloke in the pub, won't you, darling?'

Stacey's face is crimson. 'Shut up! I don't know how you can say such a thing.'

'You were all over me that night. Wouldn't leave me alone. I tried to sneak off but you followed me into the men's toilet and pulled me into the cubicle. Knickers off, tits out, your hands everywhere. It was easier to just give in and shag you rather than fight you off.'

Stacey has her hands over her ears. 'Stop it! Stop it! You liar! You absolute liar. It wasn't like that at all. You sent my friends away and told me you were getting me a taxi, but then you just plied me with more drinks and took advantage of me when I was in no fit state to stop you.'

Jarvis shakes his head slowly. 'That's not how I remember it.'

'Oh my God,' says Nina. 'You two have history? Was this before Xander?'

'No, it was when she was already married to him. He obviously wasn't giving her enough,' says Jarvis with an inflammatory smile.

'You bastard!' Stacey jumps up from the bed and lunges at Jarvis, punching him solidly in the chest.

He turns and dodges her next strike, stumbling backwards and tripping over Nina's foot.

'Hey!' she shrieks, pushing him back towards Stacey.

Suddenly, he slips on the broken glass and instinctively throws his arm out for balance.

Stacey assumes that he is trying to grab her. 'Get off me!' She hits his wounded face as hard as she can, blinding him with pain and knocking him forcefully into the jagged edge of the window.

Then there are three seconds of silence.

Three seconds of stillness.

Everyone is frozen in horror.

'Fuck,' says Jarvis, without breathing. 'Oh fuck.'

'Oh God,' says Rhiannon, slapping a hand across her mouth. 'Oh shit.'

Jarvis slowly peels himself away from the sliver of glass that has sliced into the side of his neck and slides down the wall to a sitting position on the floor. He presses his hand to his neck to stop the blood that is trickling, then pumping, soaking into his clothes, pooling into the bare floorboards. 'Help me,' he whispers. 'Please, help me.'

Nina runs to hammer at the door. 'Kim! We need an ambulance. Jarvis is bleeding. Please, it's urgent. HELP US!'

Rhiannon seizes a pillow from the bed and whips off its pillowcase, rolling it into a bandage to wrap around Jarvis's neck. 'Stay with us, now,' she says, slapping his cheek. 'Stay with us, you're going to be fine.'

'I'm sorry.' Stacey is crying. 'I didn't mean to do it. I'm sorry.' She kneels down beside Jarvis and forces an extra hand over the pillowcase but the blood won't stop, it just keeps pouring out.

'KIM! Get up here now, because we need a fucking ambulance!' Nina has both her shoes off now and is whacking the door with the heels, screaming into the wooden slab.

Jarvis's head is lolling to the side and his eyes are closed. His clothes are scarlet, soaked wet, sticky, giving off a sweet metallic smell.

'Actually, I think he's stopped bleeding now,' says Stacey, hopefully. Naively. She removes her hand from the makeshift dressing on his neck.

Rhiannon feels for a pulse. She presses his wrists in different places, then puts her palm on his chest.

Finally, she stands up on trembling legs, her own hands and clothes smeared red.

'It's too late. He's dead.'

THIRTY-EIGHT
THE WEEKEND AWAY

Saturday – the second day of the weekend away

'Oh God. Oh God. We should have gone up and let them out. We should have just called the police when I said. What the hell are we supposed to do now?' Paul is hyperventilating, gripping his chest, looking like he is on the verge of collapse. 'We could go to prison for this.'

Kim is immobile, her body, legs and arms turned to jelly. She sits, dazed, her eyes glued to the screen of the iPad as Rhiannon and Stacey lay Jarvis's body flat on the floor, and Nina is still screaming. She could turn the sound off but she knows that she will still hear her up in the attic. What happens now? What will happen with the kids, with Hayden? Kim reaches for the bottle of wine and gulps greedily at it until there is nothing left.

'This obsession of yours about getting revenge... Just look what it's led to.' There's a new vibrato in Paul's voice. 'I should never have got involved. I could have just had a normal life instead of all this... this horror. There's a man dead upstairs in my house now, and he didn't even have anything to do with Dylan.'

'He killed Mrs Coates!'

'But that's just speculation. You can't prove it.'

Kim's throat is burning from holding back the shock and the tears that will inevitably come in floods. She feels so sick, but has to keep everything down, even though her body just wants to collapse into a bed where weighted blankets will crush her and release her from this deformed idea of retribution that has possessed her whole being for years.

'Kim? Kim? What shall we do?' Paul shakes her out of her nauseous trance. He looks so young, so innocent, his face so pure and trusting. She knows that she can't let him be harmed by this. She is entirely to blame and will accept whatever punishment is necessary. Yet...

Maybe there is still a way out.

'No one knows that you are here,' Kim tells Paul. 'And we need to keep it that way. If it all goes wrong I will say it was totally down to me and you had no part in it. I'm going to go up to the attic.'

'To let them out?'

'No. I'm going to talk to them. But I want you to lock me in. Watch and record everything. And only let me out again when I ask you to.'

'No, you can't do that: it's too dangerous. They're going to be so angry with you. Look what Stacey did to Jarvis. You could get slaughtered up there.'

She shakes her head. 'I've got to do it; I've got to take that risk.' She passes the key to him. 'Come on. Bring the iPad and wait outside. I'm going in.'

* * *

The screaming has subsided by the time they reach the door; the room resounds with low sobs and consoling noises. Kim gives a perfunctory rap and waits for their reaction.

'KIM! Let us out. Jarvis is dead. This is all your fault!' Nina yells at full volume again.

Paul puts the key in the lock.

'I'm coming in,' Kim tells them. 'We need to sort all this out. Move away from the door.'

Quickly, Paul unlocks the door, and Kim pushes her way in through the slimmest gap before it is closed and locked behind her.

She's inside the room.

She notices the duvet is off the bed, on the floor by the end wall. Covering the body of Jarvis.

Rhiannon runs over to her. 'What just happened? Who's out there?' She turns the handle and pulls at the door. 'It's locked. We're locked in again. Kim, tell us, what the hell is going on?'

Kim has her back to the wall, her body tensed and ready to defend itself.

Then, suddenly, the women are all around her, with wild eyes and bloody hands and the smell of fear and death on them, jostling, shouting, putting their fingers and fists in her face and blaming her for everything when it was them, always them, who started it all that day on the beach with Dylan...

'STOP IT!' she screams.

THIRTY-NINE

THE WEEKEND AWAY

Saturday – the second day of the weekend away

It feels like some fevered nightmare, this extraordinary meeting of the childcare circle in a grotty attic room with the sea spray gusting in through the hole in the window and the cackle of gulls outside. There is glass and congealed blood on the floor; there is Jarvis's body covered with the duvet, his feet sticking out.

The women perch on the edge of the divan in a stupor. There is no fight left in them; they've used up all their adrenaline. It's as if they have just retreated from a war zone and are trying to process the horrors that they have witnessed. A disconcerting tranquillity has settled in the space between the trio and Kim, who feels able to sit on the floor with her back to the door.

'I realise that there's a lot of stuff to deal with and we've got to get things sorted out because our kids need to be collected in less than three hours.' She begins by laying out the facts.

'Who's outside the door?' Rhiannon asks.

Kim shakes her head. 'It's no one you need to worry about.

But he will call the police if things get intense in here, so you need to seriously ask yourselves if you want the police involved.'

'*We* haven't done anything wrong,' protests Nina. 'It's you who should be worried. You locked us in. You caused all this.'

'No, Nina. You smashed the window. You and Stacey pushed Jarvis into the glass.' Kim points up to the ceiling, to what looks innocently like a downlight. 'There's the security camera. I was able to access it on my iPad, so I could see and hear everything that happened. It's all been recorded, too, just in case the police need evidence.'

There's a loud gasp from Stacey as she looks upwards. 'I can't believe this is happening.'

'An innocent man is dead, and the events that led to his death – his *accidental* death – were started by you locking us in this room.' Rhiannon seems the most level-headed, but Kim needs to tell them the truth.

'Jarvis wasn't as innocent as you think. We all noticed how he looked like he'd been in a fight yesterday, and he tried to tell us that he'd fallen while jogging, didn't he? Well, the thing is, he was lying. All those police sirens and that woman who was attacked in her home – the incident that you were talking about last night – well, Jarvis did it. He smashed in an old lady's head and left her for dead.'

'What? An old lady? Like, who? And why would he attack her?' Nina asks. 'You're just talking rubbish now.'

It hits Kim even harder then, the thought that Mrs Coates is dead. The thought that she will no longer have the job that she loves in that peculiar old house. She will no longer need to cut crusts off her bread, set the mouse traps, rake out parrot mess.

She covers her face as a sudden bout of weeping takes hold, trying her best to speak between sobs. 'Mollie Coates. She died this morning from her injuries. I think you were related to her.'

'Oh. My. God.' Nina stands up and puts her hands on the top of her head. 'Aunt Mollie. Well, great-aunt to be precise.

The hospital rang me last night to say she'd been admitted and I just thought it was... well, I just thought she'd had a fall, you know, something minor. They told me I was her next of kin which was news to me. I've never had much to do with her but, still...'

'Yeah. Still,' Kim replies. 'I worked for her. Cared for her. Personal care, cleaning, cooking.'

'I didn't know you worked for her.'

'There's a lot you don't know about me. And probably a lot you didn't know about your aunt either.'

Nina nods in agreement. 'The last time I remember seeing her was at a family event when I was about nine or ten. I've never been to her house or even knew where it was. My grand-mother always used to describe her as having airs and graces, of being an obstinate character. I don't think the two of them really got on very well.'

'She was lovely,' Kim retorts. 'I wish she'd been *my* aunt.'

'Let me guess,' says Rhiannon. 'She lived on The Elms?'

'Did *you* know her?' says Kim.

'No, but I think there has been some confusion around all this. We thought that you lived there, Kim. We all thought you were rich and keeping it secret.'

Stacey looks sheepish. 'I mentioned to the others that I saw you withdrawing a load of cash.'

Kim lets out a hollow laugh. 'But that was for Mrs Coates, so that she could pay the tree surgeon.'

Nina's mouth has dropped open. 'My aunt lived on The Elms?'

'You never knew? So, who started the rumours about *me* living there?' says Kim.

'Oh God, we all just jumped to conclusions, didn't we?' Rhiannon says. 'Look, when we got the text about how much we'd pay to keep our secrets I overreacted. I sent a reply. I thought – well, we all thought, didn't we? – that you were hiding things about yourself, Kim. And I thought that if I passed on some information about you to the person who was trying to blackmail us then they would just go after you and leave the rest of us alone. So, in that text I said something like "you need to check out Kim as she's the one with all the money" and I passed on what I thought was your address on The Elms, not knowing that it was just your place of work. I'm so sorry. I didn't realise that the text would go to Jarvis. He must have used a different phone number.' Rhiannon shakes her head regretfully. 'I know that he had money problems because he asked me for a loan, so maybe he went to the address that I gave him, thinking that you could help him out financially. Maybe he was desperate? And then something went horribly wrong?'

'He killed an old lady.' Kim shudders. 'The receipt for the donation to the parrot trust definitely came from Mrs Coates's house. Remember, it was stuck to the cash that Jarvis gave you? Actually stuck on with *blood*. And he turns up on Friday with a load of injuries and a load of money at the same time as Mrs Coates is found unconscious by the tree surgeon. She was found with money all around her, in her blood. The police are involved, so presumably now it is a murder investigation.'

'The police could already be searching for Jarvis.' Nina turns frantically to look at his covered body. 'What if they come here and find him dead?'

'It was an accident!' Stacey cries. 'Caused by you locking us in, Kim.'

Kim rubs her knuckles into her eyes. 'We are all implicated. Every one of us.'

'So how do we deal with this whole fucking mess then?'

Kim holds out her hands in a calming gesture. 'Listen. The despicable thing that Jarvis has done has made it easier for us to get away with hiding his body.'

'Hide his body?' Nina is almost retching as she speaks the words.

'It's the only thing we can do.'

'But hiding a body is a crime! And what if we don't all agree to be involved?' Stacey says.

Kim shrugs. 'There are no individual options. Either we're all in or we're all out. We can go to the police and own up to Jarvis's death and face a prison sentence, which would mean that we could lose our children. Or we can hide his body and let the police think he's gone on the run. Your choice.'

'What a fucking choice,' says Nina.

'OK. We hide the body,' says Stacey.

Rhiannon nods. 'Yes. I'm in. We can't go to the police.'

'You might not like me, but we've got to be solid, and we've got to have each other's backs,' says Kim. 'We have all done some terrible things, but this will have to be our darkest secret ever. And we can never tell anyone about it.'

'How do we do it?' Stacey asks. 'How are we going to get away with it?'

'Listen carefully,' says Kim. 'I have a plan.'

FORTY

THE WEEKEND AWAY

Saturday – the second day of the weekend away

Kim stands and knocks on the door. 'Hey. I need the key. We're coming out so you can go now. You can stop recording.'

'Who is out there?' Rhiannon asks again. 'Because I thought it was only *us* that knew about all this?'

'I can't say. But it's someone trustworthy. They won't ever tell. You've just got to believe me on that.'

The key is slid under the door and Kim picks it up before they hear the sound of footsteps running down the stairs. 'Let's swear an oath,' she says, standing and holding out her right arm. 'Come on.'

Rhiannon and Stacey reluctantly stand up to join her.

'Nina? We can't do this without you.'

'Oh my God. This is just an absolute nightmare.' She rises and stands stiffly with the others who have their right hands clasped together.

Kim speaks. 'This will be our darkest secret, never to be told to anyone, ever. Agreed?'

'Agreed.' The other voices join in unison.

'OK. Now we're ready.'

* * *

They use the roll of bin bags that Nina has brought along; as a
perfectly organised events manager she wouldn't host anything
without providing a means of clearing up afterwards. Rhiannon
gets gaffa tape from the boot of her car: it's an essential in the
world of stage productions and she always carries a spare roll
everywhere. Between them all, they wrap up Jarvis's body so
that they can haul it down the stairs and outside without
smearing blood everywhere. At the end of the garden – the
place where Bobby slipped down the edge of the cliff – they
place Jarvis's body behind the shrubbery so that the children
won't see it when they return from the play arcade.

Stacey takes a bucket of hot water and detergent upstairs to
scrub away the blood from the floorboards. When the place is
clean, they clear up the broken glass, strip off their clothing and
bundle it all up into a bag with the bedding from the attic.
Stacey will dump it in a bin at the motorway services on their
way home.

Nina goes to clear out Jarvis's room.

Kim rings Neil, the tree surgeon. 'I've got bad news, I'm
afraid. Mrs Coates died this morning. The hospital said that
there will be an inquest due to her injuries. So, presumably it's
now a murder investigation.'

'I know. The police have just been in touch because they
want to ask me some more questions.' Neil groans and sighs at
the other end of the phone. 'I've got to go down to the police
station this afternoon. They said they're examining CCTV
from other houses on the road and want to rule me out as a
suspect. I'm so sorry about everything. You must be devastated.'

'It's an awful situation and I'm not back in the area until
tomorrow. But... well, thanks for your help, and I just hope they

find whoever did this.' Kim hangs up and tries to hold back the genuine wobble in her chin.

Rhiannon has Jarvis's phone. She scrolls through the contacts to find Helena, Jarvis's ex-wife, and has a look through the texts that they have sent each other over the past few weeks. Brief, perfunctory messages that have no hint of warmth or fun or affection. A marriage gone bad. Their last communication demonstrates that Helena is annoyed how Jarvis hadn't yet let her know what time she needs to collect Hayden.

Rhiannon types a text:

You can pick Hayden up at six and I'll make sure he's ready. Don't be late.

She sends it, adding the postcode of the property. 'Done,' she says to Kim. But she doesn't put the phone back; she looks through his apps, his browsing history, his other messages.

'Weird bloke. Obsessed with online bingo, roulette, poker. And – wow – all his emails are just full of sports betting. He is *seriously* in debt with it. I guessed all along that he had some kind of addiction, and looking at all this, I'd say that it was gambling.'

She clicks into the pictures folder next, to swipe through Jarvis's most recent photographs. 'Hey, do you recognise this garden? Because it's definitely not his.'

Kim goes over to have a look. 'Well, well. If I was only ninety-nine per cent certain of him being at Mrs Coates's house before, then it's one hundred per cent now. Because that's *her* garden. These are the trees that should have been pruned.' She taps on the picture to see the information about it. 'Just look at the date and time on there. It puts him right at the scene of the crime, Friday mid-afternoon before Neil turned up and found her unconscious.'

'And while he's there he finds a stash of money that he

needs – and remember that he still owed me a hundred quid at that point – and thinks he can get away with taking it.'

'Poor Mrs Coates.' Kim's eyes start to well up again.

'Nina's her only living relative. She might get to inherit everything,' says Rhiannon. 'Doesn't seem fair, really, when she's had nothing to do with her all her life. And considering that you'll be out of a job now.'

Kim sighs. 'It is what it is. Life isn't fair, generally. It hasn't been to me. But I get by, and at least I have Dulcie. I can't bear to think about what might happen to her if we don't get away with all this. And I feel so bad for Hayden.'

'I know.' Rhiannon reaches out to squeeze Kim's shoulder. 'It's terrifying to think about. But we can't let that stop us now. And remember that Hayden still has a mother who loves him, who was in the process of fighting for full custody anyway. If Jarvis had lived, he would have been locked up for murder and Hayden would have had to deal with that which would also have been hard.'

Nina returns from her task of packing up Jarvis's belongings. She puts Hayden's holdall by the door, ready for him to take to his mother's house, and – apart from a spare pair of trainers, his keys, and his phone that Rhiannon has – she's moved Jarvis's possessions into his car that is parked outside.

'Well, I think we're pretty much sorted now,' she says. 'Unless you can think of anything else.'

Kim checks the time. 'We have forty minutes before we need to collect the children. So, I'd like to use that time to discuss a different subject, and the one that I originally gathered you here for.'

The women stand with puzzled expressions on their faces.

'My brother, Dylan. It's time for me to hear all the pieces of the story.'

FORTY-ONE

THE WEEKEND AWAY

Saturday – the second day of the weekend away

There is a gravity in the room congealing with the confusion and adrenaline of the earlier events. Stacey checks her Fitbit: her heart rate is higher than ever and just won't return to normal. Nina leans her elbows on the table and drops her head into her hands.

'I set up this weekend, and carefully manipulated Nina into *organising* it so that we would all be together.' There is emotion breaking in Kim's voice. 'But I never really planned what I was going to do with you. Some kind of revenge or punishment? I'd dreamed about it for years: the chance of being here with you in the very place where my brother died. But now... Well, everything has just gone horrendously wrong.' Kim pauses to scrub the tears off her face. 'My head has been so messed up about this. It's like I hated you and wanted to inflict harm and pain on you, but I almost wanted to be friends with you, too. But... you know what? I think what I need most is just the truth. The real truth about what happened to Dylan, so that I can process it and accept it and move on.'

'Yes, but what will you do with the information?' Nina asks. 'Go to the police? Ask for the case to be reopened?'

'How can I?' Kim is baffled by Nina's stupidity. 'We are all in *this* shit now, aren't we? We have a body to hide, the final biggest secret that we will have to keep forever. So, I can assure you that whatever you tell me now about Dylan will stay between us. Absolutely. It won't be shared with the police, because our relationships with each other, with this circle of us, have to stay solid and unbroken. None of us can risk the police getting involved with anything to do with our past, present or future. After all this, we have to go away and behave impeccably. Do you understand?'

The women nod and murmur.

'So, what I want is an honest account of what happened when you came here to the dancing contest, and how Dylan ended up drowning. I have spent my life speculating and grieving and hating and it's time to put it to rest. Whatever happened on that weekend: well, I just want the truth, so that I can finally let go and get on with my life.'

No one moves; no one talks. The clock ticks oppressively and the gulls outside whine at the edge of the shore. There's a pulsing background hum, probably coming from the fridge. Finally, Nina lifts her head and speaks.

'It was me. I did it. But it wasn't intentional; it just started as a joke when we were playing. He was a lovely kid and I liked him and I am so, so sorry that he died as a result of what I did. And if it makes you feel any better, I have never forgiven myself either.'

'Oh my God.' Stacey gasps through the hand over her mouth. 'What did you do?'

'Remember, on that Friday, after we'd all been playing on the beach, I gave him my winner's medal to wear. I let him take it away with him and said he had to bring it back to me the next day, and we all arranged to meet up on the beach at five o'clock?

Well, at the Contest Party on the Saturday afternoon, you lot had abandoned me, hadn't you? I was the only one left. And although I didn't really want to go to the beach on my own, I wanted to get my medal back off Dylan, obviously, to take home and show my parents. I mean, where were you?'

'I had to leave. It was so embarrassing – an emergency – and I was so humiliated. Some of the kids from another school started laughing at me because my period had started and I was wearing white jeans and...' Stacey's face is flushing at the memory. 'I had to get away from everyone and go back to the guest house, so I just tied my jumper around me and ran back up the hill. But when I got back, I could hear noises from my dad's room next door to ours and I walked in to see what was happening and—'

'Let me guess, it was the woman who was all over him at breakfast?' says Rhiannon. 'The one that seemed to appear at quite a few of our dancing contests?'

'Yes, her. They were in bed together. Wine bottles and glasses at the side of the bed. Her bra on the floor. My dad shouted, "get out, get out" and I ran and locked myself in our room and changed into some clean clothes while I was panicking and not knowing what to do, wondering whether to ring my mum or not. And then later on Dad came and knocked on the door and said he wanted to talk to me, and I let him in but I couldn't stop crying and he was trying to say it was a mistake because he'd had too much to drink, and I kept saying that I wanted to go home even though we were supposed to be staying until Sunday, and I eventually threatened him with ringing my mum and telling her everything if we didn't leave immediately. But then, I had to find you two...'

'I was still in the theatre, but not at the party,' Rhiannon says. 'I'd sneaked backstage to the changing rooms, utterly convinced that I'd left fingerprints on the bottle of bleach and that the girls would die and I would be caught by the police. So,

I'd gone to try and clean up after myself, to wipe all traces of my crime from the scene. By the time I got out, the party had finished and you and Nina had gone. The weather was horrible and the wind was blowing up a storm. I went to the edge of the beach and saw Nina holding her shoes and dodging around in the waves, which even then were coming in pretty quick and nasty. It seemed ridiculous that she would be out there, so I shouted to her and as she ran over to me, Stacey and her dad turned up in the car, saying that they had packed everything up and we had to go home before the storm properly hit. I thought it was strange how reluctant Nina was to leave, and how strange it was that Stacey was insistent that we go right away—'

Nina cuts in. 'Obviously, I didn't want to go because of Dylan. I'd left him on the beach. I was pretty annoyed that he'd turned up and not brought my medal back – firstly he made the excuse that he couldn't find it and then he said that someone might have stolen it from him – and so I'd dug a hole and covered him up to his neck in the sand. Just messing about, though, that's all.'

'He was buried standing,' says Kim. 'When his body was found they said it was in a deep hole, feet to the bottom with his arms by his side. There would have been no chance of him being able to get out without assistance.'

'I just wanted to give him a fright,' says Nina. 'There's no way I would have intended for him to drown. I dug a hole and buried him and we were both laughing about it – God, it was a *joke*, that's all – and then I went for a paddle in the sea, thinking that I'd leave him like that for about ten minutes just to wind him up and then I'd dig him back out and send him off to go and find my medal. But when Rhiannon turned up and then Stacey and her dad came in the car and said we had to go straight away, I didn't know what to do. I went off with them thinking that... well, I don't know. That Dylan would get himself out. Or that I would find an excuse to go back to the beach. Or someone else would find him and help him, like that weird mate of his with the funny arm. I don't know. I truly don't. Honestly, I didn't expect it to turn out the way it did. And then there was the cop car, and all the waiting around in the police station while Stacey's dad was arrested.'

'We shouldn't have got in the car with him,' says Rhiannon. 'You could smell the alcohol straight away. *We* could have been killed. My mother was furious about it all and even complained to the school.'

Stacey is crying. She's biting her lip and trying to control her trembling chin. 'Why didn't you say something *then*, Nina? When we were in the police station? You could have said to the police that the boy was buried in the sand, and they would have gone to find him before the tide came in. And before the storm brought the cliff down.'

'It wasn't just me at fault though!' Nina proclaims. 'If your dad hadn't been shagging that woman then we wouldn't have had to leave. Did you really not notice his bit on the side turning up to every event that he took us to? So, really, you could say that if you hadn't caught him with her then we'd have stayed the Saturday night just like we were supposed to, wouldn't we? I would have gone back to Dylan and got him out and everything would have been all right.'

'If. If. If,' says Rhiannon. 'If I hadn't put bleach in the girls' drinks then I wouldn't have had the career I've had; if Dylan had brought Nina's medal back she wouldn't have buried him; if Stacey hadn't had a one-night stand with Jarvis he'd probably still be alive because they wouldn't have got into an argument about it... If. If. If. The list goes on. We can't change the butterfly effect. How far back do we really need to go to see where it all went wrong?'

Kim pulls in a deep breath and closes her eyes as she releases it. She wedges the heels of her hands into her eye sockets and sits calmly as everyone watches and waits for her reaction. Finally, she rubs her hands forcefully over her face.

'OK,' she says in a decisive tone. 'I'm done with it all. I've grieved enough over the years and I have to draw a line somewhere. We can't change what's happened, but I'm glad that I know the truth about Dylan now. And that truth stays in this circle because we don't need to talk about it again. But we do have all *this* mess to deal with, so we have to continue with our plan. Are we all ready?'

'We're ready,' says Rhiannon.

They put on their hats and warm coats and step outside.

FORTY-TWO

THE WEEKEND AWAY

Saturday – the second day of the weekend away

'There were rides and shooting games and machines that you could put tokens in to win things but we weren't allowed to win real money. So, I got a keyring and Hayden got a little bouncy ball. Although he's lost it. And we had burgers to eat but Coralie didn't eat all of hers so I finished it,' says Bobby breathlessly.

'It sounds fab, chick. You must have had a great time.' Nina is good at putting on a show of buoyancy.

'There was a zip-wire as high as the ceiling and I went on it hundreds of times,' says Freya. 'Dulcie only dared to do it twice.'

'Well, that's fine,' says Rhiannon. 'Not everyone likes doing the same things, and I would probably only have done it once.'

'Where's my dad?' says Hayden, his vision scouting around the entrance doors.

'He went out for a walk earlier.' Kim, blinking, can't look him in the eyes. 'Just a stroll further up the beach, to see where it goes. But that's OK, because it doesn't need everyone to come and pick you up, does it?'

Stacey scrunches her brows into a pitiful expression as she looks away.

Rhiannon moves towards Hayden to help him fasten his coat. 'Well, who wants to go and play on the sand?'

There's a united shout from the children. 'Me! I do! Yes!'

'Come on then. What are we waiting for? Let's go!' Nina jiggles the collection of buckets and spades that they have brought with them, and they set off towards the beach.

Kittiwake House is in their sights as the group sets off towards the foot of the cliff. From this perspective it looks fearless and formidable, a hulking construction that can easily withstand the easterly storm due to hit the coast later that evening.

'What about here?' says Rhiannon, shaking out the picnic rug.

'Sandcastle time!' Nina is still in her zealously positive character. 'Let's start digging.'

Kim scans the crumbling edge, trying to assess the central point of Kittiwake House's perimeter. She traces an oval shape in the sand with her heel. 'Here. What about we all dig a massive hole and then when the sea comes in it will be like a pond.'

'Yes, I will!' Coralie takes a spade and then the others follow, immersing themselves innocently into the activity as they shovel out the wet sand, throwing it into a big mound behind them.

Stacey has her back to the group and is staring out at the thrashing waves, hypnotised by their rhythm.

Kim approaches her, touching her cautiously between the shoulder blades. 'Are you OK?'

'Oh God, it just seems... awful. Look at Hayden, having fun, digging a hole that is going to be...'

'I know. How about we take a couple of the kids – including

Hayden – down for a paddle at the edge of the water? Let Rhiannon and Nina do some of the digging because... well, it needs to be deep.'

Stacey nods, trying to rid herself of the troubled expression that has claimed her face.

'Who wants to go in the sea?' Kim calls to the group. 'Take your shoes and socks off, but I'm warning you, it will be cold!'

'Me!' all the children squeal, apart from Bobby who, intent on being the best at digging, stays behind to vigorously scoop sand out of the enlarging hole.

Nina and Rhiannon are red-faced with their efforts, despite using toy plastic spades.

'This is a job and a half, isn't it?' says Nina, standing up rigidly to ease the twist in her back.

'Shall I get inside the hole, Mum, and dig it out from there?' Bobby suggests, hopping down into the cavity without waiting for an answer.

The others – four children and two adults – are cavorting in the breaking waves. To onlookers, the whole party of diggers and paddlers must look like a normal group of friends enjoying some free outdoor recreation in the school holidays, burning off energy and tiring out the kids before bed.

No one takes any notice of them. The beach is almost empty, apart from an elderly couple near the boarded-up ice-cream shack who are throwing a ball for a disinterested retriever, and a trio of hooded teenagers sitting further along the foot of the cliff furtively sharing a spliff.

At a quarter to six, the children are shivering as they brush sand off their feet. Like a thief, the tide is creeping in, inch by inch, bringing the dusk, bringing the storm.

They are the only remaining people on the beach. Kim gathers up the buckets and spades; Rhiannon folds the picnic rug. No one mentions the hole behind them, the hole that is five feet deep.

'Time to go,' says Nina, leading the way.

'We didn't see my dad, did we?' says Hayden. 'He could be back at the house by now. Or he might have gone a different way.'

No one replies to him.

And no one looks back at the waiting pit in the sand at the foot of the cliff, ready to hold its secret.

FORTY-THREE

Saturday – the second day of the weekend away

Nina has only just unlocked the door when Helena turns up. Rhiannon has met her once before, when she picked up Hayden from her house, but none of the others know her. It is almost dark though and there are no working security lights to illuminate the path or the garden.

'Mum!' Hayden throws himself into her arms for a hug while everyone else is stamping sand off their feet at the back of the house.

'Hi, precious.' She deposits a kiss on his forehead.

They file into the kitchen where everyone apart from Hayden peels off their outdoor wear.

'What a godforsaken place,' remarks Helena as she gazes around. 'Is it haunted?'

'It's free,' Nina replies. 'That's what attracted us to it. And it's not so bad when the fire is lit. Although, when we got here yesterday we seriously thought about turning round and going home—'

'But the road by the caravan park got closed due to flooding so that basically decided it,' says Rhiannon. 'They only opened it again this afternoon. What was it like when you came through?'

'It was OK. Just some big puddles. There was a tanker pumping the water away,' says Helena. She pats Hayden on the back of the head. 'Go and say goodbye to your dad.'

'I'm not sure that he's here...' Kim starts to say, but Hayden is already running towards the stairs.

'Dad! Dad, I'm going now.' His footsteps thunder along the landing and into the bedroom where he spent the previous night with his father. Minutes later, he is back in the kitchen. 'He's not there. And none of our stuff is there either.'

'Is this your bag?' Helena picks up the holdall by the door.

'He must have left it there before he went out for a walk.' Nina is back in her exuberantly helpful mode.

'Well, that's fine. I didn't want to see *him* either.' Helena laughs. 'Come on, Hayden. We've got over an hour's drive now and the weather looks like it's going to get grim again.'

'I didn't say bye to Dad though.'

'You can use my phone to text him on the way, OK?'

Nina and Rhiannon follow them outside to give the impression of being sociable, waving off their car that turns and heads back to the main road.

'I don't know how much longer I can keep this up,' says Rhiannon. 'Being positive, trying to pretend everything is normal.'

'Come on, we're nearly there. We've just got to get through tonight and then tomorrow morning we can all go home.'

'And all we have to do then is keep it a secret for the rest of our lives.'

'We've been keeping secrets for years, though, haven't we? It's all been good practice for us.'

* * *

Stacey stays with the children and they find a channel with cartoons on the television.

'You're in luck,' she tells them as she hands out bowls. 'We've got some popcorn left.'

Outside, sheets of rain are already lashing sideways, and Rhiannon and Nina run through the dark, empty town towards the beach, carrying the fireside shovel and the biggest of the children's plastic spades underneath their waterproofs. Kim has already been out and cut away the bin bags and gaffa tape from Jarvis's body, and she is waiting in the kitchen for their call. Suddenly, Jarvis's phone pings in her pocket.

Hi Dad, it's Hayden. Mum picked me up before you got back. She said we're going to the cinema tomorrow and having a McDonalds. See you on Friday. Love you. Xx

Kim is suddenly awash with remorse. Will Hayden end up like her, not knowing what happened to his father for the rest of his life, endlessly seeking closure and an opportunity to blame someone? She feels no guilt for what has happened to Jarvis – he killed a defenceless old lady after all – but his young son will have to endure grief and suffering as he deals with the knowledge of his father's crime.

Oh, this is truly horrible, she thinks as she types a text in return. But it needs to be done.

Hi dude, sorry I missed you leaving. Cinema sounds fun. Hope you have a great time. Love, Dad xxx

She sends the text just as her own phone starts to ring.

'Everything is good to go at our end,' says Rhiannon. 'There's absolutely no one around and the tide is only about twenty metres away from the hole now.'

'OK, give me two minutes to put my coat on and get outside.' Kim dons her waterproofs and switches on her torch.

* * *

At the end of the garden, she carefully pushes Jarvis's body towards the very edge of the crumbling cliff, wary of how precarious it is.

She dials Rhiannon. 'I'm ready now, so stand back. I won't hang up, so you can let me know how things have gone.'

Then, as the wind and rain try to hold her back, she gathers her energy to kneel and shove the body of Jarvis – one hand on his shoulder, one on his hip – as hard as she can, so that it rolls over once and topples, head-first, down the cliff. It's as if it doesn't make a sound. Kim hears nothing apart from the fury of the sea and the percussive thrumming of the rain on the soil and on her coat.

'Hey! Hey, can you hear me? Are you still there?' Kim pulls her phone underneath her hood, shouting over the noise.

There is no reply.

'Rhiannon! Is everything OK?' Her heart punches inside her ribs as she starts to fear that the body might be stuck somewhere halfway down on a ledge that they cannot reach.

'Rhiannon!'

Still no reply.

A hefty lash from the storm knocks her backwards, and in the fluttering beam of her torch she sees a slice of the garden's perimeter disappear. She needs to get onto the path, away from the unstable ground. Scrambling away, she takes cover under the porch, still screaming Rhiannon's name into her phone. But there's no answer, and she can only think that something has gone wrong, that their plan has failed and they will all end up getting arrested and losing their children.

'Rhiannon!'

There's a noise on the other end, a muffled grunt.

'Rhiannon! Talk to me! What's happened?'

'Hey, Kim, yeah it's all sorted now.' Rhiannon's voice breaks through to send Kim giddy with relief. 'The landing wasn't in the right place, but we've dragged it along and we're just trying to move all the sand into the hole now before the waves get any closer.'

Kim exhales, trembling. 'Don't take any chances with the tide. And get back as soon as you can. Parts of the cliff are already falling and you don't want to risk getting buried yourselves.'

It would be an ironic kind of karma if the storm were to bring a chunk of the coast down to kill them on the same beach as where Dylan met his death, she thinks.

* * *

The wind slams the door shut behind her, and she pulls off her wet garments to rub a towel over her head. Stacey comes through to meet her, raising her eyebrows in an unspoken question.

'It's done. We're nearly there,' says Kim, shaking uncontrollably.

'I've lit the fire in the living room,' says Stacey. 'You need to go and get warm.'

'I hope the others are all right. They must be freezing out there. I'm concerned that the tide will come in too quickly and cut them off...'

'Don't. We can't think that. I can't take any more than what's already happened.'

Kim goes to squat by the flames, her cheeks reddening in the heat, as the children sit unaware, watching *Alvin and the Chipmunks* while they munch on popcorn.

'Do you want to share this with me, Mummy?' Dulcie proffers her bowl.

'I'm good, petal,' Kim replies. 'You enjoy it.' Her heart melts. The warmth is breaking through.

* * *

Time is loaded with apprehension. It is another twenty-five minutes before they hear the kitchen door open for Rhiannon and Nina to lurch, soaked and exhausted, into the warm, safe space. They cannot speak. Kim and Stacey pelt them with questions. *Did anyone see you? Did you manage to bury the body completely before the sea reached you? Was the body intact from the fall down the cliff?* They only realise then that they have started referring to Jarvis as 'the body', and that what Rhiannon and Nina need most is silence and dry towels.

* * *

Sunday – the third day of the weekend away

By morning the storm is subsiding. It has claimed at least another metre of the garden and has blown the makeshift fencing away from its posts to slouch against the back wall of the house. Seagulls circle over the choppy grey sea with an eye towards the town's promenade, where pickings of chips and sandwiches will later lure them inland.

Stacey is the first one out of bed, filling the kettle and tidying away the kids' detritus in the living room.

'I couldn't sleep,' she tells Kim and Nina, who emerge half an hour later. 'I don't know if I'll ever sleep again.'

'It's nearly over.' Kim puts a teabag in a cup. 'And then we just have to forget that any of this ever happened, and hope and pray that nothing ever turns up to arouse any suspicion.'

'I've been thinking,' says Stacey. 'I'll finish it off. The final bit. It looks as if the tide is on its way out, so I'll get togged up and go while the kids are still in bed. You lot had to deal with all the storm and the crap yesterday, and I feel like this whole situation was my fault. So, I'll be the one to put an end to it.'

Nina is scrolling on her phone. 'I thought I'd better check that the road hasn't been closed again overnight. Wouldn't it just be catastrophic if we were still stuck here after all this? But it's OK. We'll be fine for driving home later.'

Stacey takes the carrier bag out of the kitchen cupboard that contains Jarvis's trainers, keys and phone, and while Kim and Nina make toast and tea she sets off to the beach for the final part of the plan.

* * *

The town is still deserted, apart from a handful of delivery vans and a high-vis-clad lad on a bicycle. It is not yet half past seven and Stacey stands on the beach, trying to work out where it was that they had dug the hole yesterday. But the cliff is different this morning, as rocks and shrubs and the whole substance of the coast's edge lies in piles along the southern aspect. The place where Jarvis was buried is covered in debris. The house has given up part of its land to hide him.

Stacey strides out in the opposite direction where the groynes have held this part of the cliff stable. She puts her head down to the wind and spray, determined and purposeful, waiting for the right place to appear.

What hope is left? she asks herself. After all this... how will Coralie turn out? What kind of teenager will she be, what kind of young woman, or mother? What traits are determined in the genes that slip through into someone's personality in spite of a decent upbringing?

She thinks about her father, here in this place eighteen

years ago and how easy it was for him to forget about her mother as he slipped into bed with another woman. And then she thinks about how she herself hadn't shied away from unfaithfulness either. It hadn't taken much to persuade her: coy smiles, beguiling banter, two drinks too many.

Is there something inherent that runs through each generation? And does it mean that there could be some negative quality in Coralie, waiting deep within her like an alien being to reveal itself at some unsuspecting time?

No! How can she think such things about her own daughter? Coralie is a perfect, pure child, not some scheming adulterer-in-waiting.

But Stacey knows that her mind will never let the thought go now. It's inevitable: it's the sort of notion that will grow as if it's had yeast added, and she won't be able to stop herself watching, comparing, analysing every little action, every little thing that Coralie says or does.

She is breathless from the pace now, a stitch in her side halting her to bend and jab her fingers under her ribs. The beach is still empty. No one would stop her if she simply walked into the sea and let the current take her. But what good would that do, apart from leave yet another child without a parent?

She remembers Jarvis's phone in the carrier bag and what she has to do.

Hi dude. I'm out for a walk on the beach and missing you already. You're a good lad and you're the best thing that ever happened to me, but I've done stuff recently that I'm not proud of and what I'm about to do now is try and put things right in some way. Enjoy being with your mother and be kind to her. I love you so much. Dad xx

She sends the text and then switches off the phone, not

wanting to have to deal with a subsequent reply or a call. There is a pile of rocks nearby, coated with barnacles and seaweed, and Stacey goes to find a suitable place, a dry windswept stone where she can leave the phone and the set of keys inside one of the trainers that are contained in her flapping carrier bag.

Shrimps dart around the rock pool, and she watches the sea life enviably for a moment, swimming free and untroubled, before she sets down Jarvis's remaining possessions.

These things may or may not be found, she realises. Just like his body.

And just like her darkest secret that she still holds on to.

PART THREE
ONE YEAR LATER

FORTY-FOUR

NINA

It's incredible what can happen in a year. A new baby has taken over their house and their lives. She's called Pearl – Bobby absolutely adores his beautiful little sister – and Nina is ecstatic with happiness and the glow of new motherhood. There's a sparkle in her eyes and a spring in her step, and every day she feels unconditionally blessed. She and her husband, Lenny, have renewed their marriage vows, and he has got a new job with a UK-based company so that they can spend more time together. Their family really does feel complete now. And, with Lenny working more time remotely so that he can pick up Bobby from school, Nina no longer needs the childcare circle.

Sometimes, things just work out right, despite adverse indications. Because who would have suspected that after the shocking events of the childcare circle weekend away, Nina's life would have taken the path that it has?

The investigation of Mollie Coates's murder was made simpler by an early morning dog-walker who discovered Jarvis's phone. The photographs of her garden, CCTV footage from other properties on The Elms, along with DNA evidence – his blood at the scene and her blood on his clothing that was found bagged up in his dustbin and on the stolen cash in his sock drawer – and statements from Kim, Rhiannon, and Neil the tree surgeon, pointed to Jarvis as the only suspect. His abandoned car, along with his trainers, phone and keys, and the text that he sent to Hayden led the police to believe that Jarvis had taken his own life.

Gossip and speculation in the school playground continued for weeks.

Almost a year later, his body has never been recovered.

Mollie Coates's last will and testament was finally read in late summer. It was an unusual arrangement, with just two beneficiaries, Nina Ronson and Kim Taylor, who, other than at the old lady's funeral, had barely seen each other since their weekend away.

The women acknowledged each other politely – at this point Nina was only nine days away from her due date – and waited quietly in a book-lined room as the sun breathed dustmote beams through the old sash windows. A thick-ankled secretary wearing a tweed skirt and black polo-neck walked in and out of a door whose brass plate declared 'Talbot Lewis Esq.', the floor creaking with every step as she transferred papers and a thick manilla envelope stained with a coffee-cup ring. There was the sense of a discussion behind the door, and the clatter of a pen pot being knocked over.

'You know, I never asked before, but it's something that has puzzled me ever since our weekend. Did you *know* Paul Eyrie?' Nina's prized client had disappeared without a trace, leaving her emails unanswered, her phone calls ringing out indefinitely. She'd had to cross out all his bookings in the hotel events diary.

Kim gave a little shake of her head and put a finger across her lips, and Nina knew then that it was a subject, just like the dark secret they shared, that could never be broached.

Outside there was the sudden sound of something metallic being dropped, and the women both turned towards the window at the same time. But it was just scaffolding being erected on the office block across the road.

'Just builders,' said Kim.

Just normal stuff; normal life happening around them; no one knowing what they'd done.

'I wondered if my aunt might have left you something. She must have cared about you,' whispered Nina, stroking her belly like it was a cat on her lap.

Kim gave a sad smile. 'She was lovely, such an eccentric character. I've really missed working for her. But I'm not really expecting anything; she never talked about putting me in her will. I actually thought she might leave it all to charity. To the parrots trust.'

'I bloody hope not.' Nina laughed quietly.

No one mentioned the childcare circle. No one mentioned Jarvis.

The secret was safe.

'Would Ms Ronson like to come through first?' The secretary was back, helpfully holding the door open.

* * *

Nina pushed herself up awkwardly into a standing position, feeling the grind of her unborn baby's head in her pelvis. The office she entered smelled of leather and fusty paper, and the white-haired man behind the desk tipped his head to indicate the chair in which she should sit.

'As the only living blood relative of Mrs Mollie Coates, you are the prime beneficiary of her estate. However, this is an unusual bequest and will involve making a choice.' Talbot Lewis examined her severely over the half-moons of his spectacles.

'OK,' said Nina. 'I'm good at choosing.' A flippant laugh was not enough to sustain a smile from Mr Lewis.

'So, as executor, I have dealt with the inheritance tax on the estate and as such, the remaining assets have been bequeathed according to Mrs Coates's wishes. I have two envelopes here.' He held them up. 'Each envelope contains a selection of Mrs Coates's effects. You get to find out the contents of each one and then you can make your choice. Whichever envelope you discard will be assigned to Miss Taylor.'

Nina nodded, finding the process bizarre. Were will readings often like this?

'So, this is Envelope One, and it contains the following. The sum of four hundred and seventy-two thousand pounds – which is the remaining amount after payment of the inheritance tax – and a collection of art which includes a drawing by Henry Moore. Also, some silverware including an Edwardian tea set. And jewellery which includes Mrs Coates's ruby engagement ring with matching brooch and bracelet. Plus, some itemised books: first editions including J. M. Barrie's *Peter Pan*; Joan Aiken's *The Wolves of Willoughby Chase*; *Tales from Hans Christian Anderson*; and Andrew Lang's *The Animal Story Book*. And finally, Mrs Coates's three wedding dresses, condition unknown.' Talbot Lewis pushed his spectacles further up his nose as he tucked the heavy piece of paper back into its envelope.

'Well, that all sounds interesting,' said Nina, mainly to fill an uneasy gap where Mr Lewis's rumbling belly could clearly be heard.

'And the next envelope, which we shall call Envelope Two, contains the following. The house known as Carmel, number four, The Elms, and the entirety of its contents, but not including the aforementioned items in Envelope One. However, there are special conditions with this choice. The beneficiary must live in the house – the property cannot be sold at any point during their lifetime – and take the best care possible of Vincent' – a raised eyebrow and a deliberate nod was inserted here – 'which I believe is an African Grey parrot, dearly loved by Mrs Coates.'

Nina sat back in her chair and folded her hands over her baby bump. She had speculated over the contents of her great-aunt's will since the event of her death, in the knowledge that she was her only living relative. And now she was being given a choice.

'I always dreamed about living on The Elms,' she said.

Mr Lewis raised his eyebrows again. 'Have you visited the property recently? Because I understand that it requires a significant programme of renovations in order to be sufficiently habitable.'

'Er, no. I'm not sure that I have ever been, unless it was when I was a small child.' Nina smiled. 'But I do know the road. There are some lovely properties in that area.'

'Well, just so that you are aware... it is a Grade II listed building, which would require a certain standard of restoration to maintain the aesthetics and this could be quite costly.'

'Ahh,' said Nina. 'Yes, I see what you mean. Would it be possible to go and have a look before I make my choice?'

'Yes, absolutely. There is nothing in the will that says you have to make a blind decision. I can let you have the keys right now. The parrot is apparently being looked after temporarily by a neighbour.'

Nina picked up the weighty set of keys. 'I'll go over there this afternoon. And I'll let you know my decision by lunchtime tomorrow.'

Talbot Lewis followed her out of his office, to where Kim remained in the waiting room, an optimistic expression on her face.

'I'm awfully sorry,' Mr Lewis turned to Kim, 'I will have to reschedule our appointment while I await further instructions.'

* * *

Nina unlocked the front door and walked into the hall. The sharp smell made her reel and for a moment she had to step back out onto the porch to take some breaths of fresh air. Pulling her top up over her mouth and nose, she resolved to go in again.

Although it was August, the place felt chilly. She looked around at the flaky walls spotted with damp, the sombre staircase spindles, the grimy-framed oil paintings that sneered down at her. She poked her head around the first door on the left, the main reception room it seemed, which held an abundance of weary furniture and mismatched clutter. A plump brown slug was making its way across the dull marble hearth of the fireplace. A square of newspaper by the bay window – presumably where the parrot cage had been sited – was spattered with grain and bird shit.

Nina returned to the hall and closed the door. She checked the next rooms. The huge kitchen looked out onto a dark jungle of a garden. A possible dining room was OK apart from a corner of the floor that had obviously been eaten by rats. Some kind of extra parlour contained an unmade bed and a stained commode which may have held the reason for the astringent smell. By the back door was a kind of utility room – maybe the place that elderly posh people called a *scullery* – where a section of the damp ceiling had fallen onto the floor. A downstairs toilet was strung with cobwebs.

There was the whole of the upstairs still to explore, but the compulsion to get back outside and gulp clean air into her lungs was too overwhelming for Nina. She stood on the front path and examined further the exterior of the place: the rotting windows, the crumbling pointing, the roof that was shedding its slates onto the garden.

Driving from the solicitor's office to come and view the

house had given her the chance to think about how exciting it would be for her and Lenny to move in with the children and spend some time updating it. Choosing paint colours, soft furnishings; maybe upcycling some of the antique pieces in a quirky, arty way.

But the deterioration of what had once been a grand residence had obviously gone beyond mere updating. Infested with vermin and riddled with copious damp and rot, it would require a team of builders and vast sums of money to properly renovate the place. And then there was the situation with the parrot. She'd never been a fan of birds as pets and these particular creatures could live for up to sixty years in captivity.

It was true that with the right treatment, the house could be worth a fortune – others around here had sold for up to two million pounds – but... there was just something lacking. She hadn't clicked with the place or got any positive vibes about the layout or its potential. She couldn't see herself living here at all, even if the kitchen was kitted out with bespoke industrial-style units and the walls painted in Farrow and Ball Bancha matt emulsion. Obviously, if she'd been bequeathed the whole of Aunt Mollie's estate without all the imperious conditions, then things might have been different.

But...

The smell. The rodents. The damp and mould. The parrot. Nina realised that this whole package of horrors would make her family ill instead of making them happy. Having to live there forever and being forbidden to sell the place. Having to deal with conservation officers from the local council and being limited on what changes they could make to the building. And – oh God, no – there were probably bats in the attic that would have some kind of preservation thing on them.

No, she decided. It would have to be a *No*. She would take Envelope One, which was still a fabulous amount of money and valuable assets. She would let Kim have the house.

Something warm and blissful accumulated in her chest, then, flooding up to her neck and jaw. It was the thought of making such an altruistic gesture, she guessed; it was the feeling that she would be selflessly performing a random act of kindness.

She had taken Kim's little brother from her all those years ago; now she could go some way to making amends by giving her a home.

Kim was probably the sort of person who liked parrots anyway.

FORTY-FIVE

RHIANNON

Sometimes a change of scenery, a completely blank page, is the only solution. When your head is full of turmoil and stress, when your daughter picks up on that disturbance, becoming fearful of leaving your side, and her class teacher is ringing up daily to report meltdowns, then a drastic reset can be the only answer.

So, Rhiannon and Katya made the impulsive decision to withdraw Freya from school and sell their home. To change their lives completely.

They moved to the Netherlands, to the cool new ecovillage where Freya's father, Hans and his new partner – both keen to save the planet – had also just purchased one of the contemporary homes on stilts there that guaranteed a personal connection to the earth. Their houses – each one uniquely designed and positioned with solar gain in mind – were climate-neutral and had a choice of recycled rainwater or compost toilets. A community food forest gave them daily access to nature and a healthy and sustainable diet, and they all became evangelical about microbiomes and cold-water swimming. Home-schooled families met regularly within the ecovillage, and Freya's mood improved as she made new friends and learned a new language.

With her father living less than fifty metres away, Freya had the opportunity to build a proper bond with him, sharing time between the two households, and the four adults found that they adored being in each other's company discussing all manner of cultural, ecological and social subjects.

Rhiannon turned down the flame under her dancing career; she had given up on the pantomimes and travelled less frequently to London for choreography projects in the West End. Her celebrity status was dwindling, and in a different country she found fresh comfort in being normal, invisible. She snoozed her social media accounts more often than not and let her website lapse completely.

Mindfulness and forest bathing were the things that gave her validity nowadays, and instead of city breaks and bars she travelled out to the Wadden Islands, to walk miles along the mudflats, marvelling at the wildlife during the day and stargazing on clear dark nights. The body of water felt different there, kinder and calmer than the sea that had lashed out below Kittiwake House, the sea that had killed Kim's brother, Dylan.

The sea that kept Jarvis's body hidden.

Rhiannon still woke regularly in the night with a racing heart, with a fist clenched hard to stop the blood pumping from Jarvis's neck. Haunted wasn't the word. The memory of that weekend had sapped her strength and unleashed a fragility which she thought could only be dealt with in a spiritual way. She craved some kind of forgiveness from a higher power that she could not access. She burned incense and lit candles and hugged trees and googled if it were possible to make confessions to a priest without being Catholic. Yet she knew deep down that she could never tell. Their secret had to be kept forever.

Finally, she tracked down Helena, Jarvis's ex-wife, on Face-

book, to ask if she would let her and Freya write a letter to
Hayden.

That would be lovely, came the reply. *Hayden often talks
about Freya and how he misses her. It would be nice to hear from
you all.*

It was such a positive step.

Freya printed off pictures of her bedroom, and Toto, their
Maine Coon cat, sitting on the front steps of their new house.
She typed a letter in a flowery font, reminding Hayden about
the childcare circle and all the things they used to do at each
other's houses. She said the zip-wire and the slot machines at
the seaside holiday had been her favourite times last year
although she was sorry about what happened with his dad. She
said that she hoped Hayden might visit them one day.

Rhiannon worked on her letter for hours before eventually
deciding to keep it concise.

Dear Hayden.

*I hope you are well, still enjoying life and school. I know that
things have been sad and confusing for you, but over here in the
Netherlands, me and Freya often talk about you and all the
nice times we had with the childcare circle. Remember the
dancing? You were so enthusiastic and your krumping and
robot moves were absolutely the best! I hope you still get chance
to do them. I miss your smiling face and your terrible jokes –
some of them I will never forget!*

*Please don't forget about us either. Keep your memories
happy ones and keep in touch if you can. Go into the future
with hope and good intentions. The world is so much better for
having you in it.*

Lots of love,

Rhiannon, your Wednesday carer.

Most of the nightmares have stopped now. A life has resumed that is completely different from the one she had before, and she is grateful to have found a comfortable place in it. Things are looking up.

And the dark secret that is held in her core has hardened and withered like a nut so that one day she may even forget it is there.

FORTY-SIX

STACEY

Moving on was challenging. For the first few months, Stacey lived in a state of shock. Insomnia. Hypertension. Panic attacks. Unexplained aches and pains. Constant arguments with Xander: he wanted to know what had made her so needy and possessive; he wanted to know why they rarely had sex. But she could never – would never – tell him.

The doctor prescribed a high dose of antidepressants after which Stacey spent some time in a semi-content limbo before rashly quitting her job. She fended off Coralie's questions about Hayden and what had happened to his father – there was so much gossip around the school playground that spread like an inkblot – until her daughter became withdrawn, nervy, tearful over every minor incident.

Something had to change.

The childcare circle had fallen apart. They didn't need each other's help any longer, and Stacey was almost incapable of caring for her own daughter let alone anyone else's. Jarvis was dead. Rhiannon had already left the country. Nina's husband did Bobby's school run nowadays. And Kim no longer worked for Mrs Coates so was free to pick up Dulcie every day.

They had all vowed never to speak about what happened that weekend, so Stacey was unable to seek counselling, unable to speak to Xander about her experience and ultimately trapped by the horror of it. How would she ever deal with the trauma and return to normal life?

Something definitely had to change.

* * *

It was a Monday morning in early July when she bumped into Kim at the school gate. There was normally a nod and a perfunctory *Hi*, but this time Stacey needed more. She had been pondering her situation, analysing, overthinking everything to do with it.

Stacey needed Kim to be her friend.

'I was wondering,' she approached Kim carefully. 'Would you fancy coming round to mine for coffee? Are you busy? I don't know what you're doing nowadays and it might be nice to have a catch-up.'

Kim seemed visibly taken aback. 'But I thought...'

'I know we agreed to hide everything that happened and not talk to each other about it, but things aren't too good with me and it's not necessarily about going over *that weekend,* but, you know, I just want to talk normally about how I feel to someone who *knows*. Do you understand?'

Kim exhaled for a long time, looking at a discarded piece of gum on the pavement. 'Yeah. I do sort of understand. We could get together for coffee if you like. When were you thinking?'

'Now?' Stacey said hopefully.

Kim checked the time. 'OK. I can do that.'

* * *

They sat in the kitchen. The washing machine was churning in the background, and the fragrance of hidden meadows from the fabric softener seeped into their space.

'Have you been in touch with anyone?' Stacey asked. 'Like, from the childcare circle?'

Kim shrugged. 'No. Only you. Have you heard anything from Nina? I've only seen her once, at Mrs Coates's funeral, and I didn't really get chance to speak to her.'

'She's pregnant. Due at the end of August.'

'Really?' Kim counted the months on her fingers. 'So that must have happened very quickly after we came back from...'

'Yes. Yes, I know.'

They sipped their coffee, and Stacey enjoyed this, taking pleasure in just being quietly with someone else who had shared the same horrific experience.

'Where are you living and working now?' she asked.

Kim ran a hand through her hair. 'Just... Same old crappy jobs, although without the work for Mrs Coates I've taken on more hours in The Blue Bean, and an extra two evenings in Bart's. We're living in the flat above the burger bar – which is where we always lived despite the rumours – wishing that we could go somewhere nicer.' She gazed enviously around at Stacey's neatly co-ordinated kitchen: the cheerful glow of the under-cupboard lighting; the glitzy mosaic splashback; the spices organised in a jaunty bamboo rack.

'I packed my job in,' said Stacey. 'I couldn't handle it anymore. I'm backwards and forwards to the doctor for medication. My head isn't right. My marriage has failed and Xander moved out last weekend, supposedly to give us both some time apart, but I'm not getting the feeling that he will come back. And I'm obsessed with the thought that Coralie will end up in the same position at some point because her genes are corrupted...'

'Her *genes* are corrupted?'

'Adulterous family members. Me. My father. Her father. And she has murderous parents.'

'Murderous? What do you mean?'

'Well, just look what I did. *I* killed Jarvis, didn't I? All this situation has been my fault.'

'It was a horrible accident and we *had* to cover it up or we could all have been convicted. Perhaps it's the secrecy that you can't cope with?'

'I'm definitely struggling with it.' Stacey's fingers pinched at her scalp as she closed her eyes. 'I feel like there's a load of skeletons and I'm trying my hardest to keep the cupboard door shut, but if I'm not careful something is going to spill out soon and the shit will really hit the fan.'

Kim examined Stacey's face, watching her erratic breathing. 'There's only one secret you need to hold in to keep us all safe.'

'You don't understand.' Stacey's eyes sprang open. 'The letters, the thing about confessing our darkest secrets, before we all went for that weekend away. I never told you mine. I never got chance to say what it was, but even if I had, I don't think I would have ever said it in front of everyone else.'

'Hey.' Kim reached out for Stacey's hand as if it was an *off* tap for the tears that were spilling onto the table. 'I thought you said it was about your dad's affair and finding him in bed with someone. That was your secret, wasn't it?'

Stacey shook her head. 'No. That wasn't my *darkest* secret. It's much, much worse than that. It's about Jarvis and his genes that could be passed on, because he was a killer too.'

'What's that got to do with anything?' asked Kim.

A little sob escaped from Stacey's mouth. 'Everything. Because Jarvis was Coralie's father.'

FORTY-SEVEN

KIM

'This is amazing!' Dulcie, seemingly oblivious to the range of pungent odours, runs from room to room flinging open the doors and squealing with delight. 'We have got all this space for ourselves. And all the garden, too.'

Kim still cannot comprehend how she ended up getting the keys and the deeds to a house on The Elms. It appeared to be a combination of kindness from Mrs Coates and a generous gesture from Nina. Maybe it was some form of guilt-induced compensation. Or hush money.

Some of the art and valuables have been removed as per the will, but most of the furniture remains as it used to be, and Kim will go later to collect Vincent from the neighbour who has been looking after him.

Her new life starts here.

'Look at you,' says Paul, his body sprawled for effect on a battered chaise longue. 'Lady of the manor. Look at *us*. Together at last, just like I always dreamed about. After all that's happened.'

Kim stands by the fire, one elbow resting on the huge marble mantelpiece. She can't stop smiling. 'I know. A pair of kids brought up in care. Who'd have thought it?'

The logs crackle. It's a nasty night outside with rain and gales whipping around the roof and chimneys. A storm from the east. But the room feels warm and homely now, lit subtly by lamps dotted around on occasional tables. Deodorising air freshener has temporarily blasted away the unpleasant aroma; Kim has vowed to get to the bottom of the problem and rectify it even if it means ripping up all the floors.

This will be their first night in the place and they have spent the day cleaning and rearranging furniture, moving any decent surplus pieces to the dining room to be sold in order to pay for essential maintenance work. Kim and Dulcie have moved their meagre possessions from the flat above Bart's Burgers, and Paul's belongings are yet to be brought in from the hired van outside.

It's a big moment for all of them.

Their lives started to change after Kim spoke to Stacey. That morning in her kitchen was a pinnacle juncture. Being entrusted voluntarily with Stacey's darkest secret spoke volumes to Kim, who had never really had any true friends apart from Paul.

But it set her thinking.

Paul didn't know that Dulcie was his daughter. Dulcie didn't know that Paul was her father. For how long should they be denied that knowledge? For ever?

For two weeks Kim wrestled with the idea of telling them, cautious of how it might impact all their lives.

Her situation was the opposite of Stacey's.

It was clear that it would not benefit Coralie or Xander to know that Jarvis was Coralie's father. It could permanently split the family and destroy Stacey. That secret was best kept hidden away for ever.

But her own situation? The more she thought about it, the more it did actually make sense. Because what would happen to Dulcie if Kim were to die suddenly? Would she be taken into care, just like she and Dylan had been all those years ago? And what might happen in the future when Dulcie reaches the age where she will inevitably question Kim about her father? Because it could seriously damage their relationship if she refuses to name him. But on the other hand, how would Paul feel about suddenly gaining a daughter? How would he react to the news that Kim had been withholding this information for years?

The questions in her head were overpowering. She concluded that there was only one way to find out.

Hey, Paul. Do you fancy coming round for a takeaway on Friday night? I could get us a curry.

She texted, knowing that he would never refuse. Even after that horrendous weekend he had still stuck by her, loving and supporting her unconditionally as the pillar of strength that he'd always been.

* * *

Dulcie was in bed. Kim lit a scented candle – something musky that masked the smell of cooking fat from the shop below – and put a Nick Drake playlist on. She was able to listen to it now without pining over Willis. Paul, normally prompt, arrived ten minutes late because the side streets where he would normally park were all chock-a-block. He made his complaints in a light-hearted, considered way so that Kim wouldn't take offence. It had happened too many times before when he'd tried to make the point that she needed to live somewhere nicer than a dodgy flat above a fast-food joint, and her reply would be the same every time: 'it's cheap and it's convenient.'

They sipped Cokes with ice and lemon and perused the Mughal Kashmir menu. This took a long time and provoked much discussion, before they eventually settled on the choices: Lamb Pasanda for Paul and Chicken Jalfrezi for Kim. With special rice and garlic naan.

'How are things with you?' Paul got himself comfortable in the shapeless armchair, tucking a cushion under his bad arm.

'Yeah, good.' Kim rubbed sweat from the top of her upper lip.

'You seem a bit... I don't know. Distressed? Distracted?'

Kim took a breath. 'I've got something to tell you. I just didn't know whether to say it now or after the food.'

Paul sat up in the chair, his expression turning serious. 'Tell me now. Or I won't be able to eat, because you're worrying me.'

Kim picked up her glass and swished the ice cubes around. She was just going to come out with it and what the hell. There was no sense in tiptoeing around. 'Dulcie is your daughter.'

Paul looked her dead in the eyes, fusing his soul to hers. His nose twitched; he pulled his gaze away and stared down to check a rough-edged fingernail for an exceedingly long time.

Kim waited, the flailing of her heart under her ribs making her feel faint. 'Talk to me.'

'I think I already knew,' he said. 'For years I speculated and hoped and wished that it would be true. I've longed for this moment, for you to tell me.'

'It was that time in Kittiwake House.'

'The *only* time. Why didn't you tell me before? I could have been involved...'

'You *have* been involved. You've been great for Dulcie and she loves you.'

'I mean involved like a father rather than an uncle. I could have provided financially, got you a decent place to live.'

'You know I'm too proud for all that.' A half-laugh spilled from Kim's mouth. This conversation was going better than she had anticipated.

'So, what's changed? Why have you decided to tell me now?'

'I don't know.' She shrugged. 'Life. Maturity. I want to be able to tell Dulcie, if that's OK with you.'

'That's brilliant.' Paul's eyes were shining. Happiness glowed out of him. 'I can support you. Whatever you need, whatever Dulcie needs. I want to be in her life – and yours too – and be the best that I can. It's all I've ever wanted.'

'We'll sort things out so that it works for all of us. Just don't go on about my crap house again,' said Kim. 'I don't want to live in one of your renovations. I want to stay here where my work is, where Dulcie's school is. Where my friends are.' She had Stacey now. They had been on playdates with the kids to the park and even had a charity fun run booked to participate in.

Paul pushed himself out of the armchair and went to sit next to her. 'What happens with *us*? I mean, is there any chance of us being, like, a family? Can we do stuff like that? Because you know how I've hoped for that to happen. I could wind down some of my property projects and free up as much time and money as you want, because I'd much rather be here than there.'

Kim let him take her hand, let it rest chastely in his. 'We could make a move towards that.' She'd thought a lot about that, too. About the possibility of being in a proper relationship with Paul. Because he wasn't just Dulcie's father. He was her best friend, confidant, partner in crime. She leaned her head onto his shoulder. She was so glad that she'd told him her secret.

Now, he knew everything about her and she knew everything about him.

. . .

It was just over a month later when the letter arrived out of the blue to tell her that she was one of two beneficiaries named in the will of Mrs Coates and that both of them would be required to attend an appointment with the solicitor. Assuming that Nina would get the bulk of the estate, she hoped for a token ornament or piece of jewellery to remember Mrs Coates by.

But by the end of September, she was – quite unbelievably – the proud owner of Carmel, number four, The Elms.

It seemed the appropriate time, the most auspicious moment to take a life-changing step. After all, the property would be far too big for just her and Dulcie to rattle around in, and the three of them had been getting on very well together for the last few weeks, spending time together at the cinema, going out for meals and walking in the forest. And every time that Kim had to work in the burger bar downstairs, Paul had come over to sit with Dulcie so that she wouldn't be alone.

It really was time to take everything up a gear.

It was time for Kim to ask Paul if he would move into the house on The Elms with them.

* * *

'What have you got in that van?' Kim asks Paul.

'Not as much as you might think.' Paul pulls up his hood and takes the keys out of his pocket. 'To be fair, I probably didn't even need to hire the van: I could have got it all in the car if I'd properly sorted it out beforehand. But I was a bit impatient to bring it all over and get moved in before you changed your mind.'

Kim laughs. 'Doubting my intentions already?'

'No, not really. I'm just so excited about it all. You know that it's what I've wanted for years.'

Kim helps him, and they traipse in and out, in and out, getting blown about by the storm and wetter with every journey as they bring Paul's boxes into the dining room to sort out at his leisure. She flips open the damp tops of a few to see what they contain: books; vinyl records; trainers and shoes; more vinyl records.

'I got a bit geeky about music,' he admits. 'There's the whole stereo system and speakers still to carry in if you'll help me do that.'

'OK,' she says as she rips disintegrating parcel tape off another box to find a tub of Lego and some soft toys, a bear with one eye. 'Shall I take your cuddly animals upstairs?'

He laughs. 'Oh God, have you found *those*? Some of that stuff has been in boxes for years and I've just moved it from place to place without sorting it. Some of it was even from the care homes. It really needs to go in the bin.'

He goes back outside to see what is left in the van, and Kim retrieves the Lego for Dulcie to play with. Underneath it, at the bottom of the box, there is a piece of red, white and blue ribbon, coiled like a snake. She takes the silky fabric between her fingers and pulls it out.

But it's not just a ribbon.

A gold medal hangs off it, heavy, dull with age. *UK Street Dance Championship* is engraved on it.

Kim stares at the word *WINNER* as the room tilts and closes in.

FORTY-EIGHT

PAUL

Before the childcare circle

From the first moment he set eyes on her, Kim was Paul's everything. Despite being only eleven years old, he just knew. Having never formed such an attachment with anyone else in his life, his soul bonded willingly and solidly to hers. He jealously observed the devotion with which she smothered Dylan; would it ever be possible that she could love him, too? Yes, there were signs – she laughed at his jokes and allowed him into her personal space – and as the three of them developed an intense, inseparable relationship he began to have hope.

With an endearing humour and positivity, Paul drew out the bitterest bits of Kim, like salt on an aubergine, mellowing her character to perfection. He devoured every morsel of warmth and caring that she offered him, all the while craving the exclusivity of her affection.

Try as he might, though, he would always be second-best to Dylan. That's what he'd thought; that's what he'd resigned himself to. He would never get that top spot.

But by springtime, by that momentous weekend in late

May, an opportunity presented itself to him that suggested everything could change.

Dylan was OK, but he could often be an irritating little kid. So, when he ended up on the beach that Friday afternoon, getting fussed over by a bunch of teenage girls, Paul watched enviously, wondering just how it was that he could win that level of attention. It was obvious that Dylan lacked the entertainment factor, yet the girls were fawning around him like he was some kind of cute pet.

Feeling excluded, Paul tried to engage in the shenanigans by doing his best impression of Jonathan Ross.

'Who's that supposed to be? Quasimodo with a lisp?' one of the girls sneered, and the rest of them roared with laughter. Everyone laughed, even Dylan. Paul watched him as he bent over like the others, snorting in amusement. The girls continued to mock him, swinging their left arms flaccidly to knock down the sandcastle they had made, and Dylan giggled even more, his face creased into an uncontrollable hysterical crumple.

'Dylan,' Paul said sternly to him, 'we're supposed to be back at the cottage in half an hour. Maybe we should leave now so that we won't be late.'

'Don't go!' The girl with dark hair hugged Dylan to her chest. 'Here, you can wear my medal if you stay a bit longer.'

Everyone was ignoring Paul, who stood awkwardly beside the group, as the girl removed a ribboned gold medallion from her neck and hooked it over Dylan's head.

'Dylan, we need to go. I'm supposed to be looking after you,' Paul tried again, leaning forward and tapping Dylan on the shoulder.

'We can look after him,' said the girl. 'You go on your own.'

'Yeah, get lost, you one-armed bandit,' said a different girl, which aroused another bout of raucous hilarity.

A handful of sand came from nowhere and hit him in the face.

'Stop it!' Paul rubbed his gritty eyes which were already tearing up. 'Leave me alone.'

'Leave *us* alone,' said the girl who had given Dylan the medal. 'We don't want you hanging round us, you freak.'

Paul couldn't see out of his right eye. He poked at the corners, trying to scrape out the sand, turning his back to the group so they wouldn't see him cry. He took a few steps away, hoping that Dylan would follow, but Dylan remained with the girls, contaminated by their spite.

What could he do? He was hurt and embarrassed, and although he was supposed to be looking after Dylan his instinct was to protect himself, to run away from those bullies and get back to the cottage.

Paul was in the television room with a wad of wet tissue over his swollen eye when Dylan returned, twenty minutes late, to strut around the cottage still wearing the gold medal.

'What do you think?' he said to Paul, flaunting the shiny disc in his face. 'Does it look like I've won the Olympics?'

'No.' Paul pushed him away. 'And it's not yours. You shouldn't have taken it.'

'I've only borrowed it. I'm meeting them tomorrow to give it back.' Dylan stood and stared at him with a newfound defiance in his eyes. 'They're my friends now. So, I won't be hanging round with a weirdo like you anymore. You and your freaky useless arm.'

There was a crushing sensation in Paul's chest as he watched Dylan skip away into the kitchen to seek out snacks. How could he treat him like this? Since arriving at Summerbone House, Paul had cherished him like a little brother, even swapping his Christmas envelope to ensure that he got a golden ticket for the holiday.

Later that evening, he watched in silence as Dylan removed

the medal from his neck and carefully folded the gleaming metal circle into the ribbon. He peeked from under his duvet as Dylan tenderly placed it on the bedside table next to his bunk before settling down to sleep. And when it was dark, when everyone was still, when their sleeping breaths had settled into a semi-conscious rhythm, Paul crept out of his own bed and took the medal to hide in his pillowcase.

There was an anomalous level of chaos the next day, fuelled by a combination of factors. A family problem causing one of the staff members to disappear outside and make endless phone calls. One of the girls from a different children's home needing a prescription for a new inhaler. The inadequate supply of choco-late-flavoured breakfast cereals. A toilet that wouldn't flush.

Dylan's missing medal didn't make it into the list of priori-ties to be dealt with. 'Just think back to when you had it last,' was the advice given to him by staff unwilling to go to the effort of a full-blown search. Paul sat quietly on the top bunk, hugging his pillow to his body as Dylan fruitlessly turned the room upside down.

The shambolic morning stretched into the afternoon. Sausages were burnt. A trip to a bowling alley was abandoned due to the wrong risk assessment being in the holiday file. Someone spilt a bottle of blue nail varnish on the lounge carpet. Dylan still couldn't find the medal.

Eventually, late in the afternoon, when the fusion of boredom and bedlam had reached breaking point, two of the youth workers walked the children into town. Half of the group was allowed to peel away into the dark and dingy enclave of the penny arcade under the strict condition that they didn't leave the building. The instructions were too easily disregarded though, and Dylan was one of those that sidled off only minutes later, to make his way to the beach and find his new friends.

Paul saw him go: a blithe breakout, his route zig-zagging between the families eating ice creams, along the promenade past the cockle van until his feet were kicking through the deep sand towards the spot where only yesterday he had frolicked and joked with his admirers. Paul followed discreetly, standing at the edge of the beach in the shadow of the safety information board, watching the thinning of the tourists as they packed up sun cream and towels and frisbees to make their way back to their accommodation.

The temperature had dropped; cloud had blocked the sun; a swelling tide was eating at deserted sand sculptures.

Then, there she was: the girl from yesterday, tossing back her dark hair, checking over her shoulder as she strode barefoot swinging her sandals in her hand. Dylan spotted her first: he jumped and waved, and scampered like a puppy towards her.

She was alone this time.

Paul couldn't hear their conversation, couldn't properly see the expression on the girl's face when she realised that Dylan hadn't brought her medal back. But her stance was one of annoyance: she rammed her heel into the sand – kick, kick, kick – one hand on her hip as she jabbed a finger into Dylan's shoulder. Paul smiled and stroked the silky ribbon of the stolen award inside his pocket.

It was hard to tell whether things were amicable or not. There was a bit of rough and tumble between the two, before the girl suddenly fell to her hands and knees and began to dig a hole like a giant crazed rabbit, aggressively throwing out the sand as she burrowed deep, deep down.

The sand piled up. The cavity expanded so that her whole head and body disappeared into it while she continued her excavations, until she reached a stratum of mud. Eventually she sat back on her haunches, seemingly finished.

But no. More horseplay ensued with a stint of tickling and rolling around – their shrill squeals reached Paul's ears – then without warning Dylan was in the hole with just his head poking out.

The girl stood and stamped the pile of sand around him, like she was planting a tree. Dylan laughed and pleaded and yelled and begged as he was encased, firmed in by the girl's feet. She stood over him for a few minutes, flicking sand into his face with her toes, before picking up her sandals and leaving him buried there. With an element of satisfaction, she sauntered into the advancing water. Stooping now and then to wash her hands and arms, she dibbled her feet at the edge of the surf as she headed away from Dylan.

What was she doing? Punishing him for not returning her medal? Surely, she would go back and get him out; she wouldn't just leave him there with the tide coming in?

Paul remained still, squatting in the dunes, intrigued by the sequence of events, unable to intervene but unable to pull his eyes away.

It was around twenty minutes later when the other two girls from the previous day's trio turned up to drag the first one from the edge of the shoreline to a waiting car, its engine idling in the *No Parking* zone on the promenade. There seemed to be minimal resistance from her, and she only glanced back once, just before she was pushed into the back seat.

Paul stood and watched the car drive away.

He walked towards the sea, towards Dylan's head which looked like a football stranded on the deserted beach. The foamy tide was only minutes away from reaching his chin. Paul could hear his cries harmonising with the seagulls.

'Paul, Paul!' sobbed the little boy, his face awash with sand and mud and tears. 'Get me out.'

Paul said nothing, but dropped his gaze to the squirming, shrieking head at his feet.

'GET ME OUT! Pull me up! I'm going to drown!'

Paul felt the first chill of water as a wave scurried up to his heels. He looked around calmly. Desolation; a bleak, empty space stretching out in both directions; vast, clumsy cliffs facing up to him. There was no one in sight: the brewing storm had drawn all the tourists to cosier havens.

'PULL ME OUT! Paul, please!'

Paul thought of Kim then: her generous spirit; her warm, enveloping hugs; her enigmatic smile. The way her presence made him tingle. How it could be just the two of them instead of the three of them. Paul and Kim. Kim and Paul. Best friends forever.

'Help me, please!'

The water fearlessly washed up again, encircling Dylan's neck. Paul jumped out of the way; he didn't want his trainers getting any wetter. There was a rumble of thunder in the distance and spits of drizzle in the air.

'PULL ME OUT! QUICK!'

Paul took a deep breath and squashed his face into an expression of pity. 'Sorry, mate. I can't help you. It's because of my freaky useless arm.'

'NO! No, don't leave...'

But Paul was already pacing away.

And the rain was already thrashing down.

And the wind was already whipping around.

And the sea was already lapping up to, and into, Dylan's gasping mouth.

* * *

There are only two boxes and Paul's stereo system to remove from the hire van. Dulcie comes skipping outside, coatless, despite the atrocious weather.

'Can I help you, Dad?' she asks, her teeth beginning to chatter in the cold.

'Here, take this one. It's not too heavy.' Paul passes her a container sealed up with parcel tape. 'You're a good girl.'

He watches as she dashes through the rain back into the house, the home that he is going to be sharing with Kim and his daughter, the two people he loves most in the world. What could be better? It's amazing to think back to how his life was all those years ago, and then to compare it with now.

Wow.

He's said it all along, though, hasn't he? You can't let your circumstances dictate your life. Everyone has the power within themselves to do anything, to change anything. You've just got to believe in yourself and see what opportunities arise and then make the most of them.

And sometimes, too, you have to keep secrets.

A LETTER FROM HAYLEY

Dear Reader,

I want to say a huge THANK YOU for choosing to read *The Childminder*, my third psychological thriller. If you enjoyed it, and would like to keep up to date with all my latest releases, just sign up at the following link. Your email address will never be shared and you can unsubscribe at any time.

www.bookouture.com/hayley-smith

I hope you enjoyed *The Childminder*, and if you did I would be so grateful if you could write a review. I'd love to hear what you think, and it makes such a difference helping new readers to discover one of my books for the first time.

You can also connect with my social media. I chat about all sorts of things – particularly books and music – and would love to hear from you.

Thanks again for reading.

Love,

Hayley

KEEP IN TOUCH WITH HAYLEY

 facebook.com/Hayley.Smith.Writer

 x.com/WriterHayley77

 instagram.com/HayleySmithWriter

ACKNOWLEDGEMENTS

Firstly, masses of appreciation must go to the wonderful team at Bookouture, and in particular my editor, Susannah Hamilton, whose creative brilliance has brought yet another of my stories to life. THANK YOU!

Thanks to my Facebook followers (and in particular, members of the Psychological Thrillers Group) for helping me to name the characters in this story. I hope you're not disappointed if you have a 'baddie' named after you!

To my family and friends who were unwittingly coerced into doing research – 'so what might happen if...' – your knowledge and support is invaluable.

Huge thanks again to Nicola for being my social media advisor and giving me a kick up the bum on 'content' and stuff. Keep on keeping on. You do so much better than I ever could.

Lizzie Morris, writing buddy for yet another book: we slogged those words out, ate the cheese and drank the wine. Cheers for everything!

And as always, the biggest thanks go to Michael who has put up with me behaving like a zombie for months while I've been immersed in plotting. You can have my complete attention now, for a short while at least!

PUBLISHING TEAM

Turning a manuscript into a book requires the efforts of many people. The publishing team at Bookouture would like to acknowledge everyone who contributed to this publication.

Audio
Alba Proko
Sinead O'Connor
Melissa Tran

Commercial
Lauren Morrissette
Hannah Richmond
Imogen Allport

Cover design
Ghost

Data and analysis
Mark Alder
Mohamed Bussuri

Editorial
Nina Winters
Nadia Michael

Made in United States
Orlando, FL
26 November 2024

54537327R00189